She wanted him still

Wanted him again, she amended. As much, or maybe more, she realized, than before he had taken her. *Taken her.* The words echoed in her consciousness. Out of place. So foreign to what she had always thought should happen between a man and a woman. She didn't think she had ever used the term in connection with making love. Now, however, she knew exactly what it meant.

Hawk had taken her. He hadn't talked to her, no whispered words of seduction. And he hadn't pretended he was doing anything other than what he had done. He had consumed her. Invaded and conquered, just as his kiss had the first day she'd met him. Taken, she repeated mentally, acknowledging the truth. But at the same time, she knew that he had taken nothing she hadn't willingly given. Nothing she didn't want him to have.

Dear Reader,

The most frequently asked question an author hears is, "Where do you get your ideas?" For this trilogy, that spark was wondering what would happen to our secret warriors now that the Cold War has ended.

What if a highly specialized black ops team is considered by the CIA to be obsolete in today's New World order? What if the men who had spent their lives carrying out incredibly dangerous missions around the globe are now an embarrassment to their own government? What if the agency that created them wants to destroy their identities, so that even if the operations they took part in come to light, they could never be traced back to their superiors?

In this trilogy, three men, all members of the CIA's elite External Security Team, are in such a position. Their identities destroyed, but with all the deadly skills they have been taught still intact, these men embark on private missions that will test not only their expertise in dealing with danger, but also their hearts. And the skills they once used to guard their country will now be employed to protect those they love.

Please watch for all the stories in this new MEN OF MYSTERY series from Harlequin Intrigue: *The Bride's Protector* (April 1999), *The Stranger She Knew* (May 1999), and *Her Baby, His Secret* (June 1999). Enjoy!

Love,

Gayle Wilson

The Bride's Protector
Gayle Wilson

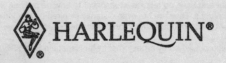

TORONTO • NEW YORK • LONDON
AMSTERDAM • PARIS • SYDNEY • HAMBURG
STOCKHOLM • ATHENS • TOKYO • MILAN • MADRID
PRAGUE • WARSAW • BUDAPEST • AUCKLAND

For my Aunt Maylia, with love and deep affection

ISBN 0-373-22509-1

THE BRIDE'S PROTECTOR

Copyright © 1999 by Mona Gay Thomas

Printed in U.S.A.

EXTERNAL SECURITY TEAM

"Standing Guard"

CAST OF CHARACTERS

Tyler Stewart—On the eve of her fairy-tale wedding, she discovers that not everything in her life is what it seems.

Lucas Hawkins—The mysterious CIA operative known only as Hawk, whom Tyler unwittingly draws into the middle of an assassination plot.

Amir al-Ahmad—The playboy bridegroom. Did he have a hand in his own father's death, or is he caught up in the same plot that threatens to destroy Hawk?

Jordan Cross—Is this CIA agent a friend, or is he playing a very dangerous double game?

Claire Heywood—A powerful Washington attorney, Claire has the influence and the resources to get to the bottom of the mystery, but will her beliefs keep her from helping her slain lover's friends?

Malcolm Truett—An Englishman with ties to Middle Eastern terrorists, or simply an innocent pawn in someone else's game?

Carl Steiner—The new head of the External Security Team appears to be dismantling the close-knit unit, whose loyalty still lies with their slain leader.

Griff Cabot—The man whose leadership tied them together and whose death threatens to destroy all that the team had once accomplished.

Prologue

This was, of course, what he did. He was the unquestioned master of a skill the CIA believed there was no longer any need for. A skill...

The man he was watching moved, and without any conscious thought, his brain directed his body to adjust the rifle the fraction of a millimeter that would again place his target in its crosshairs. He supposed that at one time he had had to think about making that alignment. But no longer.

Just as there was no longer any adrenaline rush to overcome. No tremor of hand or glint of perspiration on the motionless finger that held on the trigger. After that infinitesimal, automatic adjustment, his entire body was again absolutely motionless. And it could remain that way for endless minutes.

No nerves. No compunction concerning what he was about to do. He had made his peace with that a long time ago. And of course, in this case...

He eased in a breath, aware that the line of thinking he had begun to pursue was not an indulgence he could afford. This was simply another job. Another target. Another slow squeeze of the trigger. Danger passed. Threat resolved. Lives saved.

Just another job, he told himself again, forcing the

rhythm of his breathing back into the familiar calm of duty. Away from the images of what had been done to his friend.

It had taken him months to reach this place. To find this man. This time. This moment. *Just another job.*

His entire world was focused now on his rifle sight, sharp, clear and utterly unmoving. His finger completed the slow pull it had begun. The remarkable brain that functioned behind the ice-blue eyes, locked now on their target, was once more in complete and total control of every emotion.

The shot was true. He knew that without even watching the result. Instead, as soon as he released the trigger, his hands began the familiar tasks of picking up the casing and disassembling the custom-made, lightweight rifle. Those actions, too, were automatic and unthinking.

It was finished in a matter of seconds, less than a minute, certainly. He could hear, on some level at least, the commotion from the street below, just as he had probably unconsciously heard the shot.

He didn't think about either. Picking up the rattan case that now contained the silencer and the strapped-down, high-powered rifle with which he had just killed a man, the operative known only as Hawk descended the curving staircase that led downward from the roof where he had waited for his victim. He didn't appear to hurry. There was, after all, no need for haste.

When he reached the street, he put the case on top of his left shoulder, holding it in place with the long, brown fingers of his left hand. Dressed in the traditional headdress, which covered his dark blond hair, and a white robe, both totally unremarkable in this locale, he moved with utter and unhurried confidence through the throng that crowded the narrow streets of Baghdad. His skin was tanned darkly enough to allow him to pass for a native— at least to the casual observer.

There was nothing about his appearance that might cause anyone to give him a second glance. Nothing to cause comment. Nothing out of the ordinary. Nothing that would betray the fact that he didn't fit into this society. Just as he had never fit into any other.

It was not until he turned into the shadowed arches of an ancient building, blocks away from the roof from which he had fired the fatal shot, that he paused. He made a pretense of adjusting the case he carried, and the hard line of his mouth moved only enough to whisper the phrase he had waited months to say.

"Rest in peace, Griff," the man called Hawk said softly. "Rest in peace, my friend. The debt is paid."

Chapter One

"I knew you'd be the most beautiful bride in the world," Amir al-Ahmad said softly. His deep voice, with its slight British accent, was filled with satisfaction and a hint of possession, something Tyler Stewart had certainly noticed before.

"Turn around, my darling, so we can see every inch of you," he ordered. His full lips tilted upward beneath the dark mustache, a smile intended to soften the effect of what had been—almost—a command.

"I think *you've* seen more than enough," Tyler objected with a laugh. "The groom's not supposed to even glimpse the bride on their wedding day, and you're demanding the full runway show."

"And why should I not see the woman who will become my wife in…" Amir paused, consulting the gold Rolex he wore before he looked up at her, smiling again "…in a little more than an hour? Besides, that is *not* a custom in my country, I assure you," he said, unmoved by her objection.

Tyler knew, of course, she shouldn't be surprised. After all, her fiancé had listened to none of the objections she had tried to make throughout the course of their whirlwind courtship. Why should she think that would change now?

"Please, darling," he urged again, the false patience of

his tone clearly expressing his impatience, "we are all waiting."

Fighting a frisson of resentment, Tyler smiled at him instead of arguing. Her smile was forced, perhaps, but she was determined not to let anything spoil this day. Not Amir's tendency to ride roughshod over anyone else's suggestions. Not even the building anxiety she had felt during the last week.

Despite her repeated mental lectures, that sense of foreboding had been present the whole time her bridesmaids had clustered around her, laughing and chattering, helping her dress. Making all the old prenuptial, off-color jokes.

Just prewedding jitters, Tyler had told herself over and over. *Just nerves. Stress. All perfectly normal.*

She took a deep breath, striving for serenity. After all, Amir's request was simple enough. And he was right. Why should he be expected to observe traditions he didn't understand?

Just as she didn't understand the ones that had shaped his personality. The ones that would soon govern her life. That was probably part of her apprehension, she acknowledged. She knew so little about the culture from which he came, despite hours spent at the library trying to remedy that ignorance. And sometimes it seemed she knew even less about her fiancé himself.

Obediently, however, she made the slow pirouette he'd requested, showing off the designer gown that Amir had chosen. And paid for, of course. The yards of silk organza that made up its bell-shaped skirt and short train swung gracefully as she circled. The elegant Manhattan hotel suite, one of the two floors of rooms Amir had rented for the wedding entourage, certainly provided an appropriate background.

"Breathtaking," he said. "But I always knew you would be."

Always. The word reverberated in her mind. This was really for always.

"Thank you," she said softly. "The dress is wonderful, Amir. Thank you for that, too."

"I don't want your gratitude, Tyler. You're to be my wife. I am looking forward to having the right to take care of you," he said softly. "The privilege."

She could see the approving smiles on the faces of the watching women, but for some reason, the romantic words jarred. Maybe because that sounded like something Paul might have said. The part about taking care of her. And Paul...

Was something else she wasn't going to think about, she decided, pushing the pain of that away. It had nothing to do with today, she told herself, and shouldn't be allowed to spoil what was supposed to be a joyous occasion. The most wonderful day in a woman's life.

Deliberately, she smiled at her fiancé again, the movement less forced this time. She held his eyes, trying, as she had so many times before, to read past their opaque blackness and into the soul of the man. Maybe that was also part of the problem. She never seemed to know what he was thinking. Or feeling.

Educated at Eton and Cambridge, Amir al-Ahmad seemed almost British, even to the Saville Row suits and school ties he favored. He was handsome, in a darkly exotic way, and probably more sophisticated than anyone she had ever known. And, of course, he was also immensely wealthy. Riches beyond anything she could imagine, produced by the seemingly endless supply of oil that lay beneath the forbidding surface of his country.

According to everyone she knew, he was, therefore, everything a reasonable woman could possibly want in a husband. And apparently he had fallen head over heels in love with Tyler Stewart the first time he had seen her.

She couldn't imagine why. She had finally been forced, however, to accept that it must have happened. Which *did* make her the luckiest woman in the world, she supposed. At least that was the other thing everyone told her. And she had the evidence of her own experiences with Amir. All as charmingly romantic as the statement he had just made.

"Well, aren't you even going to look at yourself?" Cammie Torrence asked in exasperation. Her maid of honor's suggestion destroyed the awkward silence that had fallen when Tyler failed to respond to Amir's claim. Cammie took her shoulders and turned her to face the hotel suite's floor-length, gilt-framed mirror.

For the first time Tyler surveyed the finished product of this morning's efforts. At what she saw reflected there, she took another breath, this one deep enough that the white veil, gossamer sheer and touched delicately with seed pearls, lifted like a cloud around her bare shoulders.

The exquisite lace that comprised the bodice of the gown she wore was cut so that it ran straight across her chest and upper arms. The line of the material lay just above the beginning swell of her breasts. The bodice narrowed to show off the twenty-three-inch waist she worked so hard to maintain, and then spread out into those billowing yards of silk organza.

It was strange, but Tyler couldn't remember ever having been a bride before. Surely she had been. Surely at some time in the last twenty years she had been photographed for a bridal magazine, these familiar features topped by a spill of veil and a small, artfully arranged spray of flowers.

If I was, she thought, still studying her reflection with a detached and professional appraisal, *I hope I looked happier. Younger. More at peace.*

Her lips tightened against the surge of anxiety, and she watched in the mirror as the creases formed at the corners of her mouth. And she could clearly see, as she had been able to for the last few years, the fine lines etched by time into the delicate skin around those famous violet eyes.

She turned her head, unconsciously examining the still-taut line of her jaw, looking for the smallest sag and thankfully not finding it. *Not bad,* she thought. *Not too bad for an old broad.*

"What do you think?" Cammie asked softly, interrupting that unconscious assessment.

Tyler smiled at her maid of honor, catching her eyes in the glass and holding on to the friendship in them. "I think…" she began, and then her gaze shifted to the figure standing behind Cammie. Amir al-Ahmad. To whom she would be married in a little more than an hour. "I think I look like a bride," she finished.

They all laughed. Even Amir smiled, his dark eyes moving away from hers to study her reflection in the mirror. In them was again possession, which was not, she realized, the emotion she had always dreamed she would see in her bridegroom's eyes.

"Will your father approve of this?" she asked, denying that small disappointment, burying it with all the other anxieties that had been growing in her heart as this day approached. "I'm sure this is not anything like what the women in your country—"

"My father will adore you," Amir interrupted, sweeping that particular worry away with his accustomed surety.

He walked across the short span of carpet that separated them and put his hands on her upper arms, almost exactly as Cammie had done. His long brown fingers, however, closed tightly over the off-the-shoulder sleeves of the wedding gown, the rich ivory lost under their covering darkness.

"There is absolutely nothing for you to worry about. As for what is expected of the women of my country, that's really of no concern to you. Do you think I shall require that you put on *hijab?* We are not so old-fashioned as you seem to imagine."

He smiled at her again, his expression almost paternalistic. "Nothing will change about your life, Tyler. Except, after today, I shall finally have the right to make you mine."

He paused, and Tyler wondered if the others had been aware of that slight emphasis. *Finally the right to make you mine.* Which she hadn't been.

Another tradition of his country? Or, as he had hinted, an aspect of his religion? She hadn't asked. She had been grateful for his lack of sexual pressure, especially considering all the other pressures he had imposed. That had been, for some reason, the one reassuring element in the breakneck speed at which this relationship had developed.

"And," he added, "finally I shall have the right to take care of you."

Again their eyes met in the glass. Tyler wanted to say that she had been taking care of herself just fine for the last thirty-eight years, thank you very much. That she certainly didn't need anyone's help in that department. And she might have said exactly that three months ago. But now...

Now, she conceded, her confidence was shaken. She was scared. Almost as frightened as when she had shown up in Paul Tarrant's office more than two decades ago, a skinny seventeen-year-old refugee from a little hick town in Mississippi.

This was almost the same feeling. Except twenty years ago she had fervently believed that, with a little luck and a whole lot of perseverance, she would succeed. She had had stars in her eyes, incredible dreams in her heart and almost two hundred carefully hoarded dollars in her vinyl pocketbook. The difference between then and now was that she no longer had any of those things. Not even the two hundred dollars.

"I know," she said softly. "I know you will."

She pulled her gaze from his, finding her reflection again in the glass. Was that woman someone who had made a bargain with the devil for her bruised and battered soul? Or was she really, as they all told her, the luckiest woman alive?

That was a question she had wrestled with since Amir

had proposed the first time, three days after they met. Laughing, she had turned him down, of course, but her refusal hadn't made a dent in his supreme self-confidence. He'd acted exactly as if she had agreed, lavishing her with expensive gifts that she had honestly tried to refuse. She had even sent them back, but Amir had had them delivered to her again, accompanied by his secretary this time, a very charming Englishman, who had also made most of the arrangements for this wedding.

"Really, my dear," Malcolm Truett had assured her, *"it is much easier to let him have his way. He will in the end, you know. Simply because he always has. And, after all, he is very much in love with you."*

Tyler had held on to those words like a talisman during the bouts of doubt and uncertainty about this marriage, to which she had finally agreed. She needed desperately to believe it was true, and she didn't really know why she found that so hard.

Maybe it had something to do with the fine lines and creases the morning sun was so clearly illuminating in her face. Or the knowledge that there were so many other, far more beautiful women in this city. Woman who were educated. Smarter. Wittier. More at ease in social occasions. And far younger.

Why in the world would Amir al-Ahmad, who could have almost any woman in the world, have chosen a fading model as the object of his affections? Despite her very prolonged "fifteen minutes of fame," Tyler found it hard to believe she would qualify any longer as a trophy wife. At least not for someone like Amir, whose father was reputed to be one of the richest men in the world.

Why, then, would Amir have chosen her? Other than for the reason he claimed—that he was in love with her and wanted to take care of her. That was the only conclusion she had come up with, despite endless hours she had spent worrying over that question in the short weeks since she'd accepted his proposal.

"And now, my darling," Amir said, "I am going back to my suite to dress. Then I'm going downstairs to await my father's arrival. I hope you understand the honor he pays us in attending today. I want to show him how grateful we are for his kindness."

"Of course," Tyler said. She was beginning to feel like a marionette. Amir pulled the strings, and she agreed with whatever he said. But thinking that was ungrateful, of course. And petty. She hoped she was neither.

He was naturally delighted his father was coming to the ceremony. There had been some doubt about that even as late as yesterday, but Amir was his father's oldest as well as his favorite son. Tyler understood that Sheikh Rashad al-Ahmad had made a tremendous concession in leaving his country. For security reasons that was something he seldom did. But he had come to New York to be present at this wedding, despite the fact that today would be only a civil ceremony.

Although Tyler hadn't really understood the reasons for this formality, Amir insisted it was important to protect her legal rights before they traveled to his country for the religious ceremony. Besides, he said, it would give her friends a chance to attend the wedding, and it would give him a chance to show her off to the assembled international media, something that wouldn't be allowed at the other ceremony.

He would take care of everything, he had promised. Every detail. She wouldn't have to worry about a thing. Once again, she had found herself steamrollered into agreeing.

"It's much simpler to let him have his way. He will in the end, you know." Malcolm Truett had been right. The truth of that was something she had discovered more and more frequently as the weeks wound down to the wedding day.

"I'll send someone to escort you downstairs to the ballroom when it's time for the ceremony. From today, you'll have to be far more conscious of security. The price of the politics in our part of the world, I'm afraid. And the money," he added, his tone humorously self-deprecating. "I hope you understand."

She nodded, not even bothering to voice her agreement this time. How had she gotten herself into all this? she wondered.

Her eyes flicked back to the image in the glass. She didn't look much different from the confident woman who had appeared on all those magazine covers through the years. Not spineless. Or as if she had been run over by a steamroller. Or defeated.

The word appeared in her brain, and, interested in where the concept had come from, she examined it. Defeated enough by what Paul had done that she'd decided to roll over and play dead? Or defeated enough that she would let Amir's suave determination sweep her along with whatever he wanted her to do?

In the mirror, she watched him stride across the room behind her. The door was opened by one of the ever-present, eternally silent bodyguards, who followed him through it and into the hall, white robes billowing behind. She knew that that kind of security, and the restrictions it imposed, would now become part of her own life.

Never again to be able to decide the course of her day according to mood or whim... To get into a car and take off for a weekend. To go shopping on the spur of the moment. Call a girlfriend to meet for lunch. Never again to be completely alone. Completely unguarded...

"I think," she said, turning around to escape the image in the glass as much as those frightening mental pictures, "if you all don't mind, I think I'd like a few minutes alone. Just a little solitude. To settle my nerves, I guess."

"Alone?" Susan Brooker questioned. "Are you sure that—"

"I'm sure," Tyler assured her. "I just need a minute to unwind. Time to get my act together before we do this."

"Are you all right?" Cammie asked softly, her voice touched with real concern.

"I'm fine," Tyler promised, reaching out to put her hand reassuringly on her maid of honor's forearm. "I just need...a little peace and quiet."

"You aren't nervous, are you?" Cammie teased, sounding relieved. "Every woman in New York is wishing she was in your shoes, and you're shaking like a leaf."

Cammie had put her own fingers over hers, which Tyler realized *were* trembling as they rested on her friend's arm. Cammie tightened her hand reassuringly over those cold fingers.

"That man's crazy about you," she said. "It's obvious in everything he says and does. And his daddy owns a *country.* A whole country. I don't know what more you could ask for."

Cammie was almost ten years younger than she, although according to Tyler's biography the difference in their ages was not as great. Paul had kept adjusting her age downward through the years, just as he'd told all those silly stories about her background. But still, Cammie had been a model long enough to know how this business worked and to understand the insecurities inherent in it. The not-unjustified insecurities.

Marrying Amir had seemed an answer to everything. He had appeared like a godsend at the darkest moment of Tyler's life. He had been a miracle she hadn't even had strength enough to pray for. So she didn't know why, suddenly, she was overwhelmed with doubts about what she was doing.

"It's going to be all right," Cammie said more softly, squeezing her fingers again. "I promise it will be."

Tyler smiled, grasping at those reassuring, kind words just as she had held on to Malcolm Truett's through these last stressful weeks. "I know," she said. "This is just the jitters. Every bride has them. I don't know why I should be an exception."

"Maybe because you, of all people, have no reason for them. You've got the world by the tail. All you have to do is hang on. This is a *really* good thing," Cammie said, her voice full of sincerity. "*He* is."

Their eyes met. Unlike Amir's, Cammie's were clear and open and filled with understanding. She knew exactly what Tyler had faced in the last three months—the double blow of Paul's death and the revelations that had followed it. She would understand why those had been enough to destroy Tyler's confidence. In her judgment about people. And in her future.

"A good thing?" Tyler asked, smiling. "You promise me that, oh wise Martha-clone?"

"I promise," Cammie said solemnly, her voice made strong with confidence, as if she could convince Tyler by her own conviction. Her tone lightened when she continued. "Now I'm going to run all these yakking women out and let you get ready to charm the assembled masses and your new daddy-in-law," Cammie said, broadening the last words with her natural Southern accent.

That was something that she, like Tyler, had worked for years to erase, but sometimes when they were together, they fell back into the comforting rhythm, to words drawn out to too many elongated syllables, and dropped *g*'s.

"You gotta charm the pants off that old man, honey," Cammie ordered. "He might even give you your own oil field. That's real job security."

Tyler laughed, feeling better than she had all morning. Cammie was right. Amir *was* a good thing. Especially the way her life had been going. He loved her. And she...

She hesitated, thinking for the first time about what those words really meant, before she forced herself to finish the thought. And she loved him.

Of course she did, she decided, wondering why her mind had faltered over the phrase. She must. She would never have agreed to marry him otherwise. Not for the money. Not even for the security he seemed so eager to provide. That wasn't the way she had been brought up. That wasn't what marriage was all about.

She watched in gratitude as Cammie efficiently ushered everyone out of the room. After the door had closed behind them, Tyler turned back, facing her image in the full-length glass again. Despite the famous bone structure, the gleaming blue-black hair and the wide violet eyes, reassuringly the same, the woman reflected there seemed almost a stranger.

Prewedding jitters? she thought. Was that really what this was all about? Or was it something much deeper? Scarlett O'Hara holding up that turnip and shouting into the night, *"As God is my witness, I'll never be hungry again"?*

Tyler's mouth inched upward, amused by the probably too accurate comparison. Some uptown psychiatrist would have had a field day with her life, she thought. She'd never given any of them a chance, of course. That, too, wasn't the way she had been raised. Instead, she had poured all the emotions from her painful past into her determination to succeed. To leave everything else behind her. Back in Covington, Mississippi.

Up until a couple of months ago she'd really believed she had done that. But then, for more than twenty years, she had also believed in Paul Tarrant. She had trusted that he would always be there to look after her interests. He had become the caring father she had never had, the guiding hand in her long success and her most trusted friend.

Suddenly, so quickly it seemed impossible to comprehend, he was dead, the victim of a massive coronary, and she had been alone. And devastated. Just when she needed him the most, Paul was gone, and she had been left to face a career that was going nowhere. Was nowhere, she amended honestly. The woman reflected in this glass was no longer in demand. Wrong look, wrong decade, wrong something. And suddenly it had all been over.

Paul's death, coming almost at the same time she had

had that realization, had been a terrible blow, but the one that followed had been infinitely worse. She had never begrudged Paul his agent's commission, taken out of every check she received. After all, he had kept her working through the vagaries of one of the most fickle professions in the world.

She had thought from the beginning that her time in this business would be short. Only as long as her particular "look" was in demand. That's all any model could expect—except for the very privileged few who somehow hung on through trends and fads. With Paul's direction, for almost twenty years Tyler Stewart had been one of those few.

But she had never forgotten that five-room house in Covington, featured in none of the colorful biographies Paul had fabricated. That dilapidated little house where a girl named Tommie Sue Prator had once lived. And Tyler knew there was still a lot of Tommie Sue left in her. Most of it in the form of scar tissue.

Her mother had scrimped and saved to provide them the most basic necessities after her daddy had run off. Sometimes it had been a struggle just to get enough to eat. Tommie Sue had always done without things other kids took for granted, even in a place like Covington, where nobody had much. Those memories you never forgot. Deprivations your soul never recovered from.

As a result, Tyler Stewart had never taken anything for granted, especially not success. Every job she got, she had asked Paul to invest most of the money she made. That growing nest egg would provide security when this dream ended.

She thought he had done it. Thought he knew people who would know the right things to do with that money. The safe things. He had assured her over and over that it was in good hands. That he was taking care of her. Taking care of her future.

Maybe he'd tried. It had taken her a month or so after

his death before she could come to that more charitable assessment. At first the realization that there was nothing left of all that money had left her numb. Then angry. And finally just bitter.

It seemed the only thing Paul Tarrant had been good at was peddling the unique bone structure and incredible violet eyes that had transformed Tommie Sue Prator into the woman in the glass. A woman called Tyler Stewart.

She hadn't worried when the contracts had gotten fewer and fewer. She had known that was inevitable as the years took their toll, and as other girls, younger, with a fresher look, moved up to claim their rightful places at the top of the heap.

Tyler had had a great ride on that merry-go-round. She had grabbed the brass ring, and she had been more than ready to retire. Ready to do something with her life that had meaning. More meaning than smiling into a camera.

Smile, Tyler. The familiar words echoed inside her head. All those smiles. Provided willingly even when she didn't feel like smiling. Just smiling anyway to protect that future.

Just as they expected her to do today. Just as Amir would probably instruct her to do if he thought about it. After all, that was what she had done for years. Surely she could do it a little longer, and then, if she did...

Again her brain hesitated over the painful thought. But this was the reality that had brought her to this day. *If she did exactly what Amir wanted her to do, then she'd be safe again.*

Her future with him wouldn't be snatched away from her as the one she had worked so hard to provide for herself had been. The prenuptial contracts they had signed would assure that, no matter what happened, she would always be taken care of.

All she had to do was to say "I do." Simple enough. Just a couple of whispered words, and the pain of Paul's betrayal would be over and her fears about the years ahead would be ended. Erased. Then maybe the memory of her mother's short, sad life would finally stop haunting her.

Tyler closed her eyes, feeling the burn of tears behind her lids. Why was this so hard? Everyone she knew thought this marriage was wonderful. That Amir adored her. That she was the luckiest woman in the world. And all she could think was…*there's something wrong*. Wrong about all of this. About today. *It wouldn't feel this way if I were doing the right thing*. That was it, of course. No matter what anyone else said, she shouldn't *feel* like something was wrong, if what she was doing was right.

She took another deep breath, watching the veil float around her shoulders. It was one thing, however, to acknowledge that wrongness here. To confess her doubts. Alone. In her room. Away from Amir's self-confidence, which had belittled every doubt and disclaimer she made, making her feel…

Like Tommie Sue. The realization was startling, and then she knew it shouldn't have been. That was exactly how Amir treated her. Just as Paul had. *"Just smile at them, sweetheart,"* Paul would say with a laugh, *"but don't open your mouth."*

For years she had done just that. Hiding who she was beneath the way she looked. Hiding everything, because she had felt that if they ever found out, it would all be over. The dream. The security.

Paul had always made her feel that way—inadequate. Not very bright. In need of his guidance. Maybe she *had* once been all those things, but she'd thought she had outgrown those feelings. She had made herself over in her own image. Ironically, it was the same image Paul had created for her.

She wouldn't go back, she decided fiercely. Not back to being Tommie Sue. Not to feeling as if she had no right to an opinion. No right to say no. To make a decision. She couldn't marry Amir if that's what he expected.

And it's just a little late to have arrived at this conclusion, she realized in panic. About four weeks too late.

Maybe if she told him how she felt... Surely they could talk about this. Surely it wasn't too late for that. There was still time.

Tyler turned away from the mirror and hurried across the vast, empty suite. She didn't know what she could say to Amir that might make a difference, but she knew, no matter what happened today, for her own self-preservation she had to make an effort to say something.

THE MAN CALLED HAWK stared at his reflection in the wide, well-lit bathroom mirror, its edges still hazed with the fog from his shower. He had been in the process of wiping off the middle section of the glass with one of the huge towels the hotel provided, when he'd caught a glimpse of his face.

For some reason the infinitely familiar landscape of his rugged features stopped him, making him pause in his preparations for shaving the two-day growth of beard. He leaned forward, studying the harsh contours of his own face, as if the man in the mirror were a stranger.

He leaned closer, his hands resting flat on the expensive marble of the countertop, one on either side of the shell-shaped sink. The hotels Hawk normally frequented were not equipped like this. He was unaccustomed to, and a little uncomfortable with, the luxury that surrounded him.

But then this wasn't exactly a "normal" situation. Nothing about this one-night stopover in New York was normal. He was not here on an assignment. There was no mandate to carry out. No job which he would do, unquestioning, because he trusted the man who had assigned it.

That man, Griffon Cabot, was dead—killed months ago in a terrorist attack in front of the gates of CIA headquarters at Langley. With his death, the team Cabot had slowly and painstakingly built during the last fifteen years would be dismantled by the same government that had suggested its creation.

The External Security Team would be cut out of the intelligence community, as swiftly and efficiently destroyed as a malignancy under a surgeon's scalpel. That was exactly what the current government saw the team to be—a dangerous cancer that must be eradicated.

And that destruction would start, Hawk knew, with him. He had given them the perfect opportunity, of course, with his last mission. The assassination in Baghdad had not been sanctioned, and that made him a rogue. A very dangerous loose cannon, at least in the agency's eyes.

Not that he gave a damn. He knew that kill he had carried out would only be the excuse they used for their actions. Which he had known all along were inevitable. As soon as he learned Griff Cabot had been one of the victims of that massacre, Hawk had known it was over. For all of them. All the men who had worked for Griff through the years were finished with service, with love of country, with duty.

All over but the shouting, Hawk thought cynically. He suspected he was in for more than his share of that. His lips flattened, and the pale blue eyes narrowed.

Hawk, however, was no longer conscious of the image in the glass, no longer aware that it mirrored his movements. He was thinking instead, just as he had been since he'd arrived in the States last night. Thinking about what came next.

He had known this day was also inevitable, and he couldn't explain why he hadn't been better prepared for it. Maybe *not* contemplating the future was simply part of his personality—the product of that same cold control that allowed him to put everything out of his head and focus solely on a job. The same control that allowed him to be the consummate weapon his government had forged him into.

Because Hawk had been owned, trained and used by the

United States government since he'd turned seventeen. That's when, as an alternative to going to prison, a belligerent teenager named Lucas Hawkins had been offered an "opportunity" to join the military. He had been given that chance—one last chance—by a hard-assed Texas judge. Seeing the truth of that warning in the judge's cold eyes, Hawk had accepted the invitation, smart enough even then to know the old bastard was right.

It was in the Corps that he had found the family he'd never known. Found a real job. A sense of accomplishment. And the infinitely precious knowledge that he could do something of value. Something that could make him a person of worth.

Eventually, somebody had recognized the potential of the shrewd and pragmatic mind that lay beneath his unpolished exterior. He had been moved into military intelligence, and then, finally, the identity of a soldier named Lucas Hawkins had merged into that of a CIA operative known only as Hawk.

Now the government that had created him would cut him loose. With a pension for those years of service, if he was lucky. With the skills they had taught him. And with the other skills he had taught himself, he thought, thin lips twisting into the semblance of a smile. And none of those peculiar talents would translate well to the civilian world. Not unless he wanted to move to the other side of the equation, to cohabitate for a change with the bad guys. Where he could probably make a hell of a lot more money than he was making now, or ever had made, he conceded, his lips tilting fractionally at the corners again.

But what he did had never been about money. At least not after he'd met Griff Cabot and become a member of his team. By that time Hawk knew all about the lure of esprit de corps and had believed himself sophisticated enough to avoid its entrapment. He had been wrong. Proven wrong by the caliber of man Cabot was. A man whose careful and considered offer of friendship had drawn the man who would be called Hawk like a hearth fire's warmth on a long winter's night.

Now that friendship was over, and he was going to have to find something to do with the *next* forty years of his life. And for some inexplicable reason, all that was why he had ended up spending last night here. In Griff Cabot's favorite New York hotel, where they put fresh flowers and exotic fruit in your room and chocolate on the pillow of your bed when they thoughtfully turned it down.

A place he could definitely afford and a place where he just as definitely knew he didn't belong. The problem was that Hawk hadn't figured out yet exactly where he *did* belong.

Chapter Two

"My dear!" Malcolm Truett exclaimed. The Englishman's pleasant voice, normally controlled, held a note of shock. He had stepped around the corner just as Tyler got off the elevator. His widened eyes took in her full bridal regalia before he asked, "Whatever are you doing *here?*"

"Here" was another of those cultural differences, Tyler realized belatedly. Amir had rented two floors of this stately Manhattan hotel to house the members of the wedding party. The women occupied rooms on the floor above, including the suite where they had helped her dress this morning. The men of the party, including Amir, were housed on this one.

In her hurry to talk to her fiancé before he went downstairs, Tyler hadn't even thought about those restrictions. Or the reasons behind them. The implication was plain, however, in Truett's eyes and in his voice. She shouldn't be on this floor. It was off-limits. But those restrictions were part of the reason she had come.

"I need to talk to Amir," she said, smiling at his secretary, who had always been kind. "I want to catch him before he goes downstairs to meet his father. It's very important."

Truett's eyes studied her face. Their irises were almost exactly the same shade as his gray brows, now arched in surprise. His lips pursed slightly, as if in thought, before he spoke.

"Then I'm very sorry, my dear. You've just missed him, I'm afraid. I saw him leave his room not two minutes ago and get into the lift." His gaze darted toward the door of what she assumed to be Amir's suite, almost directly across the hall, and then came back to her.

Tyler hadn't thought Amir would have had time to change. It had been less than fifteen minutes since he'd left her upstairs. Maybe his father had arrived early or maybe something had come up concerning the arrangements in the hotel's grand ballroom, which was to be used for the ceremony. Whatever had happened, Tyler was bitterly disappointed to have missed him. She had steeled herself, determined to make her fiancé listen. And instead...

"Are you sure?" she asked, hearing the elevator doors begin to close behind her. She glanced over her shoulder to check that the train of her gown wasn't in their way. But that had been a foolish question, she realized, when her gaze returned to Malcolm Truett's face. Amir's secretary always knew everything. If he said he had seen Amir go downstairs, then she could be certain he had.

"Oh, quite sure," he said emphatically. "We even spoke. There were a few things Amir wanted me to take care of. Not two minutes ago, I promise you. And then he went downstairs."

He reached past her and punched the Down button for the elevator, apparently in response to the urgency of his errands. His eyes came back to her, again assessing her features.

"If there is something *I* may do, Ms. Stewart, I should be delighted to be of assistance. If this is an emergency..." Discreetly, the Englishman let the question trail.

An emergency? Was it enough of an emergency to interrupt Amir's reunion with his father? Or was it simply a resurgence of the anxiety she had lived with for weeks?

The anxiety that everyone, including Amir, had assured her would disappear from her life forever as soon as she whispered those vows. Which she was supposed to do in less than an hour.

"It's not an emergency," she admitted.

"Then may I suggest you really *must* return to your suite? The sheikh will be arriving at any moment. He may come up with Amir, since there is some time before the ceremony. I'm sure you don't want to chance having to meet him for the first time in this hallway. That might be somewhat awkward, I should think."

Truett's eyes held hers, willing her to agree. Just as Amir's always did. "However," he added, apparently not finding the expected acquiescence there, "I shall be sure to tell Amir that you wish to speak to him. In private, of course. Will that do?"

He had already made his diagnosis. The same one she had considered. *Prewedding jitters.* His prescription seemed to be simply keep the bride calm until Amir could work his magic. And get her out of the middle of the hall before the sheikh saw her.

Maybe he was right. Perhaps that would be best. When Malcolm gave him that message, Amir would come to her room. They would have some privacy, and she could pour out all the concerns and questions he hadn't listened to before. And demand some answers. Before it was too late. Because otherwise…

The thought was shocking. It was not the one that had sent her here. And at this stage, it was almost unthinkable. *Almost,* she repeated mentally. But was it more unthinkable than the other?

"Maybe that *would* be best," she agreed softly, still coming to terms with the realization that in less than an hour her choices would be far more limited than they were right now.

"I'm sure it will be," Truett said kindly. He reached behind her and this time impatiently punched both the elevator direction indicators. One for her, to go back up to her room, and apparently the other for him, to attend to Amir's errands.

"I think I should take the stairs," she suggested, "rather than wait here."

That would make an accidental meeting with Amir and his father, which Truett had implied might be imminent, less likely. As much as she needed to talk to her fiancé, this wasn't where she wanted to do it. Nor did she want to embarrass him by being where she wasn't supposed to be. That might make Amir too angry to listen to anything she had to say.

"Quite right, my dear," Truett said, his relief almost palpable. "And very wise, I might add. I can have someone escort you to your room. I'm very much afraid that I must be engaged elsewhere, but I'm sure there's someone here who…"

Truett's voice faded as he glanced back at the row of doors that stretched along the hall. There had been no traffic in the hallway since their conversation had begun. The whole floor seemed remarkably quiet. Almost empty.

But then, Tyler realized, it might very well be empty. She had no idea how many people Amir had brought with him. Most of these rooms could *be* unoccupied, as they were on the floor above.

"That won't be necessary," she said. "I'm perfectly capable of finding my way upstairs." There must have been more of a bite in the words than she was aware of— an unintended backlash of her frustration over missing Amir—because Truett apologized at once.

"Of course you are, my dear. My offer was simply a matter of courtesy, I assure you." He reached out and stabbed the buttons once more. Apparently he was dealing with his own set of frustrations.

"Well, I'm sure you have more important things to attend to," she said.

"More important than the bride herself? I think not,"

he said gallantly, "but Amir was, I'm afraid, very insistent that I handle these matters myself. But you're right about the stairs. Everyone seems to have chosen this moment to engage the lifts."

Even the al-Ahmads weren't rich or powerful enough to commandeer all the elevators, as much as they might have liked to, Tyler thought, as she started down the hall toward the exit sign. It was not until she was halfway there that she realized she couldn't get back into her own room. Not unless she wanted to go downstairs to the lobby for a key. In her agitation, she hadn't remembered to pick hers up before she left her room.

She turned and saw that Truett was almost under the exit sign at the opposite end of the corridor. She hurried down the long hall, calling his name. He turned as soon as he heard her, but when she reached him, she read annoyance in his features.

"I don't have my key," she explained, a little out of breath. "If you're on your way to the lobby, could you have them send someone up to let me into my room?"

Again there was a fraction of a second's hesitation, and the muscles in the face of Amir's secretary seemed to tighten. *He's probably thinking that he doesn't have time for this,* Tyler thought. No time to deal with whatever feminine nonsense had sent her down here—where she wasn't supposed to be. After all, Truett had *important* things to take care of. Things Amir had asked him to handle.

"Well, I wasn't *going* to the lobby," he said.

This time his tone was almost petulant. She was interfering with whatever duties he was supposed to be carrying out, and it was annoying the hell out of him.

"Wherever you *are* going," she said patiently, "could you possibly call the desk when you get there and ask them to send someone to let me into my room? I'll meet them there."

The gray eyes assessed her again. Then his fingers, thin and white, fished into the pocket of his formal striped vest and retrieved a plastic key. "This is a passkey," he said, explaining as if she were a child. "You may give it to whomever Amir sends to bring you downstairs for the ceremony. And now, if you'll excuse me, Ms. Stewart, I am afraid I really must go."

"Of course," she said, taking the key. Malcolm was the one who had made the arrangements with the hotel, for all these rooms, empty or otherwise. She supposed it shouldn't be surprising the hotel would have provided him with a passkey, which probably only worked for the rooms on these two floors.

Without waiting for her response, Amir's secretary turned and continued his journey to the stairs. He didn't look back at her, not even when he opened the door and disappeared through it.

Tyler shook her head. She was no closer to a resolution of her situation than she had been before. Coming down here had been a wild-goose chase, she thought angrily, beginning to retrace her steps to the opposite end of the hall, deliberately rejecting the exit Malcolm had taken. Considering Truett's attitude, she wondered if he would even give Amir her message.

Prewedding jitters. Even she had bought into that explanation, but now she knew that what was troubling her was something more. This encounter with Amir's secretary had reinforced what she had known, deep inside, since the beginning of this. Maybe her sense of foreboding had been a remnant of those survival skills she had learned years ago.

Skills Tommie Sue had learned, she amended, which had served her well. Except with Paul, whom she had trusted. Lesson number one, she thought. The dangers of trusting someone else to look out for her best interests.

As she walked by it, she glanced up at the door Truett's eyes had indicated was Amir's suite. And then her steps slowed until she came to a complete stop a few feet beyond it. She looked at the passkey in her hand, her mind racing.

She might not have another chance. Truett might not give Amir her message. Or her fiancé might not come in response, even if he received it. Then there wouldn't *be* a moment alone with him to sort through these growing fears and to ask her questions. Not before it was too late. Not before they came for her, to take her down to the ballroom.

Before they came for her? she thought. Why had those words rung so strongly in her head? They sounded as if she were a prisoner of some kind. Which she certainly didn't intend to be.

She turned back to the door of Amir's suite. Without giving herself time to think about all the reasons why waiting in his room to confront her fiancé might not be a good idea, including his and his father's displeasure, she pushed the passkey into the slot and watched the light blink accommodatingly. She pressed down the handle and pushed the door inward.

As it opened, her eyes seemed to focus like a camera lens on the unexpected scene before her. There were three men in the huge room she had expected to find empty, two of them dressed in the traditional *thoabs* Amir's bodyguards wore. They were standing just outside the open doors that led out onto the room's narrow terrace, which overlooked the street below.

Security, she thought, already in place for the sheikh's arrival. She didn't even realize why she had made that assumption until she heard the crack of a rifle. The sound was strangely muffled, but still she knew what it was. After all, she also had the evidence of her eyes.

She must have made some response. The robed men turned, their eyes tracking in surprise to the opening door. And then, having watched long enough to be satisfied with the effects of the shot he had just fired, the one in Western dress, the one with the rifle, finally turned toward her as well, their eyes meeting across the vastness of the suite.

Everyone seemed frozen in place for the two or three seconds it took for the heavy door to begin to close. Tyler had time to see one of the robed men start across the room. And to see the rifle the stranger held tracking away from whatever its target had been below and toward her before the door banged shut, separating her from the scene.

Since the rifle had begun to swing toward her, the primitive part of her brain had been directing Tyler to get away from the door. At the same time, it had been supplying to her bloodstream the flood of adrenaline that would make escape possible. Just as she moved, instinctive survival skills taking control, she heard the elevator bell behind her.

One of the cars Malcolm Truett had called for while they'd been talking had finally arrived. Gathering the organza skirt up in both hands, despite the passkey still clutched unthinkingly in her right, Tyler ran toward the possibility that bell represented. When she rounded the corner, the doors of an elevator, thankfully the one nearest the hall, were standing open.

Without slowing down, she slipped through the suddenly narrowing space between them. Frantically she pressed the sides of her gown down with both hands. Trying desperately not to let the bell-shaped skirt touch anything that would make those doors glide open again and begin that mindless mechanical wait for a nonexistent passenger.

She made it, except for the tail of her train, which was caught between the doors. She turned, jerking the fabric free, just as the elevator jolted, thankfully beginning its descent.

Down, she realized, looking up at the numbers above her head. Judging by the speed, the elevator was heading all the way to the lobby. Where everyone would be gathered, waiting for the ceremony to begin. The press. Members of the wedding party. Arriving guests. The sheikh and his entourage…

The sheikh? The image of that rifle focused on something in the street below was back in her head. Along with

Amir's comment about the dangers of the politics of his region. The dangers of all that money.

Had someone attacked the sheikh as he arrived? Were those men in Amir's room protecting Sheikh al-Ahmad or was something else going on? Something far more sinister? The memory of the rifle tracking away from the street toward her seemed to indicate that it was. And suddenly Malcolm Truett's words echoed in her head. *"You've just missed him, I'm afraid. I saw him leave his room not two minutes ago and get on the lift."*

Her hand reached out, almost without her conscious direction, to slap frantically at the buttons. Her eyes were still watching the numbers at the top. *Ten, nine, eight.* Had she waited too late to stop the car's descent? Surely, as slow as the damn thing had been in arriving...

The elevator slowed, again jolting slightly, and Tyler closed her eyes, her relief so strong it was almost as paralyzing as her fear. The bell chimed; the doors glided open. There was no one in the hall. She was safe. At least for the moment.

She stepped out, hesitating until the doors began closing behind her, reminding her that they would be able to tell that this particular car had stopped on the sixth floor. One of many cars, she reassured herself. All of them coming and going. Hard to trace one, especially if you weren't sure which one you needed to be tracking. Still, she knew she had to get out of here, just in case the men from Amir's room had reached the elevators before the indicator light had blinked off.

She ran to the end of the short hall that housed the elevators and stood a second looking both ways, up and down the sixth-floor hallway. Far to her left, at the end, was an exit sign. She gathered up her skirts again and ran. There was no one in the hall. No people who could be questioned about what they had seen. No one, then, who could give them any information about where she had gone.

She ran toward the promise of the stairwell, a half-formed plan in her head to try to get out of the building through the basement or service entrance. Just to get away from the hotel and this nightmare, away from whatever the hell was going on.

Gripping the organza skirt, bunched in both hands as if it were dirty laundry, she ran helter-skelter as she had when she was a child, totally focused on the promise of the exit sign ahead. And then, behind her, she heard the soft chime of the elevator bell. Her heart rate accelerated, sudden terror causing another rush of adrenaline. The exit was too far away, she realized in that split second. In this straight, empty hall she would be visible to anyone peering around that corner as she had done. And if they'd brought the rifle with them…

She realized suddenly that she still held the passkey in her right hand, its plastic clinging to her damp palm. She had wondered if it would work only on rooms on the floors Amir had rented. She couldn't even think about that possibility now.

She turned to her right, responding again to instinct and not intellect, and slid the passkey into the slot of a door. Frantically, she pushed down the handle and felt it give. She almost fell inside as the door opened.

She turned around, slamming it behind her. Fingers trembling, she twisted the night latch and pushed the safety bolt into place. Then she collapsed against the door, heart pounding wildly, heated cheek pressed against the cold, reassuringly solid barrier she'd put between herself and whoever was out there.

Even if they had heard the sound of the closing door, she prayed they wouldn't be able to tell which one of all those on this long empty hall it had been. Hopefully they hadn't rounded the corner during the seconds it had taken her to reach her decision. Hopefully they hadn't seen her disappear into this room.

All she needed was a little luck, she thought, which she

hadn't had yet. Just some luck, please God. She finally turned to examine the room she'd entered, praying it was empty. Or at least that there would be no men in *dishdashas*.

There weren't. There was only one man, and he certainly wasn't wearing one of those voluminous robes. As a matter of fact, he seemed to be wearing...nothing at all.

Almost nothing, she amended, her eyes dropping from bronzed shoulders and chest to the hotel towel that was twisted into place around his midsection, the damp terry cloth riding low on narrow hips. He didn't have a rifle. Instead, he held a very big handgun, which was pointed straight at her heart.

"Come right in," he invited, his voice almost as menacing as the gun. Cold blue eyes pierced her, their threat holding her like an insect pinned on a board, her back against his door. "Don't bother to knock. After all," he asked reasonably, "what's a little breaking and entering between friends?"

HAWK DIDN'T KNOW what the hell was going on, but he hadn't been born yesterday. More like a hundred years ago in terms of experience, and in his business, the unexpected was almost always the deadly. He didn't like surprises, not of any kind. Not even if they came wrapped in what seemed to be a pretty enticing package. He had already decided the packaging on this one was going to be interesting, even before she turned around.

Warned by the noise, he'd made it out of the bathroom, gun in hand, in time to watch her lock and bolt his door and fall against it in relief. Which meant she was running from someone. Or at least that's what he was *supposed* to think she was doing.

When she turned around, the situation had suddenly gotten a whole lot more interesting. Hawk might be aware of all the old truths about beauty being only skin-deep and the dangers of judging a book by its cover, but clear-eyed knowledge of the undeniable veracity of those didn't prevent his body's quick physical response.

"You don't understand," she said, eyes widening at the sight of the 9 mm Browning he held trained on the center of her chest.

It was a gun intended to intimidate, and apparently it was having the desired effect. The flush of color—from fear or exertion—that had been in her cheeks drained away just as soon as the violet eyes located and recognized the significance of the semiautomatic he held. Shocked, they jumped from the gun back up to his, stretching wide.

They really were violet, he thought. At least the part of the iris that remained visible after the dark pupil's dilation was a deep purplish blue.

"Then why don't you make me understand," he suggested calmly, and watched her take a long, shuddering breath.

She moistened her lips with her tongue, leaving it visible a moment before her top teeth, which were very white and even, replaced it, fastening nervously over her bottom lip. Her eyes studied his, looking for some clue that would help her know what to tell him.

Whoever she was, whatever the hell she was here for, she was good, Hawk conceded. It looked real. Even the physiological reactions—neck flush, pupil expansion, the visibly throbbing pulse in her temple—were right on target. And those things were extremely difficult to fake.

"I was running away...." she began, and then she stopped, her teeth gnawing once more on her bottom lip.

Not bad at all, Hawk complimented mentally. That indecision had been a nice touch. He said nothing in response, however. He didn't prod, letting her decide what she wanted to tell him. After she had, he'd make his own interpretation.

"I decided not to go through with it—with the wedding, I mean. And so...I ran away."

And left some poor bastard standing at the altar, Hawk thought, fighting an inclination to laugh. The sense of threat was beginning to evaporate. With its disappearance, this encounter became even more interesting. For another reason entirely.

Hawk was familiar with menace. He had a long and intimate acquaintance with death and danger. But it had been a hell of a long time since he'd been with a woman, especially one who looked like this.

Since before Griff's death, he realized, surprised by that fact now that he bothered to think about it. That had been months ago. In the meantime, determined to find the terrorist who had given the order for that attack at headquarters, he had been living like a monk. So it was no wonder he was reacting like an adolescent to a woman's presence in his room. She had an intriguing face, he admitted. And an enticing body, if a little emaciated for his tastes. Her story even made sense, considering what she was wearing.

"And they're looking for you?" he asked, deciding to prompt her, now that he had come to the conclusion she wasn't dangerous.

"I...I think so," she said, seeming to consider the question. "They were coming toward the door. I know they saw me. They must have known I'd seen them."

That sequence didn't make a whole hell of a lot of sense to Hawk, but he wasn't listening only to her words. He was reading tone. Level of stress. Evaluating, just as he had been taught. What he came up with was fear. She was scared to death. And her fear was nothing that made his well-developed instincts react with any sort of flight-or-fight impulse.

They heard the noises at the same time. Her gaze flew upward to meet his again, away from its fascinated appraisal of the Browning, and they listened together, unspeaking, to what was happening down the hall.

Someone had begun pounding on doors. Sometimes there was a pause between knocks. Sometimes there was conversation, distant and indistinct, in response to that knocking. But the one thing that became unmistakably clear as they listened was that those sounds were moving down the hallway. Coming ever closer to the door at the woman's back. The door to this room.

"Please don't let them in," she begged, her voice a whisper. "Don't let them find me. Please, please help me."

Her tongue appeared again, touched her bottom lip with a gleam of moisture and was then replaced once more by those even white teeth. Her eyes held his, the plea in them as clear as the one she had expressed.

Hawk had no intention of letting anyone into his room, of course, and that had nothing to do with her. Whoever was out there, whatever this was all about, whatever the truth behind the story she had told him, he knew they were both a lot safer with that door between them and whoever was knocking on all the others. He had no intention of opening his.

His eyes checked the safety bolt she had thrown, the one he had neglected to put on. He wondered at that aberration in his routine. But then, no one had known he was here. They couldn't have. No one could even have known he was back in the States.

Apparently the luxury of this place, unusual in his life, had overcome his habitual cautions. Or maybe that had been some end-of-mission ennui. The knowledge that all that was over, probably forever.

His normal paranoia had seemed unnecessary and even a little weird, out of place in this setting. After all, this impromptu visit to New York wasn't professional. Not an assignment. It was just a private stop, a memorial of sorts, that absolutely no one could have known about.

He had locked all the safety locks last night, of course. When he'd opened the door this morning to retrieve the copy of the *Times* he'd ordered along with his breakfast, however, he had failed to retake those extra security measures. He had expected no one but the maids to be interested in this room and its occupant.

There was no way anyone could have traced his movements during the last few weeks. He was far too careful to allow that. He was a professional at this game. He had been for a very long time. And he was also a man without an identity. Without a name. Certainly not the one he had put down in the hotel register when he'd checked in last night, the one that matched the false identification he'd handed the clerk.

So whoever was outside in the hall, knocking on doors, wasn't looking for Hawk. That didn't mean, however, that he was going to let them in. He wondered, strictly as a matter of idle curiosity, just how much of that decision was based on the color of the woman's eyes. On the entreaty in them.

"Step away from the door," he ordered softly.

The momentary indecision in those eyes seemed to indicate she was still trying to decide if she could trust him. As the knocking came closer, however, she obeyed, slipping past him and moving farther into his room. He kept the Browning trained on her. The skirt of the gown she wore brushed against his bare calves as she went by, a sensation that didn't help the uncomfortable tightness in Hawk's groin.

Neither did the subtle scent of her body, drifting to him as she moved. It had been a long time since he'd been close enough to a woman to be aware of her perfume. And women in the countries where he'd spent the last few months didn't smell anything like this, he acknowledged ruefully.

Instead of heading across the room, as he had expected her to, the woman disappeared into the bathroom where he'd just finished shaving, closing and then locking the door behind her. The firm line of Hawk's mouth tilted again into an almost forgotten alignment, amused at her expectation that the flimsy bathroom door would offer any

protection. If this one and the Browning didn't keep whoever was out there out there, then the bathroom door
wouldn't do her any good at all.

He wondered if she was really this afraid. And if so,
then why the hell she had agreed to marry the guy in the
first place. Of course, he'd seen people do all sorts of unfathomable things in the name of love. Even intelligent,
reasonable people. People like Griff. But love was something about which Hawk readily acknowledged he understood very little.

Whoever was knocking was next door now, he realized,
getting back to the business at hand, about which he understood a great deal. Hawk put his ear against the door,
hoping to overhear the questions they were asking. This
time, however, there were none. Apparently there was no
one in that room. Which meant...

The knock he'd been expecting pounded suddenly
against the outside of the door he was leaning against. He
waited a few seconds—timing the pause—before he responded. "Who is it?"

"Hotel security," an accented voice outside the door
avowed.

Hawk wondered briefly if that could be true, and then
he decided, even if it were, it didn't change anything.
There was no reason to let security into his room, and a
couple of very good ones that argued for keeping them
out. One of those reasons was hiding in his bathroom. The
other was the fact that the fewer people who saw his face,
the better Hawk liked it.

"What do you want?" he asked.

"We'd like to ask you some questions."

"Ask away," Hawk invited.

"May we come in?" A different voice. Same accent,
not quite so heavy, and a lighter tone.

"I don't see any point," Hawk advised. "I haven't done
anything that security might be interested in."

There was a hesitation. They were probably silently

communicating about the situation, thinking over what they could say to convince him to let them make a search of this room.

"We're looking for a woman," the same voice said finally.

"Aren't we all?" Hawk asked, deliberately coloring his comment with humor. Letting them hear it. There was no response. No chuckle. No acknowledgment.

"What's she done?" he asked into the void.

Another hesitation.

"We need to ask her some questions."

"Then you're wasting your time. There's no woman in this room, gentlemen, and I was about to step into the shower. So if you'll excuse me..."

"Wait a minute," the first voice said, now with a hint of aggression.

Obligingly, Hawk waited, imagining the scene outside. They were obviously still trying to decide what to do since he was being obstinate, something that apparently hadn't happened with any of the other guests on this hall. Hawk didn't like things that made him different, that made him stand out from the crowd, but he knew that in this instance, being a little conspicuous was a better option than opening the door and letting them inside. For those same two very good reasons.

"We need to check out your room, sir. We believe the woman we're looking for may be dangerous."

"They all are, son," Hawk agreed, again letting his amusement show. "And I have to tell you, I'm beginning to lose patience with you guys. I'm not hiding a woman in here, I promise you. And I don't think one's going to break into my room, so why don't you two just get on with your search and let me get back to my shower." When he suggested the last, his voice was carefully wiped clean of that hint of humor.

There was no answer, but Hawk waited patiently through the long silence. Waited until he heard the knocking begin on the next door down the hallway. At least one of the men had moved on. Maybe both. There really wasn't a whole hell of a lot they could do about his refusal to open his door.

Despite what they claimed, he didn't believe they were hotel security. The tone hadn't been right. Or the questions. Whoever they were, they had apparently realized that if they pushed him too hard, he might put in a call to the management, which would put a swift end to their ability to search. For some reason they weren't willing to risk that.

However, after the conversation he'd just had, Hawk didn't believe either of them was a jilted bridegroom, which meant, he supposed...

The blue eyes shifted to the bathroom door, which was still closed. He had answered their questions—or at least he'd made a response to their demands. *Now,* he thought, *it's time to answer mine.*

He walked across the thick carpet, his bare feet making no sound, deliberately giving her no warning. He raised his right leg, drawing the knee back with a practiced motion, and with the bottom of his bare foot, kicked open the bathroom door, breaking the lock she had turned to keep him out.

Chapter Three

When the door came slamming into the room, Tyler stumbled backward, trying to get out of its way, and almost fell into the shower stall. Her back and shoulders banged against the glass enclosure, rattling the doors, which thankfully held.

She threw her hand up to maintain her balance, and her flailing fingers dislodged the wedding dress she had hung over the top of the stall. She caught it with her knee, trying to prevent the designer gown from dropping to the floor.

It was only as she stood there, balanced on one leg, the other raised and bent at the knee, the wedding dress draped over it, that she realized how little she was wearing. She became aware of it only when the man's eyes reminded her.

It was the first time she had seen any sort of emotion in their blue depths. Anything other than cold threat. What she saw in them now wasn't cold. She quickly lowered her leg, grabbing the dress as it began to fall.

She had locked the door. What the hell kind of person would...? Then she answered her own question. The kind who had kept those men from finding her. The kind who carried a very big gun and who looked as if he knew how to use it. And the kind who wasn't even bothering to pretend his eyes weren't examining her body.

Her shaking hands lifted the bridal gown to her breasts

in an attempt to cover some of that exposed skin. Her underwear, designed to fit under the low-cut neckline of the dress, apparently wasn't doing much of that.

His eyes openly examined the strapless, skin-colored lace corselette before they moved down the length of sheer silk stockings to the white peau de soie heels. Even considering how long her legs were, that examination seemed to take forever.

Tyler had paraded down a lot of runways wearing less than she had on right now, but somehow that was very different from the one-on-one, up-close-and-very-personal assessment this man was making. Her eyes lifted longingly to the broken door, hanging a little drunkenly on its hinges.

There was a dark brown terry-cloth robe hanging on the back of it. That's what she had intended to put on when she started taking off the bridal gown. Only he hadn't given her enough time. Or the privacy a locked door would seem to demand from any civilized person.

Civilized. The possibility that he really wasn't was frightening. Between them they weren't wearing enough clothing to start a small fire. Not that she had wanted to start anything. She just wanted to get into something less conspicuous than what she'd been wearing and then she wanted to get out of here. Out of the hotel. Out of the insane situation she'd somehow gotten herself into by agreeing to marry Amir.

The man's gaze finally came back to her face, and meeting his eyes, Tyler felt her fear explode again, almost as strongly as it had been when she'd opened Amir's door. She wondered suddenly why she had believed she could trust this man. He looked as dangerous now as the men who had been standing on that narrow terrace, one of them pointing a rifle into the street.

She stood motionless, trying to read the face of this stranger to whom she had appealed for help. Trying to decide if he meant to hurt her. After all, he had kicked in the door she'd locked, and he had slowly examined her exposed body, neither of which seemed to bode well for his intentions.

"Now why don't you tell me what's *really* going on," he said.

His voice was very calm, and she realized that whatever had been in his eyes a moment ago, that smoldering blue heat, was gone. Snuffed out as easily as someone might pinch out the flame on one of those tiny candles on a child's birthday cake.

She felt a little of her tension ease, but she didn't know what to tell him. She wasn't sure what she had seen—a security operation or an assassination. And even if it were the latter, she didn't know if Amir was involved. Or who was.

She really knew nothing other than the fact that she'd seen someone in Western attire fire a shot off the terrace of Amir's suite as two of his bodyguards watched. She had no way of knowing what, if anything, that meant.

"I needed to get out of this dress," she said, trying to think what she *could* tell him. What would be safe. And true. After all, the only thing that was important now was getting out of here. The Tommie Sue part of her had been screaming that warning since before the door upstairs banged closed, separating her from the man with the rifle.

"It's too conspicuous," she added, lifting the wedding gown she still held in her left hand a fraction of an inch.

"Who were the men outside?" he asked, ignoring the gesture. Ignoring what she'd said.

"Hotel security," she suggested, remembering their claim.

"I don't think so," he retorted, but his voice was still calm. "And I don't think they were the groomsmen of any wedding party. So why don't you just tell me what's really going on before I lose patience with whatever game you're playing."

She hesitated again, still not sure what to do. She had witnessed something she knew instinctively she wasn't supposed to see. From their reaction, she believed no one was supposed to see what those men had done. She just wasn't sure telling *this* man about it was the smartest thing she could do. She didn't know who *he* was, either. What he was, she amended. Because he was obviously something outside her experience.

"I was supposed to get married," Tyler said again, deciding, even as she talked, how much of the truth to tell him and how much she should hide. As certain as she was that she had to get out of this hotel, out of the wedding, she didn't feel she could make accusations against Amir when she had no proof that he, or anybody else, had done anything wrong.

There was probably a perfectly harmless explanation of what she had seen. After all, her feelings were colored by the realization that she had made a serious mistake in agreeing to this marriage. Amir's was not a world she could enter, but that didn't mean he was guilty of—

"And?" the blue-eyed man prodded.

"And...I decided at the last minute I didn't want to go through with it. I ran away and some people, some of the wedding party, came looking for me."

She paused, assessing her audience. His eyes had not left her face after their initial, unhurried scrutiny of her body. But they revealed nothing of what he might be thinking. No clue to that and therefore no help in shaping her narrative.

"I just don't want them to find me," she finished, deciding finally that the less said about what she'd seen the better.

Maybe this man *could* help her. That's what she had thought at first. That had been her instinctive reaction to him. But now something about him bothered her—almost the same sense of wrongness that the men with the rifle had caused.

In his case, however, it wasn't the gun he held. It was something about his eyes. Their coldness.

Their…emptiness. She shivered at the unexpected descriptive her brain had suggested. *Empty,* she thought. That's exactly what they were.

"You think they would call in security to help them look?" he asked.

"Maybe," she agreed, trying to think why they might. When an explanation occurred to her, she hesitated about voicing it. After all, he didn't look very gullible. "If they thought something had happened to me," she continued. "My fiancé's very wealthy, so if they didn't know I'd run away…"

She realized suddenly that she shouldn't have told him about Amir's money. Probably not a smart move, considering the situation, but it seemed too late to back out of the story now.

"They might call in security if they thought someone might have…" She paused, wondering if she was simply giving him ideas. Out of the frying pan and into the fire?

"Abducted you?" he supplied smoothly when she hesitated.

His tone had changed again, but she still couldn't read it. Damn it, she couldn't figure him out. Not enough to know whether she could afford to tell him the truth. Whether she dared to do that and then appeal for his help. "Maybe," she agreed.

"Why would they say you're dangerous?" he asked.

"Is that what they told you?"

He nodded, his mouth shifting at the corners. Not quite a smile, but something. A change of expression, she thought. *Almost* an expression, at least, and not that cold mask.

"I'm not dangerous," she promised softly.

The subtle expression she had noticed before flickered again. Obviously he thought her claim was amusing. And she knew why. *Because he's the one with the great big gun. And because he really is dangerous.*

"Okay," he agreed, seeming to accept what she had said, although his eyes were still amused. "So what now?"

Which, unbelievably, seemed to imply he was willing to help her. Tyler took a breath, trying to think what to do. Anything but let those men find her, she decided. "Could I stay here?" she suggested. "Stay in your room?" *Into the fire.*

"You could...but I'm leaving," he said, blue eyes guileless. "I have a plane to catch."

Maybe he'd take her out of the hotel with him, she thought, grasping at possibilities. If she were wearing different clothing, with something over her head to hide her hair and part of her face... Hope began to grow. They would be looking for a bride—a bride alone—and she would have become someone else.

"I could go with you," she said.

The corners of his lips lifted minutely. "But I don't have another ticket," he said.

There was a suggestive undercurrent in his refusal, and only when she heard it did she realize how her request might have been interpreted.

"I didn't mean on the plane. Just...away from the hotel. They'll be looking for a bride. For a woman alone..."

The words trailed away because even in her mind the plan was unfinished. But surely he'd be willing to do that. It wasn't much to ask. Men were supposed to respond to women in distress. Some kind of code of chivalry.

Yeah, right, her mind jeered. *And how many men do you know who follow such a code? Especially if it puts them in danger?*

But maybe, she thought, looking into his considering eyes, maybe *he* would. Especially since he *didn't* know that the men looking for her also had guns. She wondered again if she should tell him what they'd been doing. Tell him about the rifle.

Not telling him was unfair, but there was no one else she could turn to. And there was always the possibility that she had been wrong. That she'd put the wrong interpretation on what she'd seen. That it didn't mean anything. Nothing sinister.

This man had a gun, and he looked as if he knew how to use it. If she had to pull *someone* into this, and she didn't see any other way to get out of the hotel, then surely it would be better to choose a person who seemed capable of dealing with the risk. And he did, she realized. That, too, was in his eyes.

"All right," he said unexpectedly. "Out of the hotel and into a cab. I'll drop you wherever you say. Within reason."

She nodded, willing to agree to anything. His offer was the best she was likely to get. If he would get her out of the hotel, she'd worry then about what came next.

"There's a robe behind the door," she said. "Would you hand it to me?"

Surprise flickered briefly in his eyes and was controlled. He caught the broken door with his free hand, pulling it toward him. Without releasing her gaze or his gun, he reached behind it with that same hand and took down the robe she'd asked for. He tossed it to her, and she caught it awkwardly.

She waited a moment, hoping he'd have the decency to go into the other room. Finally she hung the wedding dress across the top of shower enclosure again. Then she turned her back and slipped her arms into the sleeves of the robe. She didn't turn around until she was knotting the sash around her waist.

His eyes had lightened, and she realized he was laughing at her. Not *laughing,* she amended. She wondered if he even knew how to laugh, but there was no doubt he was amused. And she didn't understand why she had turned her back. She was comfortable with her body, at ease with showing it off. That had been an integral part of her profession, so her reaction to this one man looking at her was hard to explain.

"You planning on wearing that?" he asked. His eyes remained on hers. They didn't examine the bathrobe, even though he was obviously referring to it. "Because if so, I have to tell you that it will attract as much attention as the wedding thing."

"I thought maybe I could borrow something of yours," she suggested.

His eyes moved up and down her body, appraising, but doing it quickly this time. Asexually. Then he stepped out of the bathroom and walked over to the double closet. He pulled a small black nylon bag, duffel shaped, off the shelf and pitched it unceremoniously onto the bed.

"There's not much there," he said, "but you're welcome to anything you think might fit."

She hesitated only a second before she walked across to the foot of the king-size bed and bent to pull the bag toward her. As she did, she glanced up and found his eyes on the shadowed cleavage the corselette had been designed to create, emphasized now by her leaning position. She straightened quickly, the bag in her hand, and his eyes came up to meet hers. This time there was nothing in them but amusement.

Her mouth tightened. For some reason, despite the seriousness of her situation, Tyler was a little annoyed that amusement seemed to be the only emotion she had the ability to evoke in this man. She hadn't intended to be provocative. She had simply been reaching for the bag, but still...

Not quite sure why she was angry, she unzipped the duffel with more force than was necessary and began rummaging through its contents. He had certainly told the truth. There wasn't much here. A couple of changes of underwear—briefs and T-shirts rolled neatly together to conserve space. Two pairs of worn jeans, also rolled and not folded. A knit golf shirt. And another shirt—this one a long-sleeved white button-down. A pair of cotton knit athletic shorts. Several pairs of socks. Loafers and some well-used running shoes.

She glanced up, assessing him, wondering if the jeans would be worth trying. He was only an inch or so taller than she. Narrow hipped and flat bellied enough that they might be possible. Out of the pile she'd created on the unmade bed, she picked a pair of jeans and the white button-down, along with the running shoes and a couple of pairs of thick athletic socks.

She didn't look at him again until she had chosen the items and was ready to make the trip back into the bathroom to try them on. When she did, his eyes were uncommunicative, neither disagreeing with nor commending her choices.

"Are these okay?" she asked. "Okay to borrow? I can mail them back to you. You'll just have to give me your address."

"Throw them away."

"But the shoes are—"

"I don't want them back," he said. "Not any of it."

"You don't want to give me an address," she concluded.

"Would you give me yours?" he asked.

She wouldn't, of course. She was a woman, and he was a stranger. And besides, after what she had seen, she didn't want anyone associated with this hotel to be able to find her.

"No," she said truthfully.

He nodded. They stood a moment without speaking, eyes holding. His seemed open and honest for the first time. But they weren't, she knew in her gut. That was only for show. He had forgotten how to be open. That cold control was habitual, and she wondered what was behind it. And then decided that wasn't any of her business. That was something she didn't need to know—what had made this man so hard.

She took the items she'd picked out and retreated into

the bathroom. There was no way to lock the door this time, but then he'd already demonstrated how inadequate that would be in keeping out someone who was determined to get in. If he wanted to, there was nothing she could do to prevent him.

But as she began to dress, she realized she was no longer afraid that he might assault her. She felt a lot of emotions about the man she had appealed to for help, but fear was not one of them. Not any longer.

There had been only one brief glimpse of the man beneath the controlled facade—that moment when he'd broken down the door, demanding answers. She hadn't given him any. She still hadn't told him the truth, and he probably was aware of that, but it seemed he was willing to help her anyway.

And maybe, she thought, it was safer if he *didn't* know what she'd seen. Safer for him. Still, the urge to tell him had been almost overpowering. For some strange reason, she had really wanted to tell the man with the cold blue eyes all about it.

WHEN SHE CAME OUT of the bathroom, he was standing just beside the bed, almost where he had been before. Now, however, he was dressed in the other pair of jeans and the knit shirt, the pale blue of its faded cotton a contrast to his darkly tanned skin. The towel he had wrapped around his waist had been thrown on the bed, but the clothing she had rummaged through was no longer there. She assumed he had stuffed it back into the bag.

His hair was completely dry, and it was lighter than she'd realized at first, sun streaked and very short. On him, however, the length looked good. Almost military. He wasn't handsome. His features were too strong for that, too harsh, but he was striking. *You'd probably give him a second look,* Tyler thought. Most women would.

"What do you think?" she asked, clearing those assessments from her head. It didn't matter how he looked, as long as he was willing to help her get out of here. And after that, she would never see him again.

His eyes examined her again, but this time she had given him permission. She had used one of her stockings as a belt, threading the silk through the loops of the jeans to hold them up. She had tied the tails of the shirt in front and turned up the cuffs a couple of times. The double layer of thick socks insured that the running shoes would probably stay on her feet long enough for her to walk to a cab. She hadn't been able to do anything about her hair, except to take it down and comb it out.

"Here," he said, reaching into the closet and tossing a black baseball-style cap on the foot of the bed. A pair of mirrored sunglasses was already lying there. "Stuff your hair inside. Maybe with the glasses..." He shrugged.

She nodded, grateful for the elements he had added to her disguise, neither of which would be out of place with her outfit. Actually, what she was wearing hadn't looked all that ridiculous when she'd surveyed the finished product in the bathroom mirror.

"I don't know what to do with these," she said, holding up the bridal garments.

"Leave them," he suggested.

She almost smiled at his casual disposal of several thousand dollars worth of designer clothing. And she had thought about that, but if the wedding gown were found in his room, she would have tied him to her. Maybe put him in danger. Because then whoever was looking for her could find out his name.

"I can't," she said, again trying to think of a reason he might believe. "They're not mine," she said finally.

"Not yours?" he questioned, the hint of suspicion clear.

"They belong to a friend."

"You borrowed a wedding dress?"

Which was not all that unusual, she knew, but apparently he'd never heard of the practice. "Not exactly. It belongs to a designer friend. I wore it—" She almost said "as a favor," which would be too revealing. Indicative of the fact that she was someone whose wedding would attract a lot of media attention.

"To save money," she amended.

He nodded. Apparently that was something he understood.

"And I promised to return it," she added. "So I have to."

He seemed to be considering what to do about that, although they both knew the dress wouldn't fit into the black bag, which seemed to be all the luggage he had with him. Finally he walked over to the closet and pulled out the plastic laundry sack the hotel provided, holding it out to her. She'd have to crush the dress to make it fit, but that was better than the alternative.

She dropped the shoes into the bottom and, folding the veil, stuffed it in on top of them. The dress was a harder proposition, but by folding and pushing, she managed to get it in. She looked up when she'd finished, and he held out his hand for the sack.

"You carry the duffel," he suggested.

He was probably right. It would be obvious that the black bag didn't hold a wedding gown. Obvious to anyone who might be looking for one.

She picked up the cap and stuffed her hair into it. Then she slipped on the sunglasses he'd thrown on the foot of the bed, hiding her eyes. Finally she slung the strap of the black bag across her left shoulder, positioning it comfortably on her back.

There was nothing about her appearance that would attract attention. This kind of attire was almost a uniform for a certain segment of the urban young, and with her figure she could still pass for twenty-something. More importantly, she now looked as if she belonged with him. He was a man who would probably be attracted to a woman who would dress in this very casual way, even in the environs of this old and elegant downtown hotel.

He also looked like a man who would be attractive to such a woman. Probably attractive to any woman, she admitted. He looked dangerous. Exciting. And undeniably sexy. Tyler was a little surprised by her own admission.

"Ready?" he asked.

"As ready as I'll ever be," she agreed reluctantly, and watched him open the door.

After he checked out the hall, he signaled for her to join him. The short walk to the elevator and the ride down were thankfully uneventful. Tyler kept her face turned down, the bill of the baseball cap he'd given her shadowing her features.

Her nervousness didn't seem to have rubbed off on her companion. He acted as if what they were doing was routine. There was nothing furtive about his manner, and no one who got on the elevator gave either of them a second glance.

When the doors opened on the lobby, Tyler was aware from the volume of the noise that something was going on. For one thing, it was almost wall-to-wall people. She reached out and grabbed her escort's arm, keeping her head bent and her eyes lowered. She intended to let him lead her past anyone who might be looking for her. However, they could barely push their way off the car. The way across the lobby was blocked by the crowd.

There seemed to be a lot of noise coming from outside, too. The thrump of a helicopter circling overhead. Sirens. Tyler realized only now that she had heard those upstairs, but they were such a familiar background noise in this city that she hadn't paid much attention to the distant wail. Only, the wails weren't distant anymore. They were loud, really loud, because they all seemed to be converging on this building.

"Something's happened outside," her companion said under his breath. Tyler raised her eyes and found he was looking toward the row of glass doors under the striped awnings at the front of the lobby. When she turned, she realized he was right.

The sidewalk was crowded with people, including a lot of men in Middle Eastern garb and members of the media. There were also cops, uniformed and not. To someone who had lived in New York City as long as Tyler had, however, they were as obviously cops as if they'd been sporting badges.

"What is it?" she asked, shaken by her growing realization of what had happened, still hoping somehow she was wrong.

"Something out on the street," he said. "But it seems connected with the hotel. They're not letting anyone leave."

Her heart plummeted. Her fingers tightened convulsively on his arm, and he glanced down. She met his eyes, glad that the fear in hers would be hidden by the dark lenses. Glad that he wouldn't be able to read what else was almost certain to be in them—knowledge of exactly what was going on outside and an immediate, sharp increase in her terror, which had begun to ease with his steady confidence.

"What do we do?" she asked, desperate now to get out of here. She couldn't change what had occurred. All she could do was try to protect herself.

"See anybody you know?" her companion asked, his own eyes scanning the lobby.

The men in Amir's room? she wondered. And then her brain began to function. He meant the wedding party. Her gaze also circled the waiting throng, searching. He was right, she realized. No one was being allowed to leave the hotel.

As a result the lobby was filled with angry people, suitcases beside them as they waited for permission to leave. Permission to catch their trains or planes. She wondered if anyone had taken time to explain to them what was going on.

"By the far doors," she said, recognizing a familiar figure in the sea of strangers. It was Susan Brooker, conspicuous because of the bridesmaid's dress she wore. Susan's attention was on whatever drama was unfolding outside the glass doors.

Tyler also discovered that there were several of Amir's men in the lobby, dark eyes searching the milling crowd. And she knew who *they* were looking for. "Can't we go out the back?" she asked, trying to keep her voice steady, to control the surging panic.

"I don't think they're letting anyone out. Not from any entrance. If they were, this mob would already be gone."

Of course they weren't. She knew, even if he didn't, what the cops were looking for. They were looking for an assassin. Searching for a murderer. Murderers, she amended. Murderers whose faces she had seen. For one split second, at least.

And those men might be here in the lobby. Looking for someone who was the right height. The right build. The right—

"Come on," her companion ordered softly.

He turned, pulling her with him since her fingers were still fastened in a death grip around his arm. He plowed politely, but with purpose, through the angry crowd. They had fought their way across the lobby before Tyler realized where he was headed.

"Wait a minute," she protested when he finally stopped at the door of the Grill Room, the most casual of the hotel's five restaurants. Even if he thought they couldn't get out, she wasn't going to sit down and eat.

"I'm not going in there," she said.

"You want out of the hotel, don't you?" he asked.

"Yes," she agreed, wondering what he was planning.

"Then come on," he said.

"What are you going to do?" she asked.

"Get us out," he said simply.

It sounded as if he thought he knew exactly how to do

that. The calm surety was in his voice again, and because she didn't know what else to do, Tyler followed him.

The dark pub-style restaurant didn't seem as affected by the commotion out front as the rest of the hotel. The waiters were still moving about, and there were a few people sitting at the tables, finishing brunch or talking over coffee.

"Something in the back," Tyler's companion requested of the hostess. "And give us a few minutes alone before you send a waiter," he added softly.

The woman's eyes assessed what she could see of Tyler's face, hidden by the cap and dark glasses, and then came back to his. She smiled in understanding. "Right this way."

The table she led them to was about as far away from the hubbub out front as they could hope for, in a dark corner not far from swinging doors that apparently led to the kitchen. Tyler slipped into the chair that faced them, her back to the rest of the room. She slid the black bag off her shoulder as the hostess put down menus and left them alone. Tyler glanced up to find the blue-eyed man, watching her from across the table. His eyes, shadowed in the dimness, seemed cold again.

"Anything you want to tell me?" he said, his voice too low for anyone else to hear.

"Like what?" she asked.

He had realized her need to get out of the hotel had something to do with what was going on out front. From there, it wasn't too great a leap to arrive at the possibility that she might know something about what that was. But that was the key he was missing. He didn't know what had happened to cause the excitement, so he couldn't begin to guess what she'd seen.

"That's a hell of a lot of commotion for a runaway bride."

"That doesn't have anything to do with me," she denied.

She hated to lie to him. She wasn't good at lying, but

it probably didn't matter. He hadn't believed anything she'd said from the beginning, and yet he'd still agreed to help her.

His eyes were still trained on her face. "Eventually you'll have to trust someone," he warned softly.

"I thought you were going to get us out of here," she reminded him, ignoring the invitation to confide. But God, it was tempting. So damn tempting she had to lock her teeth into her tongue to keep the story in. He nodded, still studying her face, but thankfully he didn't push it.

"Distraction," he said. "I'll provide it and then you go. Your best shot is through that door."

He gestured to his left with a tilt of his head, not even looking in that direction. Apparently he had already checked everything out. Tyler turned to see what he meant. There was a set of double glass doors that led to a side street. Outside them, his back to the restaurant, stood a uniformed policeman.

"There's only one guy out there, and a lot of confusion," her companion stated. "He's not going to be able to handle everyone. And they'll concentrate on the front."

"What are you going to do?" Nothing he was saying made much sense, although he acted as if it did.

He ignored the question. "Don't hesitate," he ordered. "Just go. The first couple of minutes are crucial. When you get outside, mingle with the crowds. Go in whatever direction the most people seem to be headed. Get in the middle of the pack, and whatever you do, don't look back. Just walk. Your normal stride. Head up. None of that eyes-on-the-ground crap you pulled in the lobby. When you're a few blocks away, grab a cab or get on the subway."

"Where are you going?" she asked. She had thought they would go out together. He'd get a cab and drop her on his way to the airport. That had been the plan upstairs.

"I'll be heading in the opposite direction," he said. The corners of his mouth lifted slightly, just as they had before.

"I don't have any money," she said.

He stood, reaching into the front pocket of his jeans, and laid a few folded bills on the table beside her. She picked them up without looking at them and pushed them into the breast pocket of the shirt she was wearing.

"You understand what you're going to do?" he asked.

She nodded, and then, compelled by what he was doing for her, she offered an explanation he couldn't possibly understand, and probably didn't really want to hear. "I didn't have anything to do with what happened," she whispered. "I told you the truth. I want you to know that. But…I saw them."

Despite her previous intention not to involve him any more than was necessary in her danger, she hadn't been able to resist adding the last. It was an opening if he wanted to take it. Not exactly a request for his help, but an admission that there was more to this than she'd told him. *You'll have to trust somebody,* he had said. Apparently she had chosen to trust him, and she waited for his reaction.

The blue eyes rested on her face a moment, but he made no verbal response. Finally he stepped across the space that separated them and put the plastic laundry sack stuffed with the wedding dress beside her chair.

Without straightening, he gripped the arms of the chair she was sitting in, and then he leaned down—slowly, his eyes still examining her face. Tyler realized she was closer to him than she had ever been before, close enough that she could smell the hotel's soap and shampoo, the same subtle scents that had dominated the steamy bathroom upstairs.

There was something totally different, however, about the current effect of those aromas. Because now they were emanating from a strongly masculine body in very close proximity to hers.

She honestly had no idea what he intended, but she was fascinated enough that she didn't move, didn't even think about protesting his unexpected nearness. Maybe, she thought, there were some last-minute instructions he didn't want to chance anyone else overhearing.

His head began to lower. She watched, almost mesmerized, as his mouth opened, tilting to align itself to fit over hers. Only then did she realize what was about to happen.

His lips were warm. Despite the fact that they appeared hard and thin, they were unbelievably soft, lingering a heartbeat over hers before they applied pressure. When they did, the sensation was incredibly sensuous.

It created an anticipation she hadn't felt in too many years. The feelings that suddenly flooded her body had almost been forgotten—the same expectation she had felt before all the firsts in her life, so intense this time it was frightening. She had never felt anything like this when Amir kissed her. Or anyone else, she acknowledged, surprised by that realization.

After only a few seconds, his tongue pushed into her mouth, seeking contact with hers. Later she would wonder if, in that small hesitation, he had deliberately given her an opportunity to deny him. And when she didn't take it…couldn't take it…

His kiss was expert. And thorough. She had been kissed by a lot of men, but never by one who was so ruthlessly in control of what was happening. Or so sensually dominant. His hands never left the arms of her chair. His body was not making contact with hers, but his mouth ravaged until there was nothing left for her to do but respond. Respond with all the emotions that were surging through her. That was automatic. Unthinking. It was as if she had been unconsciously considering the possibility of this man kissing her the entire time she'd known him. Preparing for it.

And she wasn't ready for the kiss to be over when his head finally lifted away, the dampness his mouth had left on hers causing her lips to cling to his a second, as if they, too, were reluctant for this to be over.

In unspoken protest of his desertion, she put the fingers of her left hand against his cheek, almost desperate to hold on to him in some way. His skin was freshly shaved, but still rough under her fingertips. Completely and obviously masculine.

The blue eyes looking down into hers were unfathomable—not cold and yet not filled with the same searing heat of desire she had briefly been allowed to see before. They seemed almost questioning. As if he were as disconcerted by what had just happened between them as she was?

Slowly her thumb traced across his bottom lip, touching the gleam of moisture her tongue had left. She wanted his mouth over hers again. She was hoping his head would lower as it had before. Hoping...

Instead, abruptly breaking the spell he'd created, he straightened his elbows, lifting his body away from hers in one smooth progression and releasing the arms of her chair. Almost in the same motion, he turned and picked up the duffel bag at her side.

He slung it over his shoulder, and then, without looking at her again, he walked unhurriedly toward the doors that led to the kitchen. He pushed through them as if he had the right.

She watched him disappear, still disoriented by the unexpected kiss. By the depth of the feelings it had aroused. Need. Loneliness. Desire. And a hunger she hadn't even been aware existed until he had tantalizingly answered it.

Gradually, she began to think again, to wonder what would happen next. He hadn't told her what to expect. She had no idea what—

Even considering what he *had* told her, she hadn't been expecting the noise that erupted, and it took a second for her brain to register its meaning. But if she hadn't, the people rushing out of the kitchen would have given her all the information she needed.

From the first shout of "Fire," people in the restaurant began to respond. That warning, along with the alarm, was too much to ignore. Or else the shouted word broke the paralysis that the unexpected volume of the fire alarm had caused.

Tyler picked up the plastic bag, remembering her instructions. The first minutes would be crucial, he'd said. Because this was unexpected, of course. Even for the cops. There weren't that many people in the restaurant to begin with, but panicked, they made quite a crowd trying to push their way out that side entrance. Too many for the single cop to restrain, even if he'd had the presence of mind to try.

Despite everything that had happened, Tyler almost smiled as she moved out into the mob in the street. The same thing must be happening with the people in the lobby. They, too, it seemed, were flooding out of the hotel, their determination overpowering the flustered cops.

It had all been as easy as the blue-eyed man had promised. Everything had gone exactly as he had said it would. She resisted the impulse to look for him, keeping her head up and her eyes straight ahead, exactly as he'd told her. There was no challenge. No rifle shot. There was nothing except the normal flow of traffic and the crowds.

It took her only minutes to walk the six blocks she had decided on. Only an additional minute to hail a cab. When she was safely inside, she couldn't resist the urge to look back.

She didn't know what she had been looking for, but whatever it was, she didn't find it. There was no one following her. Not the men she had seen. No one from the wedding party. Certainly not the man with the cold blue eyes.

Chapter Four

Although Hawk had been conscious of a bone-deep fatigue throughout the short flight from New York to Virginia, he had refused to think about it. Or the reasons behind it. There was, after all, one more thing he had to do—one last step on this journey he had willingly begun more than six months ago. Then and only then would it be over.

He had concentrated so long on his quest for revenge, blocking everything else from his mind, that it was difficult to give himself permission to remember the other. To focus on Griff's life, rather than on the senseless brutality of his death. And as he walked across the tree-shaded tranquillity of the vast cemetery, its quietness crosshatched by miles and miles of simple markers, Hawk thought that maybe, in some strange way, this would be the proper place to finally do that.

Griff Cabot had known all the dark and dirty secrets the powerful of the world hide. A cold-war warrior, he had been left behind on the empty battlefield of a war that supposedly had already been won.

"We seem to be the only ones left who understand the world is still a dangerous place for freedom," Griff would say, smiling a little to lessen the reality of all he asked of the team through the years. *"Think of what you're doing as sentry duty. Standing guard over the things you love."* Standing guard. And now, for Hawk, and for the rest of

them as well, that duty, that sacred responsibility, was over.

He topped the slight rise that looked down on the area of the cemetery he sought. From where he stood, he could see a figure standing beside the small granite stone that marked Griff Cabot's grave. A woman, slender and blond, wearing a sleeveless black dress. Her hair had been gathered in a chignon low on the back of her neck, but the breeze whipped strands of it free. As he watched, she raised her hand and, turning her head, pushed an errant tendril away. Turning enough that he could see her face.

Claire Heywood, Hawk realized. Although he had never met her, there was no doubt in his mind of the identification. And no doubt that her being here was the last thing Griff would have wanted. Cabot had taken a lot of precautions to insure that there was nothing about his relationship with Claire that was open or known, nothing that could possibly expose her to his enemies.

Hawk stopped beside one of the massive trees that shaded the rise, still far enough away that he could be sure she would remain unaware of his presence. He didn't want to intrude on her grief. His own could wait. It had waited, his emotions carefully controlled, for over six months. Another few minutes wouldn't make any difference in what he had come here to do.

He watched as the woman Griff Cabot had loved reached out to touch the top of the granite marker. Using it for balance, she stooped down beside the grave and placed something on the grass. Then her hand lifted to the stone, fingers slowly tracing over the letters that had been cut into it.

Touching Griff's name, Hawk realized. His throat closed suddenly, painfully hard and tight. His lips flattened, fighting the emotional pull. He didn't want to be a witness to this. Griff Cabot had been his friend. He and the team had been the only family Hawk had ever known, sharing a bond of brotherhood stronger than that of blood, perhaps because it had been forged in secrecy and death. In their dependence on one another.

The woman at the grave bowed her head, fingers still touching the stone marker. *At least,* Hawk thought, watching her, *at least I don't have to live with regret.*

Claire Heywood had chosen to break all ties with Cabot only a few months before his death. No one on the team had talked much about it, of course, especially not Griff, but Hawk imagined most of them had come to their own conclusion about what had happened. Hawk had. He believed that two people with very differing views of the world had fallen deeply in love. And because of those differences, the relationship had been impossible.

Finally Claire's hand fell away from the face of the stone, and then she stood, looking down a long moment on the grave. She turned away and began to walk toward Hawk, another mourner in a place that had, through the years, seen millions come and go. She did not look back at the grave of the man who was, here at least, only another soldier, fallen in his country's wars.

Her eyes met Hawk's as she climbed the slope. She nodded slightly as she passed by, but they didn't speak. After all, they were strangers, and she could have no idea that he was here for the same reasons that had drawn her to this place.

Hawk waited a long time before he finally walked down to the grave. As he approached, he realized there was a blotch of what appeared to be blood on the smooth green lawn. When he reached the marker, however, Hawk saw that the spot of crimson was a rose, widely opened in the oppressive heat of the Virginia summer. A few of the petals had dropped and scattered, maybe as Claire Heywood placed it on the ground.

Hawk's lips tilted. No one would have been more amused by the romantic absurdity than Griff, he thought. And then Hawk's smile faded because he knew that wasn't true. Not true simply because the rose had been left by the woman Griff loved.

Hawk looked down at the wilted flower, again fighting the release of emotions he had so long controlled. Losing that battle, he finally allowed his blurring eyes to move upward to the letters Claire Heywood had traced in the face of the stone. Brutally new. Too sharp. Like his grief.

Below Griff's name, engraved in Latin, was a single sentence: *Dulce et decorum est pro patria mori.* A strange inscription for someone as coldly rational as Cabot. *Sweet and proper to die for your country?* Again his lips tilted as Hawk remembered Griff's hardheaded pragmatism.

He wondered who had chosen that epitaph. Someone at the agency? It sounded like them. Of course, it didn't matter what they put on the stone. Griff Cabot's memorial had been written in the lives he had touched. Including Hawk's. And in the continued strength of the country he had loved and protected.

Standing guard, Hawk thought again. And then the long brown fingers that had closed unerringly around the trigger of that rifle in Baghdad closed again over what *he* had brought to lay on Griff's grave. He bent, placing the casing of the bullet with which he had taken revenge for Cabot's murder beside the wilting rose. The pairing was as incongruous maybe as Claire and Griff's had been. But even so, they belonged together. Here, at least.

"Rest in peace, my friend," Hawk said, the same words he had whispered in Baghdad. And finally, it was truly over.

QUITE A CONTRAST to where he'd spent last night, Hawk thought, pitching the black bag onto the narrow bed. It bounced a little as it hit the sagging mattress, and his mind flashed back to the scene in the hotel room this morning. To the image of this same bag on another bed. To a woman reaching for it, the lapels of the robe she wore falling open, exposing the beginning swell of ivory breasts and the shad-owed valley between.

The tightening in his groin caused Hawk to destroy the image, to wipe it out of his mind with that practiced con-trol. Despite the length of his sexual abstinence, he still wasn't sure why he had reacted so strongly to that woman. The same way he was reacting now, simply to the memory of her.

He wasn't an adolescent. He had gone for longer periods without sex, his mind too absorbed by a mission to think about his physical needs. And after all, she was nothing like his normal taste in women. Nothing like any woman he'd ever known, he admitted. Out of his realm of expe-rience, which, he acknowledged without any pride or ar-rogance, was extensive.

Hawk's mouth tightened, remembering the way she had reacted to his insultingly prolonged appraisal of her body. Remembering his own reaction, that powerful surge of sex-ual hunger. And remembering the kiss.

That had been intended to exorcise the demons she'd created. The decision to kiss her had probably been as insulting as his deliberate examination of her body. But it had become something else. Maybe because her response had been totally unexpected.

He could still feel her fingers resting against his cheek, expressing a tenderness that was light-years away from his usual encounters with women. About as far as this dingy apartment was removed from the luxury of the hotel where he had slept last night, he thought, taking a deep breath.

This was his reality. And it was past time for him to get back to it, he decided, pushing the memory of the woman out of his head. He punched the button on his answering machine to play the single message left during the long weeks he'd been gone.

Hawk didn't have the kind of friends who left messages. It was a pastime too dangerous in their line of work. The one on the machine was short and impersonal.

''This is Mike down at Ken's Electronics. Just calling to tell you your VCR's ready.'' That was followed by a phone number, and then the computer voice of Hawk's answering machine gave a date and time. The message had been left a couple of days before. About the same time he had been boarding a plane in Athens to fly back to the States, Hawk realized.

He hadn't left a VCR for repair, of course, although there was a Ken's Electronics in this small Virginia town. And if anyone bothered to check, the repair shop would probably even have a VCR, held in the same name Hawk had used to rent this apartment. *If* anyone bothered to check.

He took another breath, trying to think. He was aware again of his fatigue—too extreme to be explained by his activities the last few days. Despite jet lag, he had even slept last night, thanks to the help of half a bottle of pretty good bourbon. That wasn't his normal remedy for insomnia, but at the time it had seemed an appropriate ending to the success of the mission he'd undertaken. Celebrating alone, in a place Griff had loved.

At least the whiskey had kept him from having to think about what came next, and eventually it had let him sleep, so he shouldn't be feeling this exhaustion. This…mental lethargy. This letdown. However, the only plan he'd been able to formulate on the flight home was to report in, take a long, hot shower and then sleep for a couple of days.

He needed the shower. It seemed years since this morning's, and a lot had happened in the meantime. His mind had insisted on replaying all of it during the plane ride. He still didn't know what had occurred to cause the excitement at the hotel. There hadn't been enough time for the papers at the airport to have gotten the story out. Besides, Hawk hadn't really cared, not beyond an idle curiosity.

The woman he had helped wasn't his responsibility. The fact that he had taken the trouble to get her out of the situation was still surprising to him, because he was not by nature given to playing Good Samaritan. The hard lips tilted at that thought. Very few people would classify Hawk as a Good Samaritan. At least not those who knew him professionally. And there weren't any who knew him any other way. The man called Hawk was a loner, by inclination and preference.

The image of the woman's face reappeared in his mind's eye, her voice sincere, almost apologetic, violet eyes pleading. *"I didn't have anything to do with what happened out there,"* she had said. *"I want you to know that. But...I saw them."*

Well, good for you, Hawk thought cynically, denying the pull of that appeal, just as he had when she'd made it. *Whatever you saw sure as hell is nothing to me. Nothing to do with me. You just keep running, sweetheart, and maybe if you're lucky, you'll even get away.*

Hawk turned from the answering machine, denying the strength of those memories: the length of long, shapely legs, the shadowed cleavage between the high breasts, even the remembrance of the way her lips had felt moving against his. There was no room in his life for those. Someone had left him a message, left it in such a way that he understood it meant trouble. Probably official trouble for him. That was nothing he hadn't been expecting.

Reluctantly Hawk left the stifling apartment where, during his brief stay, he hadn't even bothered to turn on the air-conditioning, and walked a few blocks. He picked the middle phone booth out of a row that stood on an isolated corner.

There wasn't much traffic, but his blue eyes continued to scan both it and the streets around him as he punched in a number. He wondered briefly who would answer, which of them would have gone to the trouble to call.

Not Griff, he thought, his throat tightening. Never again would Griff Cabot issue an order or debrief him after a mission. Compliment him on a job well done. Talk to him as a friend. Or issue a warning, he thought, listening to the distant ringing.

"Hawk," he said as soon as he heard someone pick up. His eyes were still searching the street around him.

"Don't even think about coming in."

Hawk recognized the deep voice. He supposed he should have known who it would be. "What's going on?" he asked.

"They know about Baghdad," Jordan Cross said.

There had been no doubt in Hawk's mind they would figure that out. His skill was its own signature, and given the target, they wouldn't have needed much help to finger him as the shooter.

"Okay," he said simply. He would have to take that heat. It had been an unsanctioned hit. Diplomatically, his target had been off-limits, and the State Department would be in an uproar.

Hawk had never even hesitated over the possible repercussions—political or personal. Not once he had been certain in his own mind that his victim had been responsible for Griff's death. And for the deaths of the others who had died in that senseless massacre. Secretaries and clerks. People who had nothing to do with the clandestine work of the CIA. A lot of innocent people who had died so those bastards could make some kind of political statement.

If it came down to it, Hawk could prove that the man he had taken out had been responsible for those deaths. He had made sure he had that proof. He thought it might buy him a little forgiveness, despite the current climate in the government about the team and its mission.

"And they've tied you to what happened at the hotel in New York this morning," Jordan continued. "Maybe just their way of justifying the knives that were already out."

There was a question implied by the last, but Hawk said nothing in response, thinking instead about the import of that. *"What happened at the hotel in New York this morn-*

ing.'' He still didn't know, and up to this point he hadn't cared.

His decision to help the woman had been quixotic and unplanned. He had the skills, so he had used them. But if he were going to get the blame for something, he figured he ought to take the trouble to find out exactly what it was he was supposed to have done.

"You do that one?" Cross asked.

A friend's voice, Hawk reminded himself. *A friend's question. No blame involved. Simply a request for the truth.*

"It wasn't me," he said. He knew, of course, what "that one" implied, so the situation he hadn't cared enough to find out about suddenly became a little clearer.

"They're putting you in the hotel. Right in the middle of the thing. They even have pictures. Watch yourself. They're dead serious about this."

"Thanks for the warning." Hawk acknowledged his debt, while ignoring the unintended irony of the adjective Jordan had used.

"We owe you," the disembodied voice responded.

"Nobody owes me anything," Hawk declared harshly. "It was personal. Just for Griff," he added softly, trying to modify the unintended sharpness of his voice.

That was true. He probably couldn't explain to anyone what Griff Cabot's friendship had meant to him. Maybe he didn't have to, he thought. Not to this man, at least.

"I just thought you should know you're not alone. You can call in a lot of favors for what you did. If you need them."

Hawk had been a loner too long to believe he would ever need anyone's help. The corners of his lips inched upward fractionally, but his voice when he spoke reflected none of that amusement. "I'll keep that in mind," he said. Then, without saying goodbye, he placed the receiver back on the hook.

They've tied you to what happened in New York this

morning. He still didn't have any idea to what—or rather to *whom*—they had tied him. Obviously something they believed they could use to get rid of him, without having to admit he had been justified in what he'd done in Iraq.

The blue eyes searched the area around the phones. Then the man called Hawk stepped away from the one he had chosen and crossed the street to the neighborhood newsstand. Once there, it wasn't hard to figure out what they had fingered him for. All the afternoon editions carried the story, even the locals.

The man called Hawk didn't make many mistakes. In his line of work, one was usually the total allotment. That first mistake was very often the last an operative got a chance to make. And he had made his, Hawk thought in disgust, scanning the long columns of text. A hell of one, apparently.

Sheer fluke? Accident? A simple case of being in the wrong place at the wrong time? Except Hawk didn't believe much in coincidences. Not even violet-eyed ones who begged for his help. Maybe especially not that kind.

He had been so damn sure no one could know he was in New York, absolutely certain no one could have traced his movements from Baghdad. And maybe they hadn't. It was always possible someone had recognized him when he checked in and decided to make the most of the opportunity. He couldn't be sure at this point how it had come about, but someone had played him for a fool.

Hawk had known she was good, had acknowledged it from the first, but still he had gone along for the ride. Not many people through the years had succeeded in taking advantage of him. Not many had had guts enough to try.

They probably had him on video, he realized. That's what Cross meant about pictures. The hotel's security cameras. A grainy black-and-white image of one of the government's top covert operatives—a highly specialized black ops agent—walking through the lobby of the hotel where this morning's assassination had been carried out.

Whoever the hell that woman was, she had gotten him. Despite his initial instinct that she hadn't been telling the truth. She had set him up, exactly as she'd been sent to do. And because of that aberration in his normally careful behavior, they were going to pin this assassination on him.

I must be getting old, Hawk thought, shaking his head in disbelief. But despite his participation in his own destruction, he thought somebody owed him an explanation. And he might as well start looking for one from the person who had suckered him in. The woman with the violet eyes.

TYLER PUT HER PURSE and the battered bag on the bed. The suitcase she'd picked out at the pawnshop where she'd hocked the wedding gown and her engagement ring looked right at home. But the Louis Vuitton purse she'd gone by her apartment to retrieve when she left the hotel looked totally out of place.

She had taken a dangerous chance, she knew, remembering the pounding at the front door as she'd climbed out the window and hurried, knees shaking, down the fire escape. It had been a long way down, especially carrying the laundry bag and the purse. But she had known she'd need some ID to show the airlines, and the purse also contained her credit cards. She had transferred the essentials to the new purse Amir had bought for the honeymoon. She hadn't thought she'd need her social security card or her credit cards, so thankfully they were still in this one.

She pushed her fingers into the mattress of the bed, feeling it sag, hearing the reminiscent, metallic creak of the springs. She had spent the first seventeen years of her life in this room. And not much had changed about it, she thought.

But change always came slowly to Covington. Despite the proliferation of fast-food places and discount stores, she had had no trouble finding her way from the interstate exit to the front door. The tree-shaded dwellings she passed on the way had seemed exactly the same, except for the colors of their paint or the variety of flowers wilting in their beds.

Even the thick humidity was exactly as she remembered. Lying in this bed, night after night, trying to sleep despite the heat. The double windows would be open to let in any stirring of the heavy air, and the tree frogs would be almost loud enough to drown out the sound of her parents' fighting. Almost loud enough.

She took a breath, pushing those memories away. She interlocked the fingers of her hands at the base of her skull, slipping them under her hair and lifting it off her neck. She could feel the perspiration underneath the heavy mass of curls. She pulled her elbows forward and then pushed them back to stretch out the tiredness that had settled between her shoulders.

As tired as she was, however, she wondered if she'd be able to sleep in the heat. Despite the money Tyler had sent home through the years, there was still no air-conditioning. Of course, Aunt Martha hadn't been much inclined to change, either. No more than the rest of Covington.

When her great-aunt had died in her sleep, at age ninety, Tyler had come home to make arrangements for the funeral. Instead of staying at the house, however, she had checked into one of the motels on the interstate. Before she returned to New York, she'd made arrangements for someone to clean the house, but she still hadn't gotten around to putting it on the market.

She didn't really understand why she hesitated. Leaving this place twenty years ago had been no less an escape than the one she had made from New York this morning. Not just an escape from Aunt Martha and her eternal predictions of hellfire and damnation, but an escape from almost everything that had happened while she lived in this room.

Her mother and father had married because she was already on the way, and they had both, at one time or another, expressed regret over their union. As a child, she had blamed herself for the unhappiness that permeated the very walls of this house. It had echoed in the darkness as she lay in this bed, night after night, trying to ignore their angry voices. Their endless quarreling.

Her father had left for good when she was five. The shouting recriminations had disappeared, replaced by a grinding poverty, of body and soul, that her mother had never escaped. That's when Aunt Martha had come to live with them. To help out, she used to tell people. To take care of the child.

Tyler took another breath, realizing she had allowed herself to be drawn again into the past. Back to the sermons and restrictions and endless punishments. To the constant reiteration that she was simply a cross her great-aunt had shouldered because it was her Christian duty. Again, it had been made abundantly clear to Tyler that she was an unwanted burden. When her mother died, she had felt she'd lost the only person who had really ever loved her. She had taken what was left in the bank account and run. As fast and as far as she could.

And yet today, when she had stood at the reservation desk at the airport, trying to think where she could go, where she'd be safe, she'd been drawn back here by the sense of sanctuary this house always seemed to provide.

When she was a little girl, playing in someone else's yard, she would often lose track of the time. Then, as shadows lengthened with the quick fall of summer night, she would run across lawns rich with the scent of mown grass, and over the rough warmth of sidewalks. Familiar textures under her bare feet.

In the distance she would hear her mother calling, and she would fly toward the sound of that beloved voice, ignoring the lights that reached from the open windows of the houses she passed. And as soon as she climbed the steps of the front porch, she would know she was safe. Safe from the shadows. From the imagined terrors of the night. Safe from everything.

Tyler had felt something of that same relief when she drove the rental car into the yard at twilight and parked it in the graveled driveway, right under the oak tree, which had once held a rope swing. Her swing. Her yard. Her mother's house.

She realized that she was still standing beside the narrow bed, and the room was in almost total darkness now. She reached out and clicked on the bedside lamp, welcoming its glow as another escape from shadows, those of memory this time.

The base of the lamp was in the shape of a ballerina, arms reaching upward toward the bulb and pointed toes arching on the tarnished brass stand. The deep rose of its shade softened the ugliness of the room, just as it always had.

Tyler ran the tips of her fingers slowly down the porcelain of the dancer's body. There had never been enough money for lessons, of course, but that hadn't kept her from dancing. Moving in a awkward parody of ballet around this crowded room. Pretending she was the ballerina on the lamp.

Despite the poverty of her existence, nothing had ever stopped Tyler from pretending. She had had so many dreams, and most of them had been born in this room. She would lie in this bed, listening to the bitter voices, and gradually block them out with the glittering, impossible visions in her imagination.

Images of what she would be when she was grown. Of where she would travel. Exotic places, always so far from this town, this house. Images of when she would finally be *somebody*. Little-girl dreams.

Which had almost all come true, she thought with a sense of wonder. Perhaps desperation *was* the mother of ambition. *Lives of quiet desperation.* She couldn't remember who had said that, but it fit the ones that had been lived in this house.

What a useless and maudlin journey into the past, she

thought, shaking her head. She walked over to the windows and pushed them open, hoping for a breeze. Instead, the familiar scent of honeysuckle whispered into the stifling room.

How long had it had been since she had tasted the single drop of sweetness at the end of a honeysuckle stamen? That had been another childhood game, one that required no expenditure of her mother's hard-earned money. Tyler had been good at those. Imagination was free, and hers had been her savior.

A trill of childish laughter floated in, the distant sound traveling clearly through the soft twilight shadows. This rural Mississippi night didn't seem any different from those of twenty years ago. The child she had once been had come home. Running from shadows. From the darkness. From her own fears and terrors.

But this time those were not imagined. She had bought an afternoon paper at the airport, almost furtive about the ordinary purchase when she had seen the headline. The assassination of Sheikh Rashad al-Ahmad had been front page news.

And only now, locked inside this house, so far from that hotel in New York, was she beginning to feel safe again. She had taken all the precautions she could think of to keep anyone from finding her. She had paid cash for the plane ticket, and it had been issued in her real name. She had used her social security card, which had never been changed, as identification.

She hadn't been Tommie Sue Prator in over twenty years, and thankfully none of the silly stories Paul had told made reference to the realities of this life. So she should be safe, she told herself. At least for tonight, and tomorrow she'd be able to think about what she should do.

She would have to go to the authorities, she had finally realized, as she read the paper on the plane. They were equipped to sort out guilt and innocence. She didn't have to accuse, but she *did* have to tell them what she'd seen.

She was standing in front of the open window, her arms crossed over her breasts, running her palms slowly up and down her upper arms as if she were cold. As if the breath of air that brought the scent of the honeysuckle into the room had been the least bit cooling.

Until she had returned to this reality, to being Tommie Sue again, she hadn't realized that the life she had been living was like some fantastic dream. Amir. The limitless wealth. His whirlwind courtship and the hurried arrangements for the wedding. His father's assassination.

Those things were from a world so far away it had no relation to the dingy wallpaper and the sagging mattresses of this one. Almost no relation to her. Certainly no relation to who she really was. They seemed literally from another universe. An alternate reality. And that realization was comforting. It added a little to the sense of sanctuary she had found.

Despite the heat, she shivered, thinking about those men on the terrace. Seeing the rifle swing away from the man who had just been killed and toward her. Determined not to give in to her fears, however, she turned away from the open windows and the outside darkness. As she did, she caught a glimpse of motion in the mirror of her great-grandmother's dresser, and it stopped her.

The face that had graced dozens of magazine covers, its paleness highlighted by the shadows behind, stared back at her from the age-clouded glass. The famous violet eyes were wide and dark, of no discernible color in the gloom.

No reason at all to be afraid here, she assured herself again, fighting another involuntary shiver. *No reason at all.*

IT HADN'T TAKEN HAWK LONG to find his mystery woman. He had some advantages, of course. Computers made this kind of search easy and fast. As always, he was surprised at the amount of information available about the lives of ordinary people. And at how simple it was to find it. He had started with the story she had told him about running away from her wedding. He had assumed it was a lie and there would be nothing in it worth pursuing. What he found was something very different.

There *had* been a wedding scheduled to take place at the hotel today, and that wedding was the reason Sheikh Rashad al-Ahmad had come to New York. To attend a civil ceremony between his oldest son and heir, Amir, and a woman named Tyler Stewart.

The slowly materializing images on the screen, appearing in answer to his requests, confirmed that Tyler Stewart was indeed the woman who had entered his hotel room. Some of the pictures were prewedding publicity shots, but most came from the covers of magazines or ad campaigns in which she'd appeared. In those she was tastefully, and yet somehow almost always provocatively posed, showing off the body he'd examined today.

Her attitude in these pictures was quite a contrast to the modesty she'd displayed when he'd broken down the door. An act? he wondered. If so, she was a damn fine actress. But he had already figured out that much, Hawk acknowledged ruefully.

As he continued to read, he realized that at least another one of his initial impressions had also been correct. Tyler Stewart was totally outside his previous experiences with women. Successful, with a long international career, she was probably very well off in her own right. Not in comparison to her bridegroom, Hawk thought, but certainly in comparison to him.

And her wedding had lured al-Ahmad the father out of his desert stronghold and right into the sights of an assassin. His son was already blaming extremists. The sheikh had been the target of coups in the past, including a couple of assassination attempts. If the hastily arranged wedding had been set up simply to provide the opportunity for another…

Then someone was working in league with the fundamentalists. Nothing Hawk read about playboy Amir al-Ahmad indicated that he was interested in pursuing *Sharia,* the Moslem equivalent of the straight and narrow. And after all, if a fundamentalist revolution succeeded in his country, as it had in Iran, no one would have more to lose than Amir. Which brought Hawk back to the other party in this wedding. Right back to Tyler Stewart.

Since no one had yet thought to cancel his clearances, Hawk had access to databases that would have been difficult for the average searcher to utilize, but he still couldn't find anything to tie Stewart to the extremists. However, information about her background before she began modeling was vague and contradictory. Apparently she had told a variety of stories about her past.

And according to the papers, no one had seen her since the assassination. The reporters who had broached the subject to Amir al-Ahmad had gotten some story about her being overcome by shock and sorrow. Which might be true.

But maybe, Hawk thought, she had done just exactly what she'd told him she was going to—get out of the hotel and away. Just exactly what she had conned him into helping her do. At the same time putting him on the hotel security tapes.

When he checked, however, there was no Tyler Stewart listed as a passenger on any of the flights out of the New York area this afternoon. He did run across a name on one of the lists that triggered a memory. Something he'd seen when he was researching her background. And when Hawk backtracked, he found it. Just what he had been looking for.

When he left the university computer center, Hawk went straight to the bus station in Alexandria, where he retrieved his emergency kit from the locker he'd rented. The small nylon gym bag contained money and everything else Hawk would need to create a new identity.

He used part of the cash to purchase a change of clothes

and some toiletries, which he stuffed into the bag. And the other thing Hawk bought with the money was a plane ticket to Mississippi. A ticket that would take him to the same city into which a woman named Tommie Sue Prator had flown this afternoon.

Chapter Five

When Tyler awoke, coming out of sleep too quickly, she had been dreaming about something she knew she should remember. Something she *wanted* to remember. She lay for a long time in the darkness, trying to reenter the fabric of her dream, before she finally admitted it was gone. Irreparably destroyed.

She wondered if that dream could have had anything to do with the man who had kissed her yesterday. She remembered, almost against her will, how his lips had felt. And his tongue, demanding, making slow, heated contact with hers, its movement as controlled and assured as the man himself.

That same heat flooded her body now, stirred by memory. Tyler stretched languidly, savoring the unaccustomed feeling. Still trying to remember if she had been dreaming about him. It had been pleasant, she knew, so she wondered why she had been drawn away. Usually when she awakened like this, jerked from sleep, it was because of a nightmare, something from which her subconscious needed to escape.

She glanced at the clock beside the bed. It was a little after four. Not yet dawn, but the lesser darkness that was its herald. She closed her eyes, but they wouldn't stay closed. The hint of disquietude she had felt on awakening was still here, hiding in the once-familiar shadows of the bedroom.

She rolled onto her side, pushing the limp feather pillow into a more comfortable position, attempting to find a cool spot on its cotton case against which to rest her cheek. She closed her eyes, thinking how easily she had once been able to block out all the unpleasantness of her life.

Now that old magic was gone, swallowed up by the darkness. By the events of yesterday. Or by the fact that the dreams she had once had no longer offered any promise for the future. They represented the past, and she had not been able yet to formulate others for the years that lay ahead.

All she had come up with was her agreement to marry Amir. She was still amazed by the depth of that self-deception. Why had it taken her so long to realize her own motives? And to know how wrong they were? She had been afraid, she admitted. Afraid of whatever came next. Of facing it alone. So she had convinced herself, or let others convince her, that marrying Amir would be smart. Safe. And even moral. Now she knew it would have been none of those things.

She pushed the sheet off her legs and sat up on the edge of the bed. She put her bare feet on the smoothness of the hardwood floor, the only cool surface in the room. With both hands, she lifted her hair off the back of her neck.

It was too hot to sleep. Too hot to get comfortable. Maybe that's why she had awakened. Maybe it was just the heat. Warm milk had been Aunt Martha's standard cure for insomnia. Although the thought was unappealing in the stifling humidity, Tyler decided it was a better solution than worry.

When she entered the dark kitchen, she walked over to the sink and opened the cabinet above it. The glasses were still there, standing upside down in the same sentinel-like rows her aunt had always placed them in. It was not until she picked one up and turned toward the refrigerator that her sleep-dazed brain remembered. All the perishables would have been thrown out.

She went back to the sink, turning on the faucet and letting the water run a few seconds before she put the glass under its stream. When she lifted the water to her lips, the first sip was as familiar as the kitchen, the taste faintly metallic. She turned around, leaning back against the edge of the counter. She lifted the glass again, her eyes drifting across the kitchen.

There were two men standing in the doorway that led onto the back porch. Watching her. Even in the darkness, she could see the gleam of the white robes they wore, although their faces were dark and featureless.

This is the nightmare, she thought. It had to be. They were totally out of place in her mother's kitchen. Out of place in this life. *Nightmare,* she thought again.

Yet some more rational part of her knew it wasn't. They were undeniably real. She could see the two shapes building out of the darkness, robes billowing slightly as they walked.

Coming toward her, she realized. She seemed paralyzed by her fear, caught in that same icy terror in which one waits for the horror of one's own nightmare to become reality.

Then, suddenly, that paralysis released. She raised her hand and threw the glass at them. In the same motion she turned, running toward the door that led to the hallway and the open windows of the bedroom. She knew she didn't have a prayer of reaching those windows before they could get to her, but she also knew she had to try.

She heard the glass shatter half a heartbeat before the first shot sounded. That bullet struck the frame of the door in front of her. She felt flecks of broken wood, which had splintered under its impact, strike her face. She threw up her arm to protect her eyes, the action only a reflex.

She seemed to be moving in slow motion, a journey through a nightmare. Two more shots followed the first, so rapidly one seemed an echo of the other. Then, finally, she was through the door and into the hall. She must have hit her arm on something. She felt it as she skidded around the corner, but despite her awareness of the blow, there was little pain. Just an aftermath of tingling nerve endings.

The bedroom doorway loomed suddenly before her, dark and inviting. A minute more of safety. She slid into it, bare feet seeking traction on the smooth wood of the ancient floor. A hand grabbed at her as she came through the opening, and she fought against its grip.

The hard fingers, closing tight as a vise over her wrist, didn't loosen even as she twisted her arm, prying at them with her other hand. It did no good. Instead, she was pulled to the side and slammed against the wall, her captor's body pressed against hers, holding her prisoner.

At least she'd tried, she thought, trapped behind the solid strength of the man who had caught her. She should have known there would be more of them. That they wouldn't let her get away this time. They had let that happen once, at the hotel. They wouldn't make that mistake again.

Her head hurt from where he had slammed her against the wall. And the arm she had hit coming through the kitchen door was beginning to burn like someone was holding a blowtorch to the back of it. The man leaning against her was too close, deliberately pushing his body into hers so she couldn't move, couldn't breathe. The hard muscles of his back ground into the softness of her breasts.

She eased a shallow inhalation into her starving lungs. Despite her fear, the automatic physiological functions hadn't stopped. Precious air. Maybe one of the last breaths she would draw. Precious, life-sustaining air that smelled like…

She opened her eyes and frantically pushed her head up a fraction of an inch, forcing it up against the back of his muscled shoulder, trying desperately to see. Trying not to hope, not even to imagine…

The man whose body was glued to the front of hers didn't make any verbal response, but suddenly, unbelievingly, there was more pressure. He was pushing her more firmly into the wall, but she had already managed to lift her head far enough that she could see his arm. Outstretched. And in his hand...

She took another breath, this one savoring. Because she had been right. The fragrance she had recognized was the faint scent of the hotel's soap and underlying that... She had to snatch another breath before she could even complete the thought. Underlying that was the very masculine, somehow familiar scent of his body. Closer even than it had been yesterday when he bent to kiss her.

She could feel against her cheek the slight coarseness of the knit shirt he wore. Could see the pale blue of its sleeve. And at the end of that, a corded arm and a hand whose long brown fingers were wrapped around a very big gun.

And that outstretched arm was as steady as it had been yesterday morning, waiting now for those men to follow her through that doorway. With his other hand, the man with the cold blue eyes reached behind him and found her arm, the one she had hit on the frame. He gripped it, right above the elbow, and squeezed gently.

She wasn't sure if that was supposed to be reassurance or a question. But she nodded, head moving against the back of his shoulder, able to move only slightly because of the pressure he was exerting to keep her there. Behind his body. Safe.

He squeezed her arm again. Silent communication. For the first time since she had seen the robed men in the kitchen, hope flooded her heart. Her almost mindless terror eased. She didn't know why he was here, a miracle as inexplicable as finding him in the hotel had been, but somehow she knew he'd keep her safe.

He had his whole concentration fixed on the doorway that led to the hall. Still waiting for someone to come through it. Suddenly he moved. His left arm came around to the front, its hand fastening under the right, which held the big gun, helping to cradle and support its weight. Then she heard what he had heard. Footsteps. Coming toward them down the hall.

She watched as he eased away from the wall, his movements soundless. Unlike whoever had been in the kitchen. But then, they didn't know they had anything to fear. They thought only she was here. Only a woman, hiding in the darkness.

When they came through the doorway, it was worse than anything she could have imagined. The size of the room magnified the sound, and the flashes from the muzzles of the guns, spitting into the darkness like lightning, terrified her. She slid down the wall, putting her hands over her ears.

It seemed to go on a long time, but she knew it lasted only seconds. When it was over, she waited, the total and complete silence left behind almost as frightening as the noise.

Nothing moved in the dark room. There was no sound except her heart, beating in her throat so loudly that it seemed if anyone were left alive after that barrage of gunfire, they would be able to hear it. Finally, she couldn't stand not knowing. She lowered her hands and slowly raised her head.

The man with the blue eyes was still there, standing just where he had been before it all started. The gun he had held was still supported by both hands. His knees were slightly bent, his attention focused on the doorway leading out of the bedroom.

There were no more footsteps there. And she found herself hoping, more fiercely than she had ever hoped for the fulfillment of any of those impossible dreams she had had when she used to sleep in this small dark room. Hoping that the men who had come into her mother's kitchen were dead.

She didn't know how she became aware of movement at the window. She was still looking at his back, the light shirt that stretched across his broad shoulders palely visible in the darkness. Suddenly she saw, peripherally and almost subliminally, that something was at the window. She turned her head, eyes wide, straining against the outside darkness. The flash of motion was white, and so she shouted a warning her brain didn't formulate, her outcry primitive. Instinctive.

"Behind you."

She must have pointed before she screamed. She must have made some betraying movement, because the bullets that sprayed the wall above her head seemed to come almost before her warning. She dropped to the floor, curled into a fetal position, hands attempting to protect her head as pieces of the wall and ceiling rained around her.

The deep cough that answered that assault was familiar now. She had heard it during the earlier exchange, firing steadily, the crack of its echo reverberating in the enclosed space. *His gun,* she thought. Tyler made herself open her eyes. She could still see the pale blue shirt. He had pivoted to face the new threat, squeezing off shots as evenly as he had before.

Two or three. Maybe four. She lost count. But the last one put an end to everything. Whoever had been outside fell into the open window, his body draped limply over the sill, half in and half out, the trailing *gutra* touching the hardwood floor.

Again the silence that fell after all the noise was too profound. She watched the blue-eyed man turn, focusing the gun on the hall again and then swinging it back to the windows. There was no more movement. No footsteps in the hall. No sound in the silence except their breathing. His and hers.

Finally he walked toward her, footsteps crunching over the debris the automatic weapon had cut from the wall and blown across the room. She watched him, long legs in worn jeans materializing out of the darkness. Slowly her gaze climbed upward to his face. His pale blue eyes seemed luminous in the predawn shadows. Her own, pupils wide, were finally able to see him clearly. Same harsh features. Slightly crooked nose.

"I thought the South was famous for hospitality," he said. His tone was prosaic, infinitely calm and touched with amusement.

Hot moisture stung her eyes. Whoever he was, he had saved her life. Again. And he acted as if what had just occurred was a minor inconvenience in what was supposed to have been a visit to a sleepy little Southern town.

She blinked back the tears, ashamed to cry in the face of his nonchalance. His acceptance of the violence that had exploded around them. Of the deaths he had caused. But then, he was used to this, she thought, shivering. Accustomed to death? He must be, to do what he had just done.

He *was* dangerous. She had known that yesterday. And he was fully capable of dealing with all this. With these people. She was not. Nothing in her life had prepared her for what had happened to her the last two days.

"Are you sure that's all of them?" she asked, holding on to the calmness in his eyes. Wanting his reassurance that this was over. She wanted it *all* to be over, but she knew it wasn't, of course. At least he was here. And as long as he was... As long as he was here, she thought again, she would be safe.

"The two of them who came in the back and the driver," he said. "He was the one at the windows. He just got here a little quicker than I anticipated."

Slowly she realized the unmistakable implications of that. "You watched them?" she asked. "You watched those men come into my house?" If he had seen them come into the house, why hadn't he done something about it before they had started shooting? Why hadn't he—

"I wasn't sure why they were here," he said. "After that garbage you told me yesterday, I figured they might have just come to woo you back for another attempt at a wedding.''

His tone was mocking. She had lied to him yesterday, and he knew it. She had told him she had nothing to do with what had happened in front of the hotel. That hadn't been true, of course. And now...

"I think you and I should talk," he said softly, almost as if he had read her thoughts. "And I think this time you should tell me the truth."

"About what happened yesterday?" she asked.

"For starters," he agreed.

"I saw them," she whispered. She had told him that before, but only at the end. And she had lied about all the other, at least lied by omission. "I saw the assassins," she continued, making her voice stronger, determined now to tell him all of it. "They were standing on the balcony looking down into the street in front of the hotel. I heard the shot. Then they turned around and...they saw me. I let the door close, and I ran."

"Who are *they?*" he asked.

"Two of them... I think they were bodyguards of my fiancé. There were so many of them that I never learned all their faces, but I had seen these two before. I didn't know the other man at all. He was...I think he was a Westerner. At least, he wasn't wearing a robe. He's the one who had the rifle."

Her rescuer nodded. The approaching dawn touched his fair hair with a shimmer of light. "Who sent you to get me?" he asked.

"Sent me?" she repeated. "Nobody sent me. I was...terrified because I'd seen them. I was trying to get away."

"Just an accident that it was *my* room you entered?"

"Yes," she whispered.

She knew as she said it that he didn't believe her. That was in his tone; mocking again. And even she thought it was strange that she would have chosen the room of this man. A man who had his own gun and knew how to use it. A man who knew how to get her out of a hotel that was surrounded by a million cops.

"Nothing like that *ever* happens by chance," he said. "Not to me."

But going into his room had, Tyler thought. His had been the nearest door. She'd had a passkey. And she'd been terrified. It had been…happenstance. Random choice. Chance.

"First you just walk in on the assassins, and then you come straight to me?" he said, his voice full of sarcasm and disbelief. "You're going to have to do better than that. Like explaining where you got a passkey."

From the beginning, she thought. Maybe if she told him all of it… "I was supposed to get married," she said, her voice trembling with the need to get it out. "To Sheikh al-Ahmad's son. But…I realized I had agreed because I was afraid. I'd just let Amir talk me into it. And suddenly I realized that everything about my life would be so…"

The hesitant explanation faded because she knew he wouldn't understand what had driven her to Amir's room yesterday. *She* hadn't understood all her reasons. She had just known, almost instinctively, that what she was about to do was wrong. But that part wasn't important to him. It wasn't the truth he had demanded.

"I realized I couldn't go through with it without talking to Amir. Without making him promise…" She shook her head, knowing that wasn't relevant, either. "I knew his father was due to arrive, but I needed to see Amir before the ceremony. So I went down to the men's floor, and Malcolm Truett, Amir's secretary, said I'd just missed him. That Amir had already gone down to meet his father. He implied I shouldn't be there. That the sheikh wouldn't like it if they came back upstairs and found me on that floor."

She took a breath, thinking about what had happened next. "But I hadn't brought the key to my room with me, and Malcolm was in a hurry to run some errand Amir had sent him on...."

She paused again, remembering that chain of events. If Malcolm had known what was going on, surely he would not have given her that passkey. It would have been too dangerous. So he couldn't have known, she realized.

"And..." the blue-eyed man prodded.

"He gave me a passkey," she said softly, still trying to make sense out of what had happened.

"Why would *he* have a passkey?"

"He arranged the hotel reservations. He was in charge of the rooms. I don't know why they would give him a key, other than convenience. Or security, maybe."

"And instead of going upstairs and using the key to get back into your own room..." her rescuer suggested, apparently having followed her disjointed narrative.

"I opened Amir's door." She hesitated, realizing that she had only assumed it was his, because Truett's eyes had moved to it when he'd told her Amir had gone downstairs. "The one Malcolm indicated was Amir's door," she corrected. "And I saw them on the terrace. I saw what they were doing."

"And they saw you?" There was no inflection in his voice.

"They saw me," she agreed softly. "I let the door close, and as it did, I heard the elevator. Malcolm had punched both buttons while we were talking. I didn't know which elevator had arrived, but I got on and when it started down, I realized I couldn't go to the lobby. I didn't know who they had shot, or even, at that point, if they had shot *any-body*. I thought it might be some kind of security thing. Protection for the sheikh. I didn't know, but by then, I had realized I couldn't do it. I couldn't marry Amir, I mean. I couldn't live like that."

The spate of words stopped again. He wouldn't care about that. About her reasons. He just wanted to know why she had pulled him into what had happened.

"So you got off the elevator…" he said.

"I slapped at the buttons, hoping it would stop. Hoping I was in time. When it did, I don't think I even knew what floor I was on. I ran toward the exit at the end of the hall. But then I heard the elevator again. The bell. I heard it behind me. I thought they were coming, so I used the passkey. I slid it into the nearest door, and…that was your room."

He said nothing. Although the room had lightened, she couldn't read his face well enough to know whether he believed her. "I wanted to tell you what I'd seen," she said. "I tried to tell you in the restaurant." *And instead of answering, you kissed me.* Somehow the remembrance of that kiss seemed even more intimate, here in the darkness of her bedroom, than it had then.

"I didn't want to get you involved," she said. "I didn't want to pull someone else into that, but you seemed to know what you were doing. You seemed so capable. So…"

Dangerous. The word echoed in her brain. It was what he had seemed tonight. He had saved her life again. She didn't know why. Or why he had followed her here. But she did know he had dealt with the situation tonight with the same cool competence he had used to get her out of the hotel. Despite Amir's men and all those cops.

Cops. As soon as she thought the word, the explanation for all those things occurred to her. And it made sense. Suddenly *something* made sense out of his presence here tonight. Of the fact that he had come all the way to Mississippi to find her. It even made sense of what he had done. It explained everything that had been so puzzling about this man from the beginning.

"*That's* why you're here," she said. He was some kind of cop, of course. It was obvious, now that she put the clues together. "I told you in the restaurant that I saw them, and when you found out what had happened, what they had done, you came here to find out exactly what I saw."

Her voice had risen with her growing excitement. That would explain everything. Why he carried a gun. His certainty about what would happen when the alarms went off. About how the cop on the street would react.

"You're..." She hesitated, thinking about who they would send. FBI? CIA? She wasn't sure, but it didn't really matter who he worked for. "You're some kind of federal agent," she said. "You're trying to find out who killed Amir's father."

She should have gone straight to the police when she left the hotel. She would have, if she hadn't been so terrified. But all she had been able to think about was getting away. Away from Amir, even if he had had nothing to do with his father's death. But now, of course...

"I'll tell them what I saw," she said. "I'll tell it to whoever you want me to." She expected some reaction, but his eyes were considering. And still cold.

His response, when it finally came, wasn't what she had expected. Again it was prosaic, in strong contrast to her sudden sense of euphoria. "You should pack a few things," he suggested.

"All right," she agreed, a little let down by his tone. But obviously he was going to take her with him. Back to New York?

"Not much. One small bag."

Those directions were as precise as the ones he had given her about getting away from the hotel yesterday. And she was more than willing to do what he told her. After all, he was one of the good guys. She'd be safe with him. Far safer than she would be here alone. Tonight had proved the fallacy of that.

"And get dressed," he said, holding his hand out. "You won't want to travel in what you're wearing."

The blue eyes, however, didn't examine the sheer nightgown. They focused instead on her face, and in the growing light of dawn, she could find nothing in them like the flare of desire she had seen yesterday.

She put her fingers into his. Hers were cold against the warmth of his hand. Soft against its callused strength. He pulled her up, but as soon as she was upright, the room began to swim. She closed her eyes, swaying toward him. He took a step nearer, pushing his body against hers. Supporting.

"You're okay. Just shock," he said. The breath from his words, as warm as his fingers, stirred against her temple. The soft words seemed to give permission, and without having the strength to resist their invitation, she accepted, leaning into his body. Resting her forehead against his cheek.

His arms didn't enclose her. He didn't touch her in any other way, and after a moment even his fingers let go of her hand. He stepped back, but he waited a moment before he turned away, maybe to make sure that she wasn't going to faint.

That would be nice, she thought, watching him walk across the room. If she fainted, maybe her head would stop hurting and her arm wouldn't feel like it was on fire.

He disappeared into the hallway, and she closed her eyes, leaning back against the wall. Unconsciously, she rubbed at the back of her arm, wincing as she touched the area that hurt the worst. An area that was wet, she realized. She glanced down and was surprised to find that the fingers of her hand had come away covered with blood. Which was also dripping off her left elbow, a small pool of it forming on the wooden floor.

Seeing that made her light-headed again, so she closed her eyes and leaned back against the wall, wondering why her arm was bleeding, wondering what she could have hit it on to do that much damage. She didn't open her eyes until she heard him come back into the room, shoes crunching on the debris.

She watched him walk over to the man hanging over

the windowsill. He reached under the headdress to check for a pulse. Apparently he didn't find one, because he gripped the back of the man's robe and pulled, jerking him up off the sill and into the room. The body crumpled bonelessly to the floor, hitting headfirst. She closed her eyes at the sickening noise, but then, curious about what he was doing, she forced them open. He was bent down beside the corpse, methodically searching it.

"Is he dead?" she asked.

"Very," he said succinctly. "They all are."

Three dead men in her mother's house. Bleeding all over Aunt Martha's spotless floors.

"What are you going to do with them?" she asked.

"Leave them." He didn't look at her.

"Maybe we should call the sheriff," she suggested hesitantly. They had to do something. You didn't just leave bodies lying around. Not in Covington, Mississippi, you didn't.

"You never know in a situation like this who you can trust."

"But why would you think that the sheriff—"

"I don't," he said. "I just don't trust many people. That's how I've managed to stay alive this long. Since that's worked well in the past, I think we'll keep playing by my rules."

The blue eyes finally lifted to her face. They were cold again, commanding obedience. And they were still full of certainty. Still absolutely sure of what he was doing.

Maybe because they were so sure, she nodded. She didn't have any choice but to play by his rules, she thought. After all, he was the one who knew what he was doing.

At her agreement, he went back to the task he'd undertaken. She wondered what he was looking for. Identification, she supposed. And she wondered suddenly if she would recognize the dead man. Could he be one of Amir's numerous bodyguards? One of the men who had been in that room yesterday?

Thinking for the first time about that possibility, Tyler pushed away from the wall, moving carefully because she didn't want to make a fool of herself by fainting. Holding her left arm against her body, the palm of her right hand cupped around the elbow, she walked over to the fallen man. There was enough light in the room now that there was no doubt.

"He's not one of them," she said. "Not one of the ones at the hotel." She had been afraid, since she had seen them so briefly, that she wouldn't be able to identify them. But there was no doubt in her mind that this man hadn't been there.

He didn't look much like a conspirator. Or a killer. He looked as if he were sleeping. Too much at peace to have died so violently. But it might just as easily have been her lying in that pool of blood, she thought. Or the man with the blue eyes.

"I don't even know your name," she said.

His eyes came up suddenly, locking with hers. They held a moment, assessing. She understood his hesitation. His caution was habitual, not personal. He was just doing his job.

"Call me Hawk," he said finally.

Not his real name. She understood that also.

"Hawk," she repeated.

"For now," he agreed, eyes holding hers.

She nodded, although she wasn't sure exactly what that meant. She had bent forward a little, arms crossed over her stomach and her shoulders hunched, giving in to the searing pain that continued to burn across the back of her arm.

"What's wrong?" Hawk asked.

Without waiting for an answer, he stood up, rising in one fluid motion, and closed the distance that separated them. Unaccountably, at his nearness she found herself thinking about yesterday, about when he'd leaned down to kiss her. About the warmth of his lips moving against hers.

"I hurt my arm," she said, looking up into his face. Remembering.

Hawk, however, apparently wasn't bothered by those same thoughts. He stuck the pistol into the waistband of his jeans, took her left arm in both hands and turned it.

Finally she looked down, pulling her gaze away from those compelling features. He was holding her upper arm toward the thin light coming in through the windows. In that position she could see the bloody slash across the back of it.

"What in the world?" she whispered.

"Looks like somebody shot you," Hawk said.

"Shot me?" The blow she had felt stumbling through the kitchen door? Could that have been—

"Or you got hit by a ricochet, maybe even one of mine. I don't suppose it makes all that much difference *how* it happened."

She looked up again at his face. His eyes were very blue, focused on hers. There was something different about them. They were not like they had ever been before. Not cold. And not heated by the sexual desire she had seen so briefly. They were full, instead, of something else.

Even as she looked at him, trying to decipher whatever was hidden in the blue depths, the control that seemed so much a part of him reasserted itself. His gaze fell, returning to the gash a bullet had plowed across the outside of her bare arm. The light, thick lashes screened his eyes. But his lips tightened, a small muscle jumping beside his mouth.

"It doesn't hurt that much. I know..." She hesitated, unsure how to phrase what she thought she should say. "I know if you did it, you didn't mean to."

Hawk's mouth relaxed slightly, his lips moving, maybe even into the beginnings of a smile, but he kept his eyes on the wound, stretching the skin around it to judge the depth. She gasped at the sudden pain and then caught her bottom lip with her teeth, determined to prevent any other reaction. He released her arm immediately.

He turned and walked back into the hall. She thought about telling him he wouldn't find anything to bandage it with, if that's what he was looking for. She wasn't sure, however, whether the people who had been hired to clean the house would have thrown away any first-aid supplies. Before she could decide, Hawk reappeared, carrying a folded dish towel. He handed it to her, but he didn't offer to look at the injury again.

"Press it against the cut until the bleeding stops. You should wash it out with some kind of antiseptic," he advised.

She nodded, obediently pressing the soft cloth against the wound. He didn't seem too concerned. If he'd had *any* experience at all with bullet wounds, it was more than she had had, so she hoped he knew what he was talking about. And maybe there were still some aspirin in the medicine chest.

"Can you manage to pack a suitcase?" he asked.

"Of course," she said.

"Then you better get dressed and do it. I parked the rental about half a mile away. I'll go get it. You be ready when I get back." The blue eyes were cold again, once more commanding her obedience. But they were still full of certainty. Still absolutely sure of what he was doing.

Still playing by his rules, she thought. But it didn't seem she really had any other choice.

BUYING INTO THE IDEA that what had happened yesterday had been a coincidence still bothered him, Hawk thought, as he jogged to where he had parked the car. For one thing, it went against all his previous experience. And against his natural cynicism.

But Hawk had also learned a long time ago to trust his instincts about people, and they were telling him now that Tyler Stewart had told him the truth. She had dragged him into the middle of that assassination by chance. A coincidence, but one that, given his past, no one else was likely to believe in.

The one time in my life I decide to play the white knight, Hawk thought, almost amused at the realization, *and where does it get me? Into a whole hell of a lot of trouble.*

The agency believed he'd made yesterday's hit. Not a totally unreasonable assumption, considering that he'd made the one in Baghdad without their approval. Maybe they thought Griff's death had driven him over the edge. Or maybe they believed he'd taken out al-Ahmad because the sheikh had ties to the terrorist Hawk had targeted.

He couldn't know what they thought or what assumptions they were acting under. But he had been warned by a man working on the inside, with access to solid information. A man he knew he could trust.

The other thing he now knew was something he should have realized all along. Instead, he had only belatedly recognized the possibilities it presented as he had listened to the halting story she told him.

What he had finally figured out was that Tyler Stewart was the one person who could prove he had had nothing to do with that assassination. If she hadn't been involved in setting him up, then she was exactly what she had claimed—an innocent bystander. And she was all that stood between him and a death sentence. Which wouldn't, of course, be the kind they handed out in any court of law.

Hawk had already had his day in court. A long time ago. "Last chance," that old Texas judge had warned him. Luckily, Hawk had believed him. He had taken the chance he'd been offered, and it had changed his life.

This time, he knew, there would be no warning. Not any beyond the one he'd already received from Jordan Cross. *Dead serious.*

Chapter Six

"Where are we going?"

It was the first question she'd asked since they'd left the house, and Hawk had been surprised by her restraint. He had been expecting her to ask a whole lot more of them.

But she trusted him, he remembered. She thought he was some fearless federal agent who had been sent to rescue her from the assassins. Sent out to bring her in so she could give the authorities a description. It was a pleasant scenario, he supposed, and if it kept her compliant and cooperative, then far be it from him to disillusion her.

"Somewhere safe," he said.

He had been trying to think where the hell that might be. There weren't many places that were "safe" when you had the full force of the United States government on your tail. And when you were traveling with a woman who apparently had half the extremists in the Middle East trying to kill her.

"By the way," Tyler Stewart said, "I want to thank you."

"Thank me for what?" he asked. He concentrated on the road a moment, and then, when she didn't answer, he glanced at her. The violet-blue eyes, wide and sincere, surrounded by that sweep of long dark lashes, were focused on his face.

"I know I should have said it all before," she said.

"Yesterday when you helped me get out of the hotel. For coming to find me. Certainly for what happened back at the house. For saving my life." She paused, the litany of his good deeds apparently finished.

At least I hope it is, Hawk thought. *I hope to hell that's all she's got to say.*

"I should have already told you how grateful I am, but…I guess this has thrown me. I've never been involved with anything like this before," she added unnecessarily.

He closed his lips, clamping them shut over the denial he wanted to make. *I came to find you because I thought you had set me up. And because I intended to force the truth about what happened yesterday out of you, any way I could.*

"If you hadn't come for me," she continued, her voice low, unconsciously intimate in the close confines of the car, "I know what would have happened back there. Even *with* you there…"

They had almost succeeded. She didn't say it, but that was certainly the truth. Hawk had almost let them get to her because he had been acting on the assumption that she had been in on the deal yesterday. They had almost succeeded, he thought again, remembering the gash the bullet had cut across the back of her arm. He didn't want her thanks. He sure as hell didn't deserve them. Because he hadn't come to save her. And because he was using her. He sure didn't want to listen to her gratitude over what he was supposedly doing *for* her.

"I thought I was safe back there," she said. "I thought they wouldn't be able to track me down."

He said nothing, keeping his eyes resolutely on the road ahead. She had been wrong about that, of course. It hadn't taken them any longer to find her than it had taken him. Even without access to the government databases he had used. At least now she seemed to understand that part of her situation.

"So I just wanted to say thank you for taking the trouble to come for me. And for what you did back there."

He hadn't lied to her, he reminded himself. She had come up with the idea that he was investigating the assassination. He just hadn't corrected it. After all, he *was* a federal agent. Not the kind she was imagining him to be, of course. Not anything at all like the kind of agent she was imagining.

"It's my job," he said. Despite his cynicism, the falseness of that lie was bitter on his tongue.

She's my ace in the hole, Hawk told himself, fighting the unfamiliar surge of guilt. *My sleeve card. The only person in the world who can prove I had nothing to do with that hit. I need you, Tyler Stewart. Not the other way around.*

"Maybe so," she said, "but...forgive me if knowing that doesn't prevent me from being grateful. They would have killed me if you hadn't been there."

A real white knight, Hawk thought, mocking himself. *Just riding in for the rescue.* He wondered why he was feeling so damn guilty about this. After all, whoever had killed the sheikh really couldn't afford to have her running around telling everyone what she'd seen. Telling *anyone,* he amended.

And it hadn't taken them long to track her down. *The bad guys,* he thought, mocking her simplistic view of the world—everything in black and white. But she was right. They would have killed her. He had a brief mental picture of her body lying on the hardwood floor of that little house, blood pooling and then slowly congealing under it.

It was as simple as that, just as black and white. The lips that had been so warm yesterday when he had put his mouth—

He cleared the memory from his head, knowing he couldn't afford to think about that. Couldn't afford to think about her in that way. It had been a mistake to allow himself to touch her, as big a mistake as playing Good Samaritan, but Hawk had believed he'd never see her again. The stolen kiss had seemed a harmless, pleasant diversion for a man who hadn't had any lately.

And it had been pleasant, he acknowledged. Too pleasant, and maybe not so harmless, because it might already have affected his judgment. Hawk couldn't afford that. He didn't have time for diversions or distractions. So he had told himself that the kiss hadn't had anything to do with bringing her with him. That his decision had nothing to do with the sexuality that had flared, so strong and unexpected, between them.

His reasons had been strictly self-interest. Self-preservation. *Just covering my ass,* he reiterated, arguing against his inherent honesty. *Nothing else.* If there was the remotest possibility he could use her to clear himself with the agency, then he couldn't let some nutcases take her out.

Nutcases. The word rang sourly through his guilt, a strange choice for someone like him. Ninety-five percent of the population of this country would probably think that term applied pretty well to Hawk himself.

The good citizens of this country didn't want to acknowledge that occasionally their government needed to eliminate someone whose potential for human destruction, or whose developing taste for it, negated his right to coexist on the planet among sane people. They wouldn't want to admit that such eliminations had been carried out in the past or to think about the possibility that, human nature being what it was, there might be a need for something like that to be done again in the future.

That wouldn't be up to Hawk, of course. Deciding when such a scenario had occurred was the job of men like Griff Cabot. Had been Griff's job, Hawk amended. Past tense.

"Apparently it isn't easy for you to accept thanks for what you do," Tyler said, interrupting that introspection.

He realized he hadn't answered her. She had taken his

prolonged silence for modesty, and her voice was touched with amusement.

"Sorry if I embarrassed you," she continued, "but... without you, I would have been in a whole lot of trouble back there."

Hawk fought the urge to look at her again, keeping his eyes on the road, as if its few curves and rises demanded his full attention. She was still in a lot of trouble. They both were. More trouble than she could probably imagine.

However, if being with him gave her comfort, some sense of safety, then he wasn't about to destroy that pleasant little fantasy. She *was* better off with him. Because he was better off with her alive, so he'd try very hard to keep her that way.

That's all it was, he told himself. Just a matter of practicality. Just good old cold-blooded pragmatism. Even if Tyler Stewart had looked like somebody's grandmother, he'd have taken her with him.

Of course, he admitted, if she'd looked like somebody's grandmother, they wouldn't be here. She wouldn't have been able to get away with wearing his clothes yesterday. Somehow, the remembrance of the way his jeans had looked, worn denim stretched over her slim derriere and down that incredible length of leg, sneaked back into his head. Sneaked in right past the need to think about where they were going to hole up.

"We're still in a lot of trouble," he warned.

That was the truth, and it was only fair she understand it. They might get into another situation where she needed to do exactly what she was told and do it quickly. She needed to understand that he was in charge. And he supposed she needed to keep believing his primary objective in all this was to keep her safe until she could make an identification of the assassins.

Ace in the hole, he thought. That's all she was. No more Good Samaritan. That was a lesson he had learned, and

Hawk never allowed himself to forget any of the lessons life taught him.

"So where are we going?" she asked again.

"Somewhere nice and quiet where I can think," Hawk said.

"Not back to New York?"

"Not yet," he said, trying to think of a reason she'd buy. "I need to be sure it's safe to bring you in. And since there are foreign nationals involved, we may need to wait a couple of days to see what shakes out. We'll hole up somewhere."

Hawk needed to know whether his picture was being splashed across the front pages. It wouldn't be the photo from his security file. They wouldn't use that one, of course. If any pictures had been released, they would have been the grainy shots from the hotel security cameras Jordan had told him about.

And if those pictures *were* in the papers, then Hawk would know that the manhunt was on. And he understood too well what kind of hunt it would be. After all, they couldn't afford to let him come to trial. He knew too many things they wouldn't want anyone to know. Hawk would never be allowed on any witness stand.

If they went public with the search for him, then it would mean a shoot-to-kill had been issued. One of those "suspect is armed and dangerous" deals. In his case, he acknowledged grimly, they'd be right.

Hawk had been more than willing to take his punishment for the unauthorized kill he'd made in Iraq. For taking down Griff's murderer. He had thought he knew what that punishment would involve. But forced retirement and a lot of unpleasantness was a long way from being the scapegoat for someone else's assassination. He remembered the pictures of Oswald being gunned down in Dallas. Those were black and whites also. Just as the grainy shots the hotel cameras produced would be.

Hawk didn't intend to be this generation's Lee Harvey

Oswald. Not if he could help it, he decided. Not if there was anything at all he could do to protect himself. And in order to do that, he knew, he also had to protect the woman beside him.

"WHERE ARE WE?" Tyler asked.

Hawk glanced at her, again feeling the impact of those remarkable eyes, despite the fact that they now reflected all she had been through the last two days. The midnight black hair was disordered, the smooth skin of her cheeks nearly devoid of color, and she was still incredibly beautiful.

At least she was awake, Hawk thought, and asking questions. Far more normal than just accepting his decisions, more normal than that implicit trust in him she'd exhibited so far.

She had slept during a lot of the long drive, and Hawk had been surprised to find himself worrying about her. In the course of the day, she had made a couple of offers to share the driving, but despite his fatigue and lack of sleep, Hawk had refused.

After what had happened in Mississippi, that unexpected barrage of gunfire in the quiet dawn, he had been expecting a state trooper to appear in his rearview mirror at any moment. He had been expecting *somebody* to show up behind them through the half-dozen states they had crossed in the course of the long day.

Hawk didn't understand why he was so edgy. It wasn't like him. He knew, at least intellectually, that there was no way they could have traced him through the ID he'd used to rent this car. Griff had supplied those identification papers, part of the kit Hawk had picked up in Alexandria. There would be no record of them with any government agency, no way in hell to trace the name on them back to the man called Hawk.

The emergency kits were something no one on the team had ever expected to have to use, but Griff had insisted they each have one. *Just in case,* Cabot had said, with that enigmatic half smile. In case of something like this, Hawk guessed.

He knew the agency would pick up his trail eventually, but it would take them a while. And the fact that no one had shown the least interest in the rental car so far was reassuring.

The last time they stopped for gas, Hawk had bought all the newspapers available at the small convenience store. He had tossed them into the back seat without taking time to read them, nothing beyond a quick scan of the headlines.

Yesterday's assassination was no longer front page headlines, not in the locals. There would be information about it inside, however, and he wanted to read everything carefully. That could wait a little longer, he had decided, knowing how close they were to the destination they had just reached.

"We're at a friend's house," Hawk explained, bringing the car to a stop at the end of the familiar road. No explanation beyond that. After all, there wasn't much more to say.

The roughness of the ride down the private road had probably awakened her. At the best of times, this was little better than a trail. Now it was potholed with washouts from the spring rains. This year, of course, no one had issued the orders for the needed repairs.

"It doesn't look as if anyone's home," she said.

Her eyes were examining the house that loomed above them. There was exhaustion in her voice. Maybe disappointment. She must have been expecting to be somewhere sanctioned and official by now. And she probably felt almost as wasted as he did, Hawk realized, in spite of the fact that she'd had some sleep. After all, she'd been shot, she had finally had to come to grips with the fact that someone was trying to kill her, and she had watched three men die. Then she'd been dragged halfway across the country by a total stranger.

By a stalwart federal agent hot on the trail of the assassins. By a hero who was supposed to be taking her somewhere she'd be safe. Where she would help him catch the bad guys. *White knight,* Hawk thought. Again the image rankled.

She turned to face him, probably because he had been simply watching her instead of answering her question. The fragile skin around her eyes was slightly discolored, yellowed like old bruises. The eyes themselves, however, were clear and bright.

And maybe a little too bright. Fever? Hawk wondered. Not this soon, he reasoned, reassuring himself. It might not happen at all, if she'd done what he'd told her and cleaned the wound with antiseptic. Even if she hadn't, it probably wouldn't make much difference. After all, the furrow the bullet had cut in her arm was little more than a deep scratch.

"No one's home," he acknowledged.

His reluctance to answer had nothing to do with her question. It was just a reality he preferred not to think about. Now, he realized, he would be forced to. He hadn't been planning on coming here when they left Mississippi. He had simply headed east, homing instinct. But when he had remembered Griff's place a few hours ago, it seemed perfect. An answer to their every need. For a few days, anyway.

This old house was what people like the Cabots called a summer home. Its irregular collection of towers and jutting roof lines perched above an isolated stretch of rock-strewn Virginia beach, looking as if it might tumble into the green churn of the Atlantic below with the first storm. It hadn't, of course. Not in the hundred years or so since it had been built.

Hawk had come here occasionally with Griff. Once or twice with the others—the members of the team. They had come to plan. Or to debrief. To celebrate.

Once Griff had brought him here after a mission that

had gone wrong. Brought him here to recuperate. That time was something else Hawk didn't want to remember, so with the ease of long practice, he pushed the thought out of his head, closing and locking mental doors that shouldn't have been opened.

The house had a modern security system, of course, the best money could buy, but Hawk knew all the codes. He was good with numbers, good at remembering them. So unless someone had taken the trouble to change things, he could get them in. And once inside, they'd be safe. It would be the perfect hideout, at least until Hawk could get a handle on what was going down.

"Come on," he ordered softly.

Without waiting for her to obey, he opened the door and climbed out of the car, legs stiff from long hours behind the wheel. He opened the back door and retrieved the suitcase she'd brought and then led the way up the steep path to the steps.

He was conscious that she was climbing slowly, lagging behind him, but he didn't look back. While she slept during the drive, Hawk had acknowledged something pretty damn disturbing. He liked looking at Tyler Stewart. Liked it a lot. And that was dangerous. Just like the kiss that never should have happened, his attraction to this woman had no place in what was going on.

This was no different than a mission. He had never allowed himself to indulge physical appetites while on assignment. That was simply another form of discipline, and Hawk understood all about discipline. It was something else, like death and danger, with which he had a long and intimate acquaintance. Abstinence was simply another aspect of that.

When he reached the top of the steps, Hawk walked across the wooden veranda and punched the code into the incongruous security pad by the front door. The doorknob turned under his hand, and relieved, he pushed it inward.

Apparently the house hadn't been sold. At least nobody had changed the codes.

The interior was dark, the air inside hinting at mildew and coastal dampness. The prospect it offered wasn't inviting, but then he hadn't expected a welcoming committee. Griff Cabot was dead. No one else was in residence. Which was exactly why they were here.

"Are you sure this is okay?" Tyler asked, her question mirroring his hesitation. She was standing on the porch behind him, looking into the house through the open door.

Hawk realized that he had hesitated on the threshold because he was dreading this confrontation. He was putting off facing his ghosts, he supposed. And she had taken her cue from his reluctance.

"You have a better idea?" he asked sharply, his voice tight and hard with the unexpected force of those emotions. Without waiting for her answer, he stepped inside. The house was exactly as he remembered, except the familiar pieces of furniture were now covered with white cotton holland covers, their massive, indistinct shapes ghostly in the dimness.

Griff's house. It would be full of reminders. Of him. Of the close-knit team he'd built. Memories of what they had accomplished together. Of friendships. Some of those already destroyed, perhaps, by what Hawk had been accused of. Not the Iraqi assassination, but the other. Going rogue. Operating outside the careful limits Cabot had set.

But worrying about that was something else he didn't have time for, Hawk told himself. The battle that was coming would demand control and a cold, clear-eyed logic. Not emotion. Not of any kind.

"Your friend's not been here in a while, I would guess," Tyler said from behind him.

Again, Hawk explained nothing and offered no information. "I'm going to pull the car into the garage. You can go on upstairs. Pick out a bedroom. I'll bring your suitcase up when I finish."

She nodded, her gaze moving slowly around the entry hall and the formal parlor that lay through the opened doors on the right. "You think your friend might have some aspirin?" she asked.

"Probably," he said. "Headache?"

She turned her head, her eyes meeting his and holding them a moment. She nodded and then looked away again, pretending to examine the shadowed furnishings.

"Your arm?" he said.

She had been holding her left elbow in the palm of her right hand again, so that her arms were crossed over her stomach. She released her hold at his question, but she didn't straighten the injured arm. "It's a little sore," she admitted.

There was pain medication here, he knew. He had been given some the last time he'd come. That time he didn't want to remember. "There's probably some kind of painkiller around," he said. "I'll find you something when I've hidden the car."

"Thank you," she said.

She started toward the staircase, its rosewood banisters curving gracefully toward the shadows of the second floor. As she walked, she again cupped her elbow, holding the arm against her body. When she reached the foot of the stairs, she released it to put her right hand on the railing, and began to climb.

Too slowly, Hawk thought. Again he felt that same touch of unease as when she had been sleeping in the car. Especially when he contrasted those careful movements to the way she had moved yesterday. There were all kinds of logical explanations for the anxiety that was stirring unpleasantly in his gut, beginning with the fact that Tyler Stewart was the one person who could clear him of al-Ahmad's assassination, and the knowledge that the assassins didn't intend for her to tell anyone what she had seen.

Those were reasons enough to be worried about the effects of her injury. Reasons enough even if he were unwilling to acknowledge the true cause of his apprehension. Hawk had buried that, too. Buried it with the feelings that being back in this house had evoked.

He realized suddenly that she had stopped on the first landing. She was looking down at him. Probably wondering what the hell he was doing standing here watching her. Just watching her, as he had in the car. That was becoming a habit, Hawk thought, angry at himself. At his lack of control.

As he had told her, there were things he needed to do. Priorities, he reminded himself. First things first. Hawk turned away, retracing his steps through the front door.

He brought the newspapers and his bag into the house this time. He spent a few minutes making sure the security system was rearmed, and checking everything out downstairs before he picked them up again, along with Tyler's suitcase, which was still sitting by the front door, and climbed the stairs to the second floor.

He called her name when he reached the top. The only answer was the slight echo the solid wood walls threw back at him. Finally he started opening doors. He put the papers and his bag in the same suite he'd occupied during those long weeks of convalescence. And he found the pain medication he'd left behind, still in the drawer of the table by the bed. There were at least a half dozen of the big white capsules left.

Taking them with him, he continued to open doors. He found her in the fourth suite. Its bedroom was large and pleasant, decorated in shades of rose. An old-fashioned mahogany four-poster dominated the center of the room.

Tyler was lying across it. She was stretched out on her right side, eyes closed. She hadn't undressed or turned back the coverlet, and she didn't move when he opened the door. Hawk walked over the faded Oriental rug and set her suitcase down at the foot of the bed. The rug was thick enough that she might not have heard him, but again Hawk felt an unaccustomed flare of anxiety. She looked exhausted. Sick. Too damn vulnerable.

"Tyler," he said softly. Slowly, in response to her name, her eyes opened.

"Did you find some aspirin?" she asked. Her tone was calm and rational, completely normal.

Hawk took a breath in relief. He didn't know why he had been so concerned. Maybe because he didn't have much experience with illness or injury. Other than his own infrequent ones—and those he usually ignored.

"Something better," he said, holding the brown plastic prescription bottle up to show her. "Pain pills."

She pushed up, propping herself on the elbow of her uninjured arm, but her movements were careful. There had been enough time, Hawk knew, for swelling and soreness to set in. Any movement probably hurt like hell.

He walked to the side of the bed, opening the bottle and rolling two of the big capsules into his hand. He held them out to her. She looked up at his face, eyes searching it quickly before they fell to the medicine.

She didn't reach for the capsules for a moment, and when she did, she used her left hand. Her fingers trembled slightly when she picked them off his outstretched palm, but he was relieved to see her use the arm at all.

"Could I have some water, please?" she asked softly.

He nodded and headed to the bathroom. He remembered swallowing the pills dry, as large as they were. Reaching for them in the middle of the night, hand trembling as hers had done, when the pain had gotten too bad to endure.

By the time he got back with the water, she had managed to sit up, shoulders propped against the pillows she'd stacked together against the headboard. However, her head was back and her eyes were again closed.

In the low light from the bedside lamp, Hawk could see the tracery of blue veins in the thin, nearly transparent skin of her eyelids, and even the small network of lines around them. He had never noticed those before, and they, too, made her seem vulnerable. More…real, somehow. No longer like the images he'd seen on the computer screen, but just a woman, like any other woman he'd ever known.

"Tyler," he said, offering the glass.

Her eyes opened immediately. She had been holding the capsules in her right hand, and she put them into her mouth before she reached for the water. She drank all of it, drank it as if she had been really thirsty.

Fever? Hawk wondered again, resisting the urge to put his fingers against her forehead to find out. That was another temptation it would be better to avoid.

"Thank you," she said, finally looking up at him.

"I brought your suitcase up," he said, without acknowledging her thanks. Belatedly, he was wondering if he should have given her two of the capsules. That was the prescribed dosage for him, for his weight. Not for her thin fragility.

These pills had been pretty potent, he remembered. He had spent a lot of time sleeping during the weeks he'd been forced to take them. Of course, that sleep might simply have been another form of escape, and not so much the result of the medication.

"Thanks," she said again, her eyes were still on his face.

She seemed to be waiting for whatever else he intended to say. Only, Hawk couldn't think of anything else. All he could think of was how fragile she seemed. How damned vulnerable.

"I should probably look at your arm," he suggested.

Her eyes widened slightly, again searching his. That had surprised her. And it made him examine his own motives. He had a vested interest in her health, he reminded himself. And since there was no one else around to take care of her…

"You need some help getting your clothes off?" he asked.

She was still watching his face. Slowly her lips tilted,

and the surprise that had been in her eyes was replaced by amusement.

"I think I'd be worried if that offer had come from anyone else," she said. "Other than you," she added softly. "Thanks, but I can still manage my own clothes." She had cleared the amusement from her voice, but it lingered in her eyes. "But before you go, you could put my suitcase on the bed for me?"

Hawk hadn't thought about how his offer might be interpreted. He had been surprised by the quiet humor that had infused her response. Or by its implication. For a second, he had been at a loss about how to respond. But her request for the case seemed to make a response unnecessary. And it gave him an excuse to move. Away from her. Away from the charged atmosphere.

Or maybe that was only in his head, he thought, as he walked to the foot of the bed and picked up the bag. Maybe there had been no other connotation in her words, and when he repeated them mentally, he couldn't really find anything sexual. But he had felt it. It had been in her eyes.

Still thinking about exactly what he had seen there, he set the suitcase down on the bed beside her. He unzipped it before he looked up. Her eyes were impassive now. Calm and ordinary.

"Thank you," she said again, smiling at him. There was no provocation in this smile. When he didn't return it, after a moment her eyes fell and, one-handed, she began going through the clothing in the bag. She didn't look up at him again.

Hawk watched a few seconds longer, and then, realizing that he was doing it again, he turned and left the bedroom, closing the door behind him to give her some privacy.

Chapter Seven

When Hawk knocked on that same door almost thirty minutes later, he had managed a hot shower and had finally changed out of the clothes he'd been wearing for the last two days. Despite the cumulative effects of the lack of sleep, he felt better, more like himself. And more in control.

Tyler gave him permission to enter, and when he did, he was relieved to find she was sitting up in the bed. The pillows were still stacked behind her, but this time she had folded the comforter down across the foot of the bed. The sheet had been pulled up to her waist.

She was wearing a sleeveless nightgown, not, of course, the same one she'd been wearing this morning. That had been blue. He remembered he'd had a hell of a time keeping his eyes off the low neckline that edged just below the beginning swell of her breasts. This one was white, and the fabric seemed a little more substantial. At least he couldn't see either the shape or the rose-tinged darkness of her nipples through it.

When he realized what he'd been thinking, Hawk pulled his attention back to her face. Too damn pale. And she was cradling the injured arm again, the elbow resting once more in the steadying palm of her right hand.

"Ready for me to take a look at that?" Hawk asked, gesturing toward her body with a lift of his chin. He could see that the wound was covered by a thick gauze pad, heavily stained with blood. It was dark, however, and not fresh. Which meant this was probably the same pad she had put over it before they left Mississippi this morning.

She nodded, shifting her weight to make a place for him to sit on the bed beside her. That wasn't what he'd intended, but he supposed it was natural in this situation. It would allow him to get close enough to examine the injury without making her move any more than was necessary. It would also put him close enough to examine a lot of other things, he thought. Too close for comfort. Finally, however, he eased down on the bed beside her.

She raised her eyes to his, still trusting. Depending on him to take care of her. To take care of everything. Almost annoyed by that unquestioning trust, Hawk deliberately broke the contact by looking down at her arm.

"It's going to hurt like hell when I take this off," he warned. He was touching the corner of the gauze pad, and his fingers looked very dark in contrast to its whiteness.

"I know," she said.

"You want it quick or slow?" he asked.

His mother used to ask him that when he was a kid. Back when she'd still been taking care of him and not the other way around. She had always asked that same question before she pulled off a bandage. Hawk always chose quick, but he was that kind. The "do what you have to do and I'll deal with it" kind.

He looked up from the stained gauze to find Tyler's lips tilting again, their upward alignment subtle, almost a smile. And what he found in her eyes was what he had seen there before.

Despite the harshness of his features, there was apparently something about him that women found intriguing. Hawk had seen this same unspoken invitation in a lot of eyes through the years. Had seen it too many times to be mistaken about what it meant.

"Either way," she said softly. "I don't have a prefer-ence. Whichever way you want to do it is fine with me."

He wondered if that was supposed to be the double en-tendre his brain was suggesting. Even if it were, however, he had already made his decision about that. Not the time or the place. Not the woman. Definitely not the situation.

He grasped the gauze he had touched so lightly before and jerked it off. The cloth ripped from the gash with a sound that was audible. As was her gasp of pain. When he looked up, she had locked those even white teeth into her bottom lip, and her eyes were brimming with tears.

"Sorry," Hawk said, disgusted with himself. He had done that deliberately, and it had been nothing less than an act of cruelty, like kicking a kitten. He even knew *why* he had done it. Because he needed to destroy whatever image seemed to be building up in her mind about who and what he was.

He was no Good Samaritan. Nobody's white knight. She needed to figure that out, and maybe, he thought, she needed a little help doing it. When she had, there would be no more of the kind of invitation he had just read in her eyes.

"It's okay," she said softly. "Quick is better, I guess."

There was no anger in her voice. She didn't seem to be blaming him for the pain he'd just inflicted. Maybe she hadn't realized he was bastard enough to want to hurt her because he believed she was attracted to him. Or maybe, he thought, inherently honest, he had hurt her because she was a temptation he was having a hard time denying.

Angry with himself even if she wasn't, Hawk looked down at the wound. His lips flattened at what he saw. Because he'd ripped off the bandage, the slash was oozing blood again.

The area around it was red and swollen. He put his fingers, gently this time, next to the damaged skin. They looked as out of place against the cream of her arm as they had touching the white gauze. He could feel the heat of infection beneath the smooth surface.

"Did you wash this out with antiseptic?" he asked. He didn't add, *like I told you to,* but it was implied. And she would know it.

"I couldn't find anything. I tried to clean it with soap and water, but apparently…"

He didn't look up. Instead, he pressed the swollen areas around the gash, using her breathing to gauge how sore it was. Her soft inhalations were uneven, sometimes sharply drawn, but none as obvious as the first gasp had been.

"I brought some salve," he said finally. The wound wasn't too badly infected, he decided. More painful than dangerous. "That should help it heal. Maybe even help with the soreness."

Hawk opened the first-aid kit and took the antibiotic ointment out. He slipped his left hand under her arm, lifting and turning it toward him. Her skin was still cool, incredibly soft against the hardness of his fingers. He ignored the sensation and squeezed a thick thread of salve along the track the bullet had made. Then, with his right forefinger, he rubbed the ointment into the torn flesh. He became aware that she was holding her breath as he worked. It took him a couple of seconds to realize he'd been doing the same thing.

"Almost through," he said in reassurance, as he recapped the tube of salve and laid it back in the kit. Using his teeth, he tore the top off one of the cellophane envelopes that held sterile dressings and awkwardly removed a new piece of gauze. He laid the dressing over the gash, pressing it into the salve to make sure it would stay. Finally, he put a strip of adhesive tape across the top and bottom.

"We'll see how it looks in the morning." He replaced the tape in the kit and turned back to find that she was looking down at his handiwork.

"Boy Scouts?" she asked, her eyes lifting from the neat

bandage to his. That same smile played around her lips again.

"I was *never* a Boy Scout," he said, holding her eyes. Another warning, if she was smart enough to take it.

"Military?" she suggested, apparently undaunted by his tone. Her eyes held, waiting for an answer. Almost demanding one.

"The less you know about me, the better."

"You could tell me, but then you'd have to kill me. I saw that movie." Her voice was rich with amusement, and the smile had widened.

Playing games, Hawk thought, inexplicably angered by the fact that she could smile. Could still think this was all some big adventure. Despite the fact that she had a bullet wound in her arm. Despite the fact that some very ruthless people were trying to kill her so she wouldn't be able to identify them. Despite the fact that she was being used by a government assassin trying to clear himself of a murder charge.

She couldn't know that, of course. She didn't know anything about him, about who he was, and that was exactly the way Hawk intended to keep it.

"I guess I owe you another thank-you," she said. "The list of things I owe you for is getting pretty long."

"You don't owe me anything," he said. He closed the lid to the first-aid kit with a snap and stood up. The quicker he got out of here and let her get some rest, the better. The better for both of them. Of course, he still had a few things to take care of before he could allow himself to make up any lost sleep.

"Why is that so hard for you?" she asked softly. His eyes, when he looked up, must have reflected his question because she added, clarifying, "Why is it so hard for you to accept thanks for what you do?"

Because whatever I do is strictly motivated by self-interest. Hawk wondered what she would say if he told her that. "You better get some sleep," he said instead. "The pain pills should help."

She held his eyes so that he was again forced to break the contact. He turned and walked back across the faded carpet to the door. She didn't speak again until his hand was on the knob.

"Marines?"

He turned, slanting a look at her over his shoulder. From this distance, the effects of the last thirty-six hours weren't that evident. She looked a lot like the bride who'd invaded his hotel suite. Almost too beautiful to be real.

"A few good men," she said. "I think that would probably appeal to you. I think it certainly fits."

There had been the slightest slur to her words. Apparently, the capsules he'd given her were taking effect. He'd check on her when he came back upstairs—before he chose one of the beds up here and passed out on it. She'd be asleep by then. That would be safer. A whole lot safer for both of them, he decided.

A few good men. For some reason the phrase kept repeating in his consciousness as he went down the stairs, taking them two at a time despite his tiredness. But that was not something that applied to him, Hawk thought. He was not in that category. And he never had been.

HAWK HAD CONSIDERED the wisdom of making this call a long time before he finally dialed the number. But an offer of help had been extended. At the time, Hawk had believed he'd never have to take advantage of it. He didn't like being obligated to anybody. However, he needed information the newspapers hadn't provided. He had read them all, sitting in Griff's study as the summer darkness finally closed in.

And there was really no reason not to call, he'd finally decided. The phone line from the summer house would be secure, and he knew that whatever line Jordan Cross was using would be secure as well. He would never have given him this number if it weren't, Hawk thought, listening to the distant ringing.

As soon as Cross answered, Hawk asked, without identifying himself, "Your offer still good?" He had decided on no preliminaries. He needed a couple of favors, and if Jordan had developed any qualms in the last twenty-four hours, Hawk wanted to know about them. He thought he'd be able to tell by Jordan's first unguarded reaction. What Hawk heard, however, was only silence. It went on long enough to make him uncomfortable. Just before he decided to break the connection, Jordan spoke.

"Of course," he said. "Whatever you need. You know that."

This time the silence was on Hawk's end as he tried to decide how sincere that agreement had been. But he really didn't have all that many options, he told himself. There was no room in this situation for his stubborn pride, because his was not the only life at stake. If it had been, he acknowledged, he'd never have made this call. And, he admitted, that was another effect on this situation that Tyler had had. Because of her, Hawk could no longer afford to be a loner.

"Just information," he said finally.

"Shoot."

"How'd you hear they had fingered me for New York?"

"There was talk here. It appeared to be solid."

Here would mean within the CIA. "Someone on the team mention it?" he asked.

"As a matter of fact…" Jordan hesitated, maybe trying to remember. "A couple of people. There was speculation that it had something to do with what you'd done in Iraq."

"Who knew about Iraq?"

"It didn't take much to figure that out. I knew it had to be you as soon as the news broke. Most of the team would know. Most of the company would probably suspect we had something to do with the hit, given Griff's death and the guy's reputation."

"And the one in New York?"

"You showed up on the security tapes."

"Why would the company review those tapes?"

"I don't know. Maybe they didn't. Maybe that came from outside. Whoever made you, it didn't take long for the fact you had been in that hotel that morning to get around."

Any leaks within the agency—the "company" to insiders—were deliberate, just as they were in the rest of the government.

"We figured that *if* you did it, al-Ahmad must have been involved in the Langley massacre. Maybe financial backing or something."

"He wasn't involved," Hawk said, his voice full of surety. He had gotten the man responsible for that. The one in Baghdad. The one who had given the orders. As far as he had been able to discover, there had been no one else in on the deal in any way.

"Then maybe they just plan to use what happened in New York to bring you down. Then they won't have to admit they were going to let Griff's killer get away with it and were even going to punish the man who had decided he wasn't."

Hawk had known that's how the agency would react and had accepted it. But coming after him personally, as Jordan had warned him they were after New York, was something he hadn't counted on and didn't understand.

"They haven't released the pictures from the hotel cameras," Hawk said. Those pictures had been one thing he'd been looking for when he'd bought the newspapers. And he hadn't found them.

"It's coming," Jordan said softly, probably knowing this was the worst news Hawk could receive. "Somehow Amir al-Ahmad found out that the hotel has pictures of whoever set off the fire alarms. He wants them made public. He's demanding we go all out to find that man."

"So why haven't they?" Hawk asked.

"The company's making sure no one can possibly trace the man in those pictures back to the agency. If anyone does, there are bound to be accusations of a CIA plot. Given the volatility of the region, there's no telling what reaction that might set off."

"They really think I hit the sheikh?"

"Maybe," Jordan said. "They know it was you in Baghdad."

Still, in spite of whatever pressure Amir al-Ahmad was exerting, there seemed to be no reason the CIA would go public with a hunt for one of its own agents—and a lot of reasons not to. Especially given the things Hawk knew.

"Any other rumors about New York?" he asked. "About who might really have been involved?"

"You're the only rumor circulating here on that one, my friend," Cross told him. His voice was slightly amused. "The sheikh's son is claiming the assassination was an attempted coup. The fundamentalists hit the sheikh. The son's out of the country. Perfect opportunity for them to take over. He may be right. We don't have any reports of anything happening in his country, but al-Ahmad had for years been resisting attempts by the extremists to loosen his control. And there *have* been two previous attempts on his life."

The stakes in that struggle were very high, Hawk knew. The income from the oil produced ran into the billions of dollars annually, most of that becoming the personal property of the al-Ahmad family. Although the standard of living in their country was fairly high, there was no doubt the royal family benefitted far more than the people from that valuable natural resource. The extremists wanted to change that situation.

In the last year or so, al-Ahmad had lived as almost a prisoner to his wealth. And the strategy had apparently worked. Until he had agreed to come to the States to attend his son's wedding. A serious error in judgment.

"I need some background," Hawk said, remembering

what Tyler had told him. "What do you know about Amir al-Ahmad?"

"That he lives well," Jordan said. "His tastes run to expensive toys and beautiful women. The model for a bachelor playboy. Most people were surprised he was planning to settle down. Everybody figured there must have been pressure from the old man, but the bride didn't seem to be someone the sheikh would have picked out. Wrong religion. Wrong nationality."

"His father was coming to the wedding," Hawk said.

"To everyone's surprise. However, he and the son were close. Amir was being groomed to take over, but not for a while. The sheikh was a vigorous man in his late fifties. He could have lived another thirty years or so."

With Amir waiting in the wings, Hawk thought. "The son have any ties to the extremists?" Hawk asked.

"Not except as a target," Jordan said. Then, because he was smart, the point of that question hit him. "You think he had something to do with his father's death?"

"I don't know," Hawk said.

"Maybe the company does," Jordan suggested.

"Maybe," Hawk said, thinking about the possibilities. "Could you put together a file for me? Everything that's public on both Ahmads. And everything the company's got that's not."

Again there was the smallest hesitation. Hawk felt that prickling of unease until he heard Cross's suggestion.

"I can ask Jake Holt. I don't have to tell him who it's for." Jake was another of Cabot's team, and the kind of search Hawk had just requested was his specialty. By the time Holt got through, there wouldn't be a shred of information in any file on the al-Ahmads he hadn't dug out.

"Okay," Hawk agreed.

"Anything else?" Jordan asked.

Hawk hesitated, knowing in his gut there was too much about this whole thing that didn't add up.

"There was a witness," he said.

The pause was longer this time, but the implications were obvious. "A witness to the assassination?" Jordan said.

"Someone who saw three men in one of the rooms Amir al-Ahmad had rented. She saw one of them fire a rifle off that balcony. A witness who isn't mentioned in any of the papers, although someone was searching the hotel for her within minutes."

"Can she identify the men she saw?"

"It's possible," Hawk said, wishing that he'd taken more care with his pronouns.

"It may not matter," Jordan warned. "Not as far as the company's concerned."

Hawk understood the warning. They intended to rein Hawk in, one way or another.

"It might matter to them if I go public," Hawk suggested.

There was silence at the other end. Hawk could imagine what Jordan Cross was thinking.

"You don't mean that," Jordan said finally.

"I don't owe anybody any loyalty," Hawk said, remembering the years Cabot had worked to put this team in place, and how quickly after his death they had decided to dismantle it. "Not anymore. They're setting me up to take the heat for something they know I didn't do."

"Maybe they don't know," Cross said.

"Then there's too much they don't know," Hawk said bitterly. "About me. About what we did."

"Get out," Jordan suggested. "Just get out of the country and stay out. Disappear. You can do that."

"And have them send somebody like you after me?" Hawk asked, his voice mocking, but unamused.

"It won't be me. I can promise you that."

The corners of Hawk's lips lifted a little at the quiet assurance. "But it *will* be somebody," he said. "I know how that works. And in the meantime…" For some reason Hawk hesitated, reluctant to mention that he had the witness with him, although he had trusted this man with his life on more than one occasion. "I'll check back with you in a day or two," he said.

"Ask for a meeting."

"They'd never go for it," Hawk said, thinking for the first time about the possibility.

"They might. If you can really produce a witness who saw someone else pull the trigger..." Jordan paused, letting the suggestion sink in.

It was risky, but it might work. They wouldn't want Hawk talking. He was one of the people who really knew too much. Too much about things the government didn't want the public to find out about. Things the press would love to get hold of. As a matter of fact, Hawk realized, the media might be a valuable ally, if it came down to that kind of battle.

"I'll think about it," Hawk promised, knowing now that it had been suggested, he really would. Going public about the secrets he'd willingly kept all these years went against every principle he had lived by. And besides, a meeting with the agency would solve both his problems. It would provide a forum where Tyler could clear him of al-Ahmad's assassination, and then... Then the agency could provide some real protection for her from the assassins. Whoever they were.

Hawk knew it would be tricky to arrange a face-to-face without putting himself in a position where he no longer had any control. He wasn't sure of the agency's agenda where he was concerned. Still, it was an idea worth considering. Especially when he realized that right now he didn't have another one.

"By the way," Hawk said, "I need an ID on some bodies."

"Bodies?" Jordan repeated. "Plural?"

"I left three of them in a vacant house in a little town called Covington. That's in Mississippi. Maybe somebody's discovered them by now. If not, give the locals an anonymous tip that they should be looking. Then see if you can find out who they worked for.''

"Connected to the assassination?"

"I think so," Hawk said. He would be willing to bet that the three worked for Amir al-Ahmad, considering that two of his bodyguards had apparently been in on the hit against the sheikh, and it had been made from one of Amir's rooms. That was according to Tyler. But none of that had been in any of the papers, either.

"You *think* so?"

"That's why I need an ID," Hawk said.

"You kill 'em?"

"Only because they were trying real hard to kill me," Hawk said innocently, and listened to another brief silence.

"How do I reach you when I have something?" Cross asked.

"I'll call you."

"Give me twenty-four hours."

"I owe you," Hawk said softly, knowing how true that was.

"You don't owe me anything," Jordan said. "I told you. You can call in a lot of favors. Count this as one of them."

Hawk thought about expressing his gratitude, not just for what Cross was doing, but for the fact that he still believed in him. In spite of what the agency was suggesting.

Instead of giving in to that impulse, Hawk put the phone gently back in its cradle and sat a moment, thinking about the conversation. At least he had put something into motion. And for tonight, this seemed to be all he could do. His brain dull with fatigue, he couldn't think of anything else.

His gaze moved over the surface of Griff's desk. It was as neat and ordered as the man himself. Hawk's eyes circled the room: to an overstuffed sofa, invitingly placed in front of the fireplace; floor-to-ceiling bookshelves crammed with leather-bound volumes; carefully chosen paintings. All of it tasteful. Reflecting the Cabot wealth. But there was almost nothing personal, Hawk realized. Nothing really of Griff.

There was one silver-framed photo on the desk. It was a color snapshot of a child. A little girl, a blue-eyed blonde, who looked about six years old. Her age was pretty easy to determine because the broad grin revealed two missing front teeth.

Not Griff's child, Hawk knew. Cabot had never married, despite the fact that he had been in love with Claire Heywood for years. A man in Griff's position made a lot of enemies. Some of them ruthless enough to use a loved one. For blackmail. Or as a target for retaliation.

That was one reason most of the members of the team didn't have dependents. Or, like Cabot, took care to see that any emotional ties they formed remained hidden, the people they cared about safe. Maybe that explained why there was nothing of Claire in this room. Or maybe, Hawk realized, that was simply because Griff didn't want any reminders of what had happened between them.

The ending of their relationship had been Claire's decision, Hawk knew. It would never have been Cabot's. Not unless he thought that who he was might endanger her in some way. But Griff had been very careful to see that didn't happen.

Hawk picked up the picture of the child, studying the face a moment before he realized what he was looking at. He had believed that there were no pictures here of the woman Griff Cabot had loved. He'd been wrong. But few people would ever associate this snaggle-toothed little girl with Claire Heywood today, Hawk thought, as he put the photo back on the desk. That this picture was still here, despite the severing of their relationship, was a gesture as enigmatic as Cabot himself had been. Cool, pragmatic, infinitely careful, and yet...

Romantic, Hawk's brain supplied. It was not a word he

would ever before have applied to his friend. He had thought they were cut from the same cloth. Cynical. Realistic about the world they lived in. It was surprising to realize Hawk hadn't understood all the facets of the man he had worked with so closely. The only man he had ever considered a friend.

BEFORE HE WENT UPSTAIRS, Hawk made a final check of the house. As he did, he acknowledged that he couldn't remember ever being this tired, this burned out. It was not just lack of sleep, he knew, although the effects of the few hours he'd grabbed on the flight from Virginia had long ago worn off. Hawk had been shortchanged on sleep a lot of times, and he knew what that felt like. This was deeper. As much mental as physical.

Part of it was letdown from the end of his months-long quest to find Cabot's murderer. That desire had been a white-hot flame that flared so brightly it had kept him going, almost without having to think. Now he was, and none of the things he was thinking about were pleasant.

Like the realization that the agency he worked for was ready to betray him. To sic the dogs on him. Despite what he had done for them through the years, they were playing with Hawk's life, because he had disobeyed an order.

An order that hadn't made any sense in the first place, he thought, turning off the light when he reached the top of the staircase and plunging the house into darkness. All except for the faint glow coming from down the hall. From the bedroom Tyler Stewart had chosen.

He needed to check on her before he crashed, he remembered. He had promised himself he would. She'd be asleep by now. He'd take one last look. Check for fever. Then he'd turn off the lamp beside her bed and leave her alone.

One last job to perform. Then he would relax his vigilance, shut off the analytical mind, which insisted on going over and over the events of the last two days, and sleep. One final duty.

HER HEAD WAS TURNED slightly to the side on the pillow. She was still holding the elbow of the injured left arm protectively in the palm of her other hand. And she was so beautiful.

Nobody who had been through what she had the last two days should look like this. That was exactly what he had been thinking in the car today. Her mouth should fall open as she slept, the muscles in her face lax and unattractive. There should even be the occasional soft snore. A trickle of saliva.

There damn well should be something that made her as human as the rest of us, Hawk thought. And there wasn't. His lips tightened, remembering how she'd looked when he'd stolen those forbidden glances at the passenger seat. Just like she did now. Like some damn sleeping beauty. Fairy-tale princess. *A model,* he thought in disbelief. Just my luck to get my ass caught in a crack with a woman like this.

Except, surprisingly, he had found she had a brain. And guts. He would have to give her that, he admitted. She might not have managed on her own to escape this morning, but she'd given them a run for their money. She hadn't rolled over and played dead. She hadn't done that at the hotel, either. And for somebody whose life was as far removed from all this as hers must have been, that was something.

Despite his tiredness, Hawk hesitated a few minutes longer, standing just inside the door of the bedroom. The soft light from the lamp highlighted the high cheekbone turned toward him, emphasizing the intriguing hollow underneath. It exposed the shadows of exhaustion around her eyes, her long lashes resting against them like a fan.

The light also played over the delicate curve of her jaw. It gleamed in the blue-black hair, which was spread like a skein of tangled silk over the pillows. Even against their whiteness, her skin looked like alabaster. Almost translucent.

He thought about closing the door and leaving. Safest thing, he told himself again, but he had come here to check on her. To make sure she was all right. And it was all just a matter of discipline. Another job. One last duty before he could sleep, he reiterated. He crossed the thick carpet toward the bed, his footsteps soundless.

The sleeper didn't stir. The fan of lashes didn't quiver, and her breathing was deep and regular, moving the small, perfect breasts slowly up and down under the fabric of her gown.

When he reached the bed, Hawk stood for another moment looking down at her. From here, he could see again the subtle signs of maturity revealed in her face. The telltale effects of the years. She must be at least in her late thirties, he thought, judging by those lines and creases.

Not as young as he'd imagined in the beginning. He had thought she was a girl when he'd first seen her. She wasn't, of course. She was a woman. The only problem was Hawk liked women. Preferred them, in fact. He always had.

Almost without thinking, he put the back of his bent fingers against her cheek. And was relieved to find the skin was cool. Incredibly smooth. Despite his touch, she didn't awaken. The capsules he'd given her had done their job. Between their effects, her exhaustion and the injury, she was out like a light. Good for the duration.

Hawk removed his fingers and stood beside the bed, his hands hanging loosely at his side. Controlled. Then, his eyes never leaving the face of the woman, he bent forward and turned off the lamp on the table, plunging this room, too, into darkness. He took a step backward, away from the bed. Away from the temptation she represented.

But he didn't leave. After a few seconds, his eyes had adjusted to the lack of light in the room. The first thing they picked out of the gloom was the pale perfection of her profile, framed by that black-as-midnight hair. Then the slender column of her throat. Exposed. Vulnerable. And finally, almost naturally somehow, they found again the regular rise and fall of her breasts.

Unaware of the passage of time, Hawk didn't know how long he stood watching her sleep. Thinking about things he couldn't afford to think about. Things he knew he had no right to think about. Imagining things that could never happen.

And feeling the growing response of his body to those images. A hard, aching surge of longing. Desire. Need.

He needed a woman. Any woman would do. Any woman's body would ease the physical need, put an end to this painful ache, too-long denied. *Any woman would do.*

But he wanted *this* one. *This* woman. He had wanted her from the beginning. And now, finally, standing in the darkness watching her sleep, he acknowledged that.

The man called Hawk had, however, learned a lot of lessons through the years about controlling both need and want. He would control this. And as soon as he could, he would get her into the hands of someone who would offer her more protection from the people who were hunting her than he could.

Nobody's white knight, he thought again. He never had been, and no matter what she believed about him, Hawk knew the truth. All the truths about the man he really was.

One of those truths was that right now Tyler Stewart needed protection from him as much as she did from the assassins. And the sooner he got her off his hands, the better it would be for both of them.

Chapter Eight

"I think we should try for a meeting," Hawk said into the phone. The morning sun washed the desk he was sitting behind in light, reflecting off the glass that covered the image in the small silver frame.

"What changed your mind?" Jordan Cross asked.

Hawk knew the answer, of course, but it was something he would never confess. Not considering the things that were likely to result from the meeting he'd just suggested.

"It seems the smartest thing to do," he said, instead of explaining. "Once they put my picture out, any chance of making a deal is over. And the witness needs protection. The real kind. The kind they can provide."

That was a decision he had reached last night, after hours spent tossing and turning. The vision of Tyler Stewart, the thought of her vulnerability, kept intruding between him and the sleep he needed.

If Amir al-Ahmad had been involved in his father's death, then he now had the means to send out an army of assassins to find his fiancée, a woman whose face was too well-known to allow her to simply disappear. So damn beautiful and because of that, so vulnerable. Hawk would willingly give his life to keep Tyler safe, but with those odds, he had finally been forced to the conclusion that, despite his experience at this kind of game, that might not be enough.

He also knew that eventually the government would find him, no matter how skillfully he played hide-and-seek. Especially if they chose to go public with the search by releasing the pictures from the hotel cameras. Hawk understood what that would mean. Every law enforcement officer in the country would be after him.

Using his own psychological profile against him, the agency would eventually find a pattern of behavior he wasn't aware of. They would use everything in the bag of tricks they had access to and all their experts to figure out what Hawk would do next. Where he would go. And there was always the possibility that when they found him, if she were still with him, Tyler might get hurt. That was a chance Hawk wasn't willing to take.

"You want me to set it up?"

A friend's offer, of course, but if Jordan tried to act as a go-between, the agency would know they had been in contact. No matter what story the two of them came up with, the company would suspect Cross's loyalty lay more with the team than with them. And Hawk would no longer have access to the information Jordan was providing.

"I don't want you tied to me," Hawk said.

"They're going to deep-six the team. We both know that. My name's bound to be high on their list of people they can do without." Jordan was too smart never to have crossed the boundary between playing by the rules and questioning them. That was one reason Griff had valued him so highly.

"Yeah, but keep your nose clean and you may still get that sweet government pension," Hawk said.

The laughter on the other end indicated Jordan's appreciation of the sarcasm, as well as his knowledge of the exact size of that pension.

"Besides," Hawk added, "you're my inside line. I don't want to risk that. I may need you later. More than I need you as negotiator now."

"So who did you have in mind?"

"It's got to be somebody with no connections to the team," he answered. "But somebody who's very familiar with how things work. Someone they can't bully. Maybe even…someone they're afraid of. Someone we can trust."

"You don't want much, do you?" Jordan said, his voice filled with amusement at Hawk's list.

"I just want a slightly more equal playing field," Hawk replied softly, thinking about the truth of that.

"They aren't afraid of many people," Cross said, his voice serious again. That was another reality they were both aware of. "A lawyer, maybe?" he suggested. "Somebody with a lot of clout. Ex-congressman who's gone into private practice, but still has influence on the Hill."

"Maybe," Hawk conceded, considering those possibilities. Unconsciously, his gaze lifted, looking right into the blue eyes of the child in the silver-framed photograph.

"You have somebody in mind?" the voice on the other end of the line asked. "Somebody who's going to make the company think twice about whatever action they take where you're concerned?"

He had had this same thought before, Hawk realized. Just a general idea then. Not personalized. He had already realized there was only one possible ally the agency feared who might also be interested in fighting this one-sided battle.

"Claire Heywood," Hawk said softly.

He wasn't sure he had intended to voice that name aloud, but it was too late to take it back. The quiet on the other end of the phone line stretched across several slow heartbeats. And with Jordan's silence Hawk realized how impossible the suggestion was. *Griff will kill me if I involve her in this,* he thought.

Then, suddenly, overpoweringly, Hawk was again aware of that sense of loss. Griff Cabot would never know what he had done. But *he* would know. And he would never forgive himself if anything went wrong. "Bad idea," Hawk said.

"No," Jordan Cross replied, finally responding to a name he had obviously never expected. "Actually…" He hesitated before he went on. "Actually, it's a very good idea. But she's out of the country. She has been…since Griff's death, I think."

"She's back," Hawk said softly. "I saw her at the grave."

The silence was almost as prolonged as before. "She's just not…" Cross paused again, probably thinking about the difficulties inherent in that choice. "Not someone I would ever have come up with," he said finally.

"Forget it. She won't agree," Hawk said flatly, sorry now he had allowed it to go this far, even one person beyond himself. Pulling Claire Heywood into his situation was not something he could ever allow to happen.

Maybe Hawk had not fully understood the reasons behind the lengths Cabot went to in order to keep his relationship with the woman he loved separate from his professional life. Now he did. But he also knew he couldn't sacrifice Claire Heywood, not even to protect Tyler.

"I think she might," Jordan said. "If the approach is right. She's perfect, damn it, and you know it."

There was a trace of excitement in Cross's voice. And Heywood *was* perfect. She had the right tools and impeccable credentials, just as Hawk had laid them out before he had even thought of her in conjunction with this.

The only child of the union between one of the most respected journalists in the capital and a wealthy Washington socialite, who just happened to be the daughter of a former head of the CIA, Claire Heywood was also a highly regarded lawyer. She was often called in as a consultant by the networks to comment on any story they were running that had both legal and political overtones.

Perhaps at first that had been because she was her father's daughter, but her insider's understanding of Washington was undisputed. And Claire was not only popular with the public, her insight, intelligence and honesty were also respected by the elite of both parties.

And since half the power brokers in the capital had also jiggled her as an infant on their knees, she had unquestioned access to the conclaves of influence, including those within the tight-knit intelligence community. Which was where she had met Griff Cabot. Where they had begun a relationship that had ended only when she had broken it off, more than a year ago.

"No," Hawk said softly, remembering that relationship.

Claire Heywood might be a perfect go-between, but she was also off-limits. Griff had placed her off-limits; therefore, she still was. Hawk's lips flattened, and he pulled his eyes away from the photograph, denying the temptation.

Tyler Stewart was standing in the door of Griff's study, watching him. She had found a robe somewhere. It was a dark navy velour, obviously a man's garment. She had belted it tightly around her slim waist, and it almost touched the top of her feet, which were slender and bare.

Her black hair was loose, its natural curl unrestrained. The color of her eyes was intensified by the dark blue of the robe. Still slightly shadowed, they were focused on him now and smiling.

"May I come in?" she asked politely.

Hawk felt his body respond, his arousal incredibly quick and powerful. He nodded permission before he spoke again into the phone he was holding. "I'll talk to you later," he said to Cross. "Something's just come up."

He saw Tyler's smile widen and then dissolve into laughter at the unintended sexual connotation. He couldn't remember having seen her laugh before, and he couldn't take his eyes off her face. He hadn't been able to, not since he'd looked up and found her in the doorway.

"Maybe I'll have something definite for you by then," Jordan said. "I'll try."

Hawk put the receiver down, almost before the sound of the last word had faded, no longer thinking about what they'd been discussing. After his nod of permission, Tyler had walked over to the desk. She stood before him, looking down at the stack of newspapers he'd read before he went upstairs last night.

She had just showered. He could smell the soap. Now that she was this close, he could tell that her hair was damp, the moisture adding highlights to the midnight strands. She was wearing no makeup, and she was so beautiful he wanted to pull the too-large, too-masculine robe off her body, which he suspected might be nude underneath, and make love to her.

Here. On the top of Griff's big desk. Or on the softness of the Oriental rug. It didn't matter. He just wanted to push into her, to feel her body move under his. Responding to him. Answering every demand. More than answering. Matching them. Exceeding them.

"Good morning," she said softly, her eyes on his face.

Hawk realized he had simply been watching her, imagining the same things he had forbidden himself to think about last night as he had stood by her bed. Things he couldn't afford to think about.

"Did you sleep?" he asked. Safe topic for conversation.

"Like the dead," she said, and then suddenly her smile widened. "Not such a good analogy, I guess. Not after yesterday."

He held her gaze, not wanting to make small talk. Thinking, against his will, about exactly what he did want.

"Those are some pretty powerful pills you gave me," she said after a moment.

"How's the arm?" he asked.

She touched the back of her left arm lightly with her fingers, running them up and down against the softness of the velour. "Sore," she admitted.

"Want me to take another look at it?" he asked.

Whatever had been there yesterday was suddenly back in her eyes, and after a few seconds, she shook her head, making him wonder if he'd been right about what she was wearing under that robe. Not wearing, he amended.

"Maybe later," she offered. "We probably should change the dressing eventually. Put on some more salve."

"Okay," he said.

They were both remembering. He knew he was. Touching her skin, his fingers on the soft silken underside of her arm. Sitting beside her on a bed. The conjunction of Tyler Stewart and bed in his mind was not a safe one, but despite his vaunted self-discipline, he was having a hard time denying the appeal of that combination.

Maybe that appeal was in his eyes because suddenly hers fell, the fan of dark lashes shielding whatever she had been thinking. "Did I make the papers?" she asked, turning the top one on the stack toward her.

He knew she didn't care about whatever was in the papers. It had simply been something to say. And that had nothing to do with what was happening between them. Except, of course, it did. A lot to do with why there could be nothing between them.

At his continued silence, her eyes lifted again. "Hawk?" she questioned softly, examining his face. "Is something wrong?"

Everything you believe about me, he thought, but instead of telling her that, he shook his head. No explanations. He had already decided that. And no confession. If he succeeded in setting up the meeting he'd asked Jordan to work on, she'd know all of it soon enough.

She waited a moment, eyes still on his, but Hawk's face gave nothing away, the control too ingrained to be destroyed by his dread of what she would feel when she found out who and what he was. And why he had really come to find her.

Finally her eyes went back to the paper, and he watched her begin to read. He didn't bother to wonder which one she'd chosen. They all carried essentially the same story.

"So I'm in seclusion. Grief stricken over the sheikh's

death,'' she said, her eyes still scanning the columns of text. "How long does Amir think he can get away with that?"

"Just until they find you," Hawk said.

Her eyes came up, no longer smiling. The remembrance of what had happened in Mississippi was in them.

"He was in on it," Tyler said. "He had to have been. My God, he *was* involved in his own father's death."

SHE SUPPOSED she had to have known all along that Amir was involved. Malcolm had told her he had just left the room. The same room where the assassins had been waiting.

"They know the shot came from the hotel," she said. "I thought they could trace the path of a bullet. They should be able to figure out it came from Amir's room."

"In those circumstances, from that height and at that angle, it would be hard to prove exactly where a bullet came from. It must have gone nearly straight down. Besides, even tracing it to a floor wouldn't prove Amir had anything to do with the assassination. He's blaming it on the religious extremists in his country who had targeted the sheikh before. And they *could* have infiltrated Amir's entourage. Bought somebody off."

"But you don't believe that?" she asked.

"Not really. If he had just left that room, then he had to have known what was going on."

She nodded. That was the same conclusion she had come to, as incredible as it seemed. "Why would he kill his own father?"

She realized, even as she asked, how ridiculous that question was. People killed members of their families every day. Mothers killed their own children. And for far less reason than the billions of dollars and the almost unlimited power that were involved here.

"Dumb question," she said, without giving Hawk time to answer. "It was all about the money. I guess he just didn't have enough.'' Her tone was bitter, thinking of what she had seen Amir spend in the last six weeks. A lot of it had been lavished on her, on the wedding. Now she knew why, of course.

She laughed, shaking her head at her gullibility. ''I always wondered why he picked me,'' she said. ''But I guess I just didn't…'' She hesitated, embarrassed to admit that she hadn't wanted to question his proposal. That she had wanted so much to believe that he loved her. That he wanted to take care of her.

''Why would you wonder?'' Hawk asked.

Apparently Hawk hadn't figured this part out yet. But then he wasn't the one who had all along felt that sense of wrongness. Those feelings she had tried so hard to ignore. Sadly, she had succeeded in blocking them from her mind. At least up to the final morning. The morning of the wedding.

''Out of all the women he could have chosen, I always wondered why he would want me,'' she said. ''Now I know.'' At last she understood what had really been going on with Amir's determined courtship. She supposed it *was* better to know, even if the knowledge was painful. ''He needed someone who would agree to marry him quickly and without asking too many inconvenient questions about the arrangements. Someone…''

She paused again, recognizing finally that she had been absolutely perfect for Amir's plan. She didn't know exactly how much Amir had known about her situation when he met her. But obviously, it had been enough to realize she would be a potential target. And eventually she had shared everything that had gone on in her life. Paul's betrayal. The loss of her career and her savings.

So Amir would have realized how vulnerable she would be to his flattery. How worried about the future. Insecure about her ability to make a living. *''Just smile at them, sweetheart, but don't open your mouth.''*

''Almost any woman would have jumped at the

chance," Hawk said softly. "You had no reason to doubt his motives."

"A few," she said bitterly. "If I'd stopped to think it all out." But there was no doubt Amir's rush to get her to the altar had been balm to her battered self-esteem. *God,* she thought, *I was such easy prey.*

"I wonder what he would have done about the wedding if his father hadn't agreed to come to New York," she said.

She knew now that had been the whole point of that civil ceremony. All Amir's talk about showing her off was to cover his real motive. Which was getting his father out of his protected stronghold so he could be killed. Putting his father in a situation where *he* was vulnerable.

"If his father *hadn't* agreed to come, what story do you suppose he would have given to the press about why the ceremony had to be cancelled?" she asked. It was rhetorical, of course. Because none of it mattered now.

"Maybe it wouldn't have been called off," Hawk said. "He had nothing to lose."

"Marrying a woman he didn't love?" she asked. Amir hadn't loved her, of course. That was something else she had felt all along. Felt and ignored. Denied as much as she'd denied her own lack of feeling for him.

"A civil marriage wouldn't have been binding on him. It would have given you no rights. He could divorce you at any time."

"And all the prenuptial contracts we signed were to have gone into force when the religious ceremony took place," Tyler admitted. "It never would have. He would never have gone through with that, would he?"

"Probably not," Hawk agreed softly.

"I made it so easy for him," Tyler said bitterly. "I thought he wanted to take care of me. All he really wanted..." *Was to use me.* The words were in her head, but it was painful to admit that she had let herself be used again. First by Paul and then by Amir.

"Anyone who has the capacity to trust can be taken advantage of," Hawk said.

"The capacity to trust?" she repeated. "I guess that's one way of putting it."

She remembered what Hawk had said the first day. The day at the hotel. *You have to trust somebody.* In this situation she knew she did. And she would rather put her trust in Hawk than in anyone else right now. After all, he was the one who had come to find her. The one who had saved her life. Twice.

"As soon as I'm sure it's safe," he said, "I'll take you in and you can tell them what you saw. When you've done that, it should take some of the pressure off. Ahmad will realize he has nothing to gain by...hunting you down."

"What I saw doesn't prove Amir was involved," she said.

"Maybe not. If you're thinking of the kind of proof that can be taken to a court of law. You should realize, however, that even if you could prove he was involved, he'll probably never be charged."

"Why not?"

"Ahmad's head of state now. Diplomatically, he's off-limits. And he'll deny it, of course. He'll blame the assassination on the extremists. Or on a CIA plot," Hawk said, his lips twisting. "The agency's always a convenient scapegoat for the odd assassination or two."

"He'll get away with murder? The murder of his own father?"

"Probably," Hawk agreed.

"Then why do I have to testify?" she asked. She should have known this was the way the world worked. For people like Amir, anyway. People with that much money.

"You need to tell what you saw to prove to him that you can't hurt him. Not officially, anyway."

"And unofficially?" she asked.

"Maybe. Maybe some people will continue to believe he was involved. Most won't give a damn. It will be just a little added celebrity. Make him more interesting. After all, he has enough money to buy forgiveness for almost anything.''

"Even for murder?'' she asked.

"Far more than enough for murder,'' Hawk said, his eyes again cold and hard.

The capacity to trust, she thought. This man had lost that long ago. He knew how the world really worked, and that made him more cynical than she would ever be, despite the betrayals in her life. But still, she thought, finding comfort in the realization, Hawk believed some things were worth fighting for. Justice. The law. He must, or he wouldn't be who and what he was.

"All you have to do is tell them what you saw,'' he said again. "Tell them about the man who pulled the trigger and about the others in the room. Then they'll put you somewhere safe until it's over.''

"*They'll* put me somewhere safe?'' she repeated. *Not Hawk. Not any longer.* She would no longer be his responsibility, and she supposed he would be glad.

"Something like witness protection,'' he explained.

"And I won't see you again?'' she asked.

"Probably not,'' he said. There was no regret in his eyes or in his face. It was a simple statement of fact.

Hawk had a job to do. And he was doing it to the best of his ability. As he would for anyone in her situation. At least he had no ulterior motives where she was concerned. Not of any kind, apparently. Not even the ones she had found herself thinking more and more about, the longer she was around him.

But Hawk's disinterest had been pretty obvious. Despite the feelings that had been building up in her head about him. More self-delusion, she supposed. Or a very one-sided dream. A fantasy. And it was about time she grew out of those, too.

"THIS IS NOT MY AREA of expertise,'' Claire Heywood stated, after she'd listened to her caller's explanation.

"Perhaps if you'd told my secretary what this was about—"

"He's innocent." The deep voice on the other end of the line interrupted her polite rejection. "He's being targeted by some powerful people to take the blame for something he didn't do. I think *that's* within your area of expertise, isn't it?"

Claire lay down the pen with which she'd been making a series of meaningless doodles as she listened. This man had insisted on talking to her personally, refusing to provide any information to her secretary. Normally, Jane would have gotten rid of him, simply on the basis of his reluctance to reveal who he was or what he wanted to talk about.

However, he had made his request so persuasively, in such an impassioned manner, that the usually immovable Jane had given in. Maybe he had managed that miracle through the undeniably appealing quality of his voice.

Claire had known almost from the beginning of his spiel that she wasn't going to touch this case, but for some reason she had listened anyway. *Just a sucker for an attractive male voice,* she thought, her lips tilting a little. She had listened this long because it had been a while since she'd really enjoyed hearing a man's voice. Since before Griff's death.

Suddenly, thinking about him, her sense of loss and anger, all the regret she had felt over the things she had said, surged upward from where she'd enclosed them. Escaping from that tight little box where she had determinedly buried her feelings about Griffon Cabot.

She remembered the jolt of excitement she'd felt the first time *he* called her. Her body had reacted as soon as she recognized his voice, which had been as deep and pleasant as this one. It, too, had been touched with this same hint of Southern accent, the kind that spelled old money and good schools.

"Or doesn't that mean anything in this town anymore?" the man on the phone asked.

"Everyone's entitled to a presumption of innocence," Claire said. Somehow her fingers had found the damn pen again. This time she had drawn a box on the pad in front of her, and then placed a smaller one inside it. She recognized the symbolism.

"Except nobody seems willing to make that presumption in this case," he said.

"I'm sorry. Really I am, but I can't help your friend. I can give you a list of names, some very fine lawyers who would be much more—"

"They're going to release his picture," the voice on the phone said. "Which will start a manhunt. Despite the fact that they probably know he had nothing to do with this assassination."

With this *assassination*. The middle word in that phrase had been emphasized, and it triggered the association he had obviously been trying for.

"*This* assassination?" Claire questioned. Her voice was very low, but she couldn't have prevented herself from asking if her life depended on it. He was probably counting on that.

"He's a friend of mine. And our circle of friends is…limited. We've always looked out for one another's interests. I think maybe you understand what I'm talking about."

The words beat at Claire's consciousness, making her think about things she didn't want to think about. *Griff's team?* she wondered. *Can that possibly be what this is about?*

She had wondered when she'd heard about the earlier assassination. The one in Baghdad. She had considered the possibility that Griff's people had been involved. Because, of course, it had been rumored in the intelligence community that the terrorist in Iraq was the man who had been responsible for the attack in which Griff had been killed. And now this man seemed to be implying…

"I'm not the lawyer your friend needs," she said truthfully. "However much I might *like* to help him…" She hesitated deliberately, hoping he would understand why she couldn't do what he'd asked. "You want the best representation for your friend, I'm sure."

"I'm not talking about *legal* representation," he said.

That threw her. She had thought that's where this was leading. What else could they possibly want from her?

"Then…I'm afraid I don't understand," she said.

"Why don't we meet somewhere, and I can explain it to you," he suggested.

"I don't think—"

"Somewhere public." He broke into her refusal. "Wherever you say. You can trust me, Ms. Heywood. After all, we had a mutual friend. A very good friend."

Had a mutual friend. Past tense. The quiet words echoed as the others had. She hadn't been mistaken. This *was* about Griff. About a member of his team.

That had been something Griff had eventually told her about. Eventually and not immediately, of course, because he must have known she wouldn't approve. Griff believed the kinds of things they did were necessary for national security, but Claire had never bought into his reasoning.

It was an argument they had had time and time again, with Griff reasonably, logically and calmly defending his decisions. Acknowledging that he would make the same kinds of decisions in the future if the nation's security demanded them. And always she had argued in favor of other actions, other options.

And yet when she had heard about the death of the man in Iraq, there had been no regret in her heart. No outrage that someone had killed him. She had felt only gratitude to whichever of those men had taken revenge for Griff's death. For the death of a good man. *A very good friend.*

"The Lincoln Memorial," she said softly, her agreement surprising her as much as it probably would him. As it would have surprised anyone who knew her. "The foot of the statue. Three o'clock."

She put down the phone without waiting for his confirmation. She was still holding the pen, she realized. Because her fingers were trembling, she laid it down on the pad, beside the series of boxes she had drawn as she listened, each one smaller and more tightly enclosed than the last.

She put her head in her hands and closed her eyes, fighting the sting of tears. She had sworn she wouldn't cry. No tears for Griff. Or for her. Or for anyone else. Because she knew that her tears wouldn't change anything.

Nothing would change. She didn't believe in an eye for an eye. Since childhood she had been taught that was wrong. Still, when she had heard someone had killed that bastard in Baghdad, there had been a surge of exaltation so strong it had almost frightened her. An age-old, primitive desire for revenge. And she had recognized at that moment that she might even have done it had she had the expertise or the opportunity.

But there was no one to whom she could ever have made that admission. Like her attendance at this meeting she'd just arranged, no one who knew her would believe the thought of tracking down Griff's murderer had even crossed her mind.

But whoever he was, the man who had pulled that trigger in Baghdad, she knew exactly how he felt. And if the man they were accusing of the sheikh's death was the same one, and if, as her caller suggested, he *was* being set up in retaliation for what he'd done for Griff…

She sat for a few minutes staring out the window of her office, situated in the heart of the most powerful nation in the world. A strength protected, Griff had insisted, by men such as these.

They weren't interested in her legal expertise. They were smart enough to know that would be worthless in this case. So that meant they wanted something else. They wanted what she *could* give them. An insider's knowledge? She knew people who would know what was really going on. She thought of her grandfather. After all, as they said in Washington, there was no one as well connected as an old spook.

And her father. Of course, her connection there might be important to them also, she realized. The press was an incredibly potent force, especially in this world dominated by politics and intrigue. Even the Griff Cabots of this world recognized that. Now all she had to decide was whether she was willing to use those connections on behalf of Griff's friend.

Chapter Nine

"There's a witness who will testify that she saw the real assassins," Jordan Cross said. "A witness who can identify those men, none of whom were my friend."

It was the same voice, Claire thought, but somehow it was even more compelling in person. And the man was as intriguing as his voice. He was tall and dark, almost as handsome as Griff. His eyes, dead-of-winter gray, should have been cold as sleet. They were passionate instead, full of intelligence and purpose. Intent on making her believe that she should help them.

"Then he needs to turn himself in to the authorities and let her do just that. As soon as he can," Claire suggested calmly, fighting his power.

They were standing in the shadowed memorial, right at Mr. Lincoln's feet. The place was crawling with tourists, cranky kids in tow, snapping endless photographs, most of them across the breathtaking vista of the reflecting pool.

No one seemed to be paying them the slightest attention. Except, Claire had noticed, for the occasional feminine glance that touched on her companion and then came back, lingering a few seconds longer than was absolutely necessary on his face. She didn't blame them. Jordan Cross was as good to look at as he was to listen to. That was the name he had used when he'd introduced himself, but she couldn't know if it was his real one.

"There are a couple of problems with doing that," Jordan said softly. The gray eyes circled the crowd around them and then returned to hers. "For one thing, they don't intend to give him a chance to talk. Not even to prove his innocence."

"Why not?" Claire asked.

His well-shaped lips tightened as he continued to hold her gaze, considering, perhaps, what to tell her. "They ordered him to stay out of Iraq. He didn't. Someone had killed a friend of his. Maybe the only friend Hawk ever had."

He obviously thought that what the man he called Hawk had done was honorable. Therefore, he was willing to use any weapon he had to protect him, even Claire's feelings for Griff.

"He'll come in and take the heat for what he did in Baghdad," Cross continued. "But he wants to bring in the witness to al-Ahmad's assassination. She testifies to Hawk's innocence, and then they put her in witness protection."

"He must realize that…" Claire took a breath, trying to think how to phrase what had to be said.

"He's prepared to accept punishment that's appropriate."

"Prison?" she asked.

"Why should he go to prison? He executed a murderer. The agency knows that. Their hands haven't always been so clean."

"Maybe they're turning over a new leaf," she suggested.

"But you don't change the rules in the middle of the game. Especially if someone's been playing that game as long as Hawk."

"I think they can change the rules whenever they want to," she reminded him softly. "It's their game. Who's going to stop them?"

"That's where you come in," he said, smiling at her.

His smile was undeniably powerful. And suddenly Claire found herself wondering exactly what kinds of jobs Jordan Cross himself had done for Griff.

"I don't understand what you think I can do," she said.

"Hawk knows a lot of things the agency wouldn't be eager to have become public."

"So we threaten that he'll make them public? The same kinds of things this man Hawk did in Baghdad?" Her feelings about those were probably revealed in her tone, because he reacted.

"You really have no idea, Ms. Heywood, about the *kinds* of things Hawk has done for this country."

"I'm sorry, Mr. Cross, but my ideas about national policy differed from Griff's. They differed a great deal. So don't expect me to feel gratitude for Hawk's contributions."

"Is that why you broke with Griff? Because you didn't approve of what we did?" There was a thread of anger in Jordan's voice. For the first time the gray eyes were as cold as she had imagined they could be.

"Whatever was between Griff Cabot and me is none of your business."

Angered by his criticism, the same one she had made of herself often enough after Griff's death, she started across the floor of the memorial toward the steps. His hand on her elbow stopped her. His grip wasn't hard enough to bruise, but she was surprised he would touch her like that. She couldn't ever remember being forcibly detained. Not in her entire life.

"We're not playing games, Ms. Heywood," he said, his voice very low, his mouth close to her ear so no one around them could hear what he said. "A man's life is at stake. A good man, whether you want to believe that or not. A man whose neck is in this noose because he went after Griff's killer. And you should remember that Cabot and the others were just that terrorist's latest victims. They wouldn't have been his last, I can promise you. Whatever your politics, however deeply you feel about them, you can't possibly believe that preventing that murderer from killing again wasn't justified.''

Claire had stopped because she didn't have a choice. But what he said was compelling. Especially given his obvious conviction. And especially for someone who prided herself on dealing with the truths that lay hidden under all the convoluted rationales of national politics.

"What do you want from me?'' she asked, held now not by the grip of his hand, but by his sincerity. She wondered again in what capacity Jordan Cross had functioned for Griff's team.

"We want you to act as a go-between. Set up a forum where Hawk can make his case. Get them to promise two things—protection for the witness and to let Hawk walk out when the meeting's over. In exchange, he gives them his oath to keep quiet about what he knows.''

"Would he go public?'' she asked. Keeping that trust was the essence of the relationship the team shared. Even she knew enough about Griff's work to understand that.

"I'd bet my life he wouldn't,'' Jordan said, his lips relaxing suddenly into a smile. "But they won't know that. And with Hawk's background...I don't think, even with all they know about each of us, they can be completely sure he won't.''

"If this works, I want to be there,'' Claire said. "At the meeting.'' From the quickly concealed reaction in his eyes she realized she had surprised him. Probably because he thought there was an element of danger involved. She didn't care. She wanted to meet the man who had killed the terrorist in Iraq. She wanted to make her own judgment.

Jordan nodded slowly, only after he'd considered his options. "That might not be a bad idea. It offers Hawk more protection. It might even make our witness feel more comfortable to have another woman there.''

"A woman?''

"Hawk tracked her down just in time to keep the real assassins from killing her. She's been with him since."

"With him where?"

"I don't know," Cross said. "He hasn't told me."

"Doesn't he trust you?" she asked, challenging.

"I didn't need to know," Jordan Cross said, smiling. "The only thing I do need to know is if you are willing to help him."

"I'm not exactly willing," she stated.

"I know," he said, holding her eyes.

"But...I'll see what I can do," she said softly.

There was a long silence, and finally Jordan broke it. "I don't know if it's important to you, but Griff wasn't often wrong about people. He wasn't wrong about Hawk. And I knew he hadn't made a mistake when he chose you."

She wasn't exactly sure what that meant, but she could tell from his tone and from what was in his eyes that it was supposed to be a compliment. "Thank you," she said finally, her voice as low as his had been.

"How long will it take you to contact them?" he asked.

"One phone call," she said.

She had surprised him again. Maybe he hadn't thought she'd know who to call. She had her grandfather to thank for that information. And her grandfather's name would be a powerful introduction to the person she would need to contact to set up this meeting.

"Then I'll call you tonight," Cross said.

He released her arm and turned, striding across the floor of the memorial. His figure was almost immediately swallowed up in the crowd of tourists coming up the stairs. Claire watched until he had disappeared, his words echoing in her head. *"I knew he hadn't made a mistake when he chose you."*

It had been almost flattering to be included in that circle. The people Griff Cabot had chosen. And of them all, only she, apparently, had ever failed to live up to Griff's expectations. Now, it seemed, she was going to be given a second chance.

"SHE WANTS TO BE IN on the meeting," Jordan said.

"Too risky."

"That's the only way she'll do it."

"Then we don't do it," Hawk said, more than willing to let this whole plan drop. He hadn't dreamed Cross would go to Claire Heywood. He had thought Jordan understood that she was off-limits, that Hawk had changed his mind. He had found out only when he called Jordan tonight that he'd been wrong.

"You want your witness in protection?" Jordan asked.

"Yes," Hawk said.

"Then this is how we do it."

Jordan was waiting for him to respond, he knew, but Hawk didn't like either of the choices. They had had no right to involve Claire Heywood in this, although it seemed she was willing to be involved. And if she *did* manage to set this up, then Tyler would be protected.

"By the way," Jordan said into his silence, "they found no bodies in that house in Mississippi. Apparently when your assailants didn't report back, somebody came out and collected the corpses. They even cleaned up the mess."

"Efficient bastards, aren't they?" Hawk said.

"They've got lots of money. And lots of willing helpers. Speaking of helpers, NYPD's officially releasing the shots from the security videos tomorrow. You know what that means."

Hawk did, of course. All of it. He had gone over and over the options. There hadn't been that many to begin with. A nationwide manhunt would restrict his movements more than they were restricted now. Eventually, he knew, someone at the agency would remember this place. Maybe even remember that he had been brought here to recuperate after that botched mission. And when they did, someone would come out to check.

Or some of Amir al-Ahmad's money would buy that information. Just as they probably already had his picture. Maybe even his name. If you're willing to throw enough money at something, you can always shake loose someone who is willing to talk, Hawk thought.

If those bodies in Mississippi had been retrieved, then they knew Tyler Stewart was no longer alone and defenseless. Someone in al-Ahmad's group had probably already put two and two together and figured out who was with her. Track Hawk down, and they'd find her. And when the law put out those bulletins tomorrow…

He and Tyler needed to get out of here, he realized again, but he knew there was really no place to go. And in less than twenty-four hours his face would be almost as familiar to the public as Tyler Stewart's was now.

"Tell her to do it," he said softly.

"Claire's office," Jordan said. "Noon tomorrow. There's a parking garage below and a basement entry." He gave the address and the codes for entering the garage. "Park in spot 121 and take the elevator to the sixth floor. They'll be in her office."

"How did she arrange that?" Hawk asked, amused at the thought of them coming to her.

"I didn't ask," Jordan said. "I wasn't sure I wanted to know." The deep voice was filled with amusement. And admiration.

Griff would kill me, Hawk thought again, but this time the thought of Griff's displeasure had nothing to do with the possibility of involving Claire Heywood with his enemies.

HAWK WASN'T SURE how he had ended up here, standing again at midnight outside the door of the room where Tyler was sleeping. Maybe it had been Jordan's phone call. The realization that it was all winding down. Very soon looking after Tyler Stewart would be someone else's responsibility.

Hawk knew, because he was aware of how those things worked, that when it was, he'd never see her again.

So maybe that's why he was here. Because right now she was still his. His to protect. *Standing guard over the things you love.* Griff's words, which had once meant something entirely different to him, echoed in his head.

But they were as true now as they had been when his total loyalty had been to a friend. To his country. Hawk had never failed either of them. Never failed in doing his duty. He wouldn't fail here.

He reminded himself that nothing had happened last night. He had stood beside her bed, watching her sleep, and then he had left. Tonight would be the same. He would check to make sure she was all right and he'd leave. It was all a matter of discipline, he told himself as he opened the door.

The lamp beside the bed was on again. Tyler had fallen asleep tonight while reading, her shoulders propped on the pile of pillows she had stacked against the headboard. The newspapers she had brought up from Griff's study were spread out on the bed around her. There was a glass half-full of water on the bedside table, beside the opened bottle of the pain medication he'd left here yesterday.

Hawk's eyes came back to the sleeping woman. Her right hand again cupped the elbow of her left arm. Still sore. Painful enough that she had taken more of the capsules. And if she slept sitting up like this all night, he thought, that wouldn't be the only discomfort. She would probably sleep a lot better if—

Bad idea, he told himself harshly, fighting the image that had appeared in his head. *Leave her the hell alone,* he ordered. If she wasn't comfortable, there was nothing he could do about it. Nothing he should do. What he *should* do was leave. Back out of this room and close the door between them. He couldn't afford another mistake. He had made enough of them already where she was concerned.

He should never have played Good Samaritan. Never have kissed her. Never allowed himself to even think about doing it again. Or about any of the other things he had imagined last night as he stood in this same dark room, watching her sleep.

But she would sleep more comfortably if he gathered up the scattered papers. Maybe removed one of those pillows from behind her shoulders. He could do that without waking her, especially with the pills she'd taken. Then he'd leave.

That's all, he told himself, taking a step forward. And then another, his eyes never leaving her face. Slow, silent footsteps, until at last he was standing beside her bed. Exactly where he had been last night. Fighting the same battle he had fought then.

Slowly he reached out and picked up one of the papers. She didn't stir, despite the soft rustle of the pages. He gathered the rest of them off the counterpane, not bothering to stack or refold. When he had them all, he bent and put them down beside the bed. When he straightened, he realized that, despite the noise, she was still sleeping as soundly as she had been when he entered the room. As soundly as last night.

Then he reached out again, big fingers moving with deliberate slowness, highly disciplined, and switched off the bedside lamp. He waited in the darkness until his eyes adjusted, her face floating up out of the shadows. Infinitely beautiful. Peaceful.

One last task, he thought, stepping nearer the bed. He bent toward her. She wouldn't wake up, not with the effect of the capsules. She would never know he'd been here. She hadn't known last night.

Hawk slipped his right arm under her shoulders, lifting them. At the same time he pulled the top pillow out with his left hand. Removed it with infinite care and patience.

Suddenly her breathing changed. Her lips parted. Her tongue appeared between them, easing out to touch the top one with moisture. She turned her head, her hair brushing against his neck.

With her first movement, Hawk froze, his arm still behind her back. Her eyes didn't open, however. And after an endless wait, he took a breath in relief. She had settled back into sleep, her cheek resting now against his shoulder. She didn't move again, other than the measured regularity of her breathing.

She hadn't awakened, only stirred in her sleep. But now, he realized, if he removed his arm, her head would be against the headboard. He needed to move her a little farther down the bed.

He pulled back the sheet with his left hand and slipped his left arm under the crook of her knees. He lifted, right arm under her back, surprised at how little she weighed. She was so thin she was almost…fragile.

Hawk laid her back on the bed, her dark head settled on a single pillow. *Better,* he thought, carefully sliding his left arm from beneath her knees. Remembering to take another breath.

He glanced to his left, his eyes searching in the darkness for the sheet he'd pulled away. She'd get a better night's sleep this way, he thought again, congratulating himself on his success. Preparing to ease his other arm from behind her back.

Instead, her right arm lifted and her hand found the back of Hawk's neck. The movement was slow, almost languid. Sleepy. But her fingers touched his hair, and then they opened, sliding upward, widened to cup the back of his head.

Hawk froze, not daring to breathe. He was still bending over her, one arm beneath her shoulders. When he looked back toward the head of the bed, almost dreading what he'd find, her eyes were open. Focused on his face. There was no surprise in them. No dismay at finding him here. No shock that he was bending over her in the inviting darkness of her bedroom. Her lips moved again. This time their corners edged upward. Tilted. She was smiling at him, he realized.

The fingers that were at the back of his head shifted, no longer drifting through the short, thick hair, but applying pressure. Downward pressure. Her face moved slightly, chin lifting toward his. Her mouth opened. Inviting also. Promising. Both beautiful and vulnerable.

Hawk's head lowered in response. There was no conscious decision involved. There were no cautions left in his brain. Because Hawk was no longer thinking. He was feeling. Needing and wanting. Responding to an enticement that he knew was probably drug induced. It didn't matter. It was far too late to withdraw. His mouth found hers, and the contact between them was as powerful as it had been before, that first time he'd foolishly allowed himself to kiss her.

Heat and movement. Incredible hunger. His. And hers. There was nothing one-sided about what was happening. Hawk was aware of that. If he hadn't been, he might have found the strength to stop. He didn't, because it was obvious she didn't want him to stop.

Instead, her desire matched his. Her tongue explored, challenged, taunted. Her lips released, more tempting in their small denial, and then as quickly found his mouth again, renewing the contact between them with the same hot surge of need he had felt before, simply standing beside the bed watching her sleep.

She wanted this. There was no doubt about that. Wanted his mouth over hers. Wanted him... *Wanted him?* Sanity reared its ugly head. Only two days ago, she was supposed to marry someone else. Maybe, dazed by sleep, she thought...

Infuriated at the possibility that she might not know who he was, Hawk raised his head, pushing strongly against the slender fingers threaded through his hair. Her eyes opened again. What was in them now was clearly shock. Her lips were parted, and he fought the urge to cover them with his.

What the hell does it matter who she thinks *she's kissing?* he wondered savagely. The reality was she was kissing *him.* He was the one who was here in the darkness. Her small breasts were rising and falling against *his* chest, her fingers locked in *his* hair. What kind of stupid bastard would question that reality?

This kind. The kind of bastard *he* was, Hawk thought, watching her eyes widen at the anger in his face. Seeing the tip of her tongue ease between the trembling lips. Wanting it moving again under his.

"I'm not Ahmad," he said, his voice harsh with need.

He wanted to see that knowledge in the depths of her eyes. To read it in her face. The words were only a whisper, but they seemed to echo in the darkness, filling the small loneliness of space he had created between his mouth and her lips.

"I know," she said. "I know you're not Amir."

Her hand slipped from behind his head to cup his cheek. Her thumb caressed the tightness of the muscle beside his mouth. Even under that gentle pressure, it didn't relax. The tension didn't ease. None of the tension between them.

"I don't want there to be any mistake," Hawk said, his voice cold. Her eyes searched his face, and even in the darkness he could see the pain in them.

"Hawk," she whispered.

He wasn't sure if his name was protest or affirmation. Confirmation that what he had just accused her of was untrue, or proof that she knew exactly who he was. Not the fiancé she had almost certainly been sleeping with only a couple of days ago.

That realization hit him hard, nausea stirring at the thought of someone else making love to her. Of her responding to another man as she had been responding to him. Inviting someone else—

"What's wrong?" she asked, just as she had today. Her

fingers moved against his cheek, nails scoring lightly over his skin as they traced downward. "What's wrong?" she repeated more softly, pressing her thumb again into the tension at the corner of his mouth.

"Did you love him?" he asked.

Her hand fell away from his face. It curled against her throat. The knob of bone in her wrist was very prominent. Thin. Like a child's bone. Fragile and vulnerable.

"No," she whispered. Her eyes didn't avoid his.

"You agreed to marry him." That had been in the back of Hawk's mind all along, almost from the moment she had entered his room, begging for his help.

"It wasn't for the money."

"Then why?" he asked. Other than the fact that he had that much money, why would she agree to marry a man she didn't love?

"Because I was afraid."

The words were only a breath, but he was so close that he heard them. Too close. He could smell the fragrance of her body, released by the warmth of the bed or by the heat of the kiss they had shared.

"Afraid of what?"

He wasn't really thinking anymore about what she was saying. He had accepted her denial because he wanted to believe it. Needed to believe. Because he wanted to touch her. To put his fingers around that childlike wrist. To put his lips against her throat, exactly where her hand lay, fingers curved inward and relaxed. Trusting. He wanted to bury his face in the shadowed softness between the rise and fall of her small breasts.

He wanted her. His body ached with how much he wanted to bury himself within her. Deep and hard and tight. And as wet as only he could make her. He could. He knew that. Had never doubted it.

I know you're not Amir, she had said. And then his name. The only name she knew. Hawk. The single syllable had slipped out of her mouth as smoothly as he wanted to push into her body.

"Afraid of what came next, I guess," she whispered finally. "Afraid of the rest of my life. Of what it was going to be. Afraid of being alone. Afraid…there were no more dreams."

Hawk didn't have any idea what she was talking about. There *were* no more dreams. He had known that for a long time. Since before his mother died. No more dreams. Not in this world. Not in Hawk's life, at least.

"Dreams?" he asked. He had intended the word to be mocking, but it sounded only questioning, his voice almost as soft as hers.

"Dreams," she repeated. "I thought there were no more dreams left to come true. But…I guess maybe I was wrong."

Her hand moved, fingers touching his face again. The tips of them slid over his cheek, then lightly traced the outline of his lips. She was watching him, watching her hand move against his mouth. Then her thumb found his eyelid, and she brushed it across the short thick lashes.

He turned his head, avoiding her touch. Avoiding the tenderness it communicated more clearly than words.

"Make love to me," she whispered.

This wasn't the way it was supposed to be, Hawk thought. This was something that should never have been allowed to happen between the two of them.

No more dreams… That had reverberated in his head, echoing all that he already knew. All that life had taught a man called Hawk.

But maybe, just maybe, she *was* wrong, he thought, his mouth lowering slowly to destroy the emptiness between them. Maybe they both were.

Chapter Ten

When her eyelids finally drifted upward again, Hawk was watching her, blue eyes luminous in the darkness. She had seen them like that once before, she remembered. The night he had come to her mother's house in Mississippi. Had come to find her and to keep her safe.

Now he was lying beside her in the bed where they had just made love. Where she had begged him to make love to her. Two days ago he had been a stranger, and she had been about to marry another man. And now...

His features were set, his expression unreadable. But his gaze traveled slowly over her face, almost as if he'd never seen her before. Maybe he was as disconcerted by what had just happened between them as she was.

Two strangers. Who had met by chance. In circumstances that had nothing to do with love. That had far more to do with death and dying. His world and not hers. And he was still almost a stranger. A man she knew only as Hawk.

"Your arm hurt?" he asked.

Only with his question did she realize that it did, and that she was holding it. Like a reprimanded child, she removed her fingers from the gauze he had put over the gash.

"It's a little sore," she admitted.

"I guess this didn't help."

"Not my arm," she said softly, finally smiling at him.

"You didn't take the pain capsules," he said.

"I took one when I lay down to read the papers. Two had knocked me out last night. I decided I didn't want to be that drugged. Just…pleasantly unaware that anything hurt."

"Is that what this was all about?" he asked.

It took her a minute to put it together.

"You think I asked you to make love to me because I took a pain pill?" she asked, her voice climbing at the end of the question. She found it incredible that he didn't understand.

"Did you?"

"No," she said quickly, because that hadn't been the reason, of course. However, with his question, she did wonder if she would have been so open about what she felt if she hadn't taken that capsule. "Maybe it made it easier," she acknowledged.

"Easier?"

"Easier for me to admit what I wanted," she said. "But… I think I've wanted you to make love to me almost since the beginning. At least since you kissed me."

His eyes came up, locking suddenly with hers. She didn't flinch from their assessment. What she had told him was the truth. And she wasn't ashamed of it.

That was something she hadn't admitted then, not even to herself, or maybe she hadn't known, given everything else that had been going on. But she had been attracted to him in the hotel that day. She had wondered then what this would be like—Hawk's lovemaking—and now she knew.

And she wanted him still. Wanted him again, she amended. As much, or maybe more, she realized, than before he had taken her. *Taken her.* The words echoed in her consciousness. Out of place. So foreign to what she had always thought should happen between a man and a woman. She didn't think she had ever used the term in connection with making love. Now, however, she knew exactly what it meant.

Hawk had taken her. He hadn't talked to her, hadn't whispered words of seduction. And he hadn't pretended that he was doing anything other than what he had done. He had consumed her. Invaded and conquered, just as his kiss had the first day she'd met him. *Taken,* she repeated mentally, acknowledging the truth of what had happened between them.

But at the same time, she knew that he had taken nothing she hadn't willingly given. Nothing she didn't intend for him to have. Eventually. It was just that the way he had made love to her was so different. Powerful and unrestrained.

He was different from any other man she had ever known, of course. Harder. More cynical. Maybe even smarter—except apparently about knowing what she felt.

"Maybe we should try for slow," she suggested, her voice low and husky from thinking about the possibility. This was the image she had gotten when he had asked that question: *Do you want it quick or slow?* The thought of making love to him had been in her brain, triggered by those words, although she had known that wasn't what he meant.

Quick or slow? A choice between the almost primitive force his lovemaking had just been or the tantalizing tenderness she believed he could be capable of. She had no reason to think that, and she wondered why she did. He was not a gentle man. She had known it all along, and nothing that had happened between them had contradicted her initial judgment.

"It's…been a long time," he said. "I didn't mean to be rough."

The confession surprised her. Hawk would have no trouble finding a woman, of course, so his abstinence would have been by choice. And it seemed a strange choice for a man like him.

"I didn't mean that," she said. "I want you to make love to me again. And just…give me a little more time to enjoy it," she added, the soft suggestion teasing. She smiled at him, but the line of his mouth didn't move, the blue eyes still searching her face. Apparently whatever he found there was reassuring.

"You didn't enjoy that?" he asked, his voice suddenly more relaxed than she'd ever heard it, its timbre totally changed by the undeniable thread of amusement. "Are you trying to tell me that wasn't satisfactory?"

He would know better. Her responses had left no doubt about how much she had enjoyed his lovemaking. "I'm going to assume that's a rhetorical question," she said.

He held her eyes a few seconds longer, and then, without answering, he rolled onto his back. He put his hands, fingers interlocked, behind his head. His gaze seemed to be examining the ceiling as intently as it had her face.

She turned on her right side, propping herself on her elbow, high enough above him that she could see most of his body. The same broad shoulders and chest she had seen at the hotel, long, smooth muscles lying under tanned skin. Flat stomach.

Her eyes moved downward, examining what the towel had covered that day. Nothing was hidden now. There was nothing about his body she hadn't been made aware of. Nothing about hers he didn't know intimately.

Her fingers lifted, touching the mat of coarse hair on his chest. They moved almost as if asking permission. After what had happened between them, she shouldn't have to ask. Permission had definitely been granted, she decided. Reciprocal permission.

He turned his head in response to the small caress. She smiled at him again, moving her hand slowly, enjoying the texture of the dark, hair-roughened skin. The muscled firmness underneath. The feel of his nipples, hardening under her fingers. She liked touching him, savored the realization that she had the right to do that now.

"So how about slow?" she said again, her voice deliberately teasing. She didn't understand his hesitation in responding to her invitation.

"What did you mean before about dreams?" he asked.

But that conversation seemed to have happened a long time ago, and it was hard to remember exactly what she had been thinking. As a matter of fact, it had been pretty damned difficult to think at all just then.

He had asked about Amir. Why she had agreed to marry him. And foolishly, she had tried to explain. There was no *real* explanation of what she had done, of course. She had already admitted that. And this—what had happened tonight—was more proof of how wrong she had been.

It was almost ironic. Just as she had decided this particular dream was the one that would never come true, out of all the other seemingly impossible ones that already had, she had stumbled across this man.

This man, she thought. A man called Hawk. About whom she knew nothing. From whom she would learn nothing. Nothing he didn't want her to know. Nothing about who he really was.

All she knew was that he matched those long-ago dreams. Those cherished girlhood fantasies she had never openly confessed to anyone. Dreams of finding someone this strong. This *good*.

Her lips tilted when she realized the unintended sexual connotation of that word. That was certainly true, as she had reason to know, but it wasn't what she meant.

Just *good*, she thought. Old-fashioned, one-of-the-good-guys kind of goodness. White hat. Hero. She wondered what Hawk would say if she called him that. Her smile widened as she thought about his probable reaction.

"There's something funny about those dreams?" he asked.

She realized he was still watching her. Waiting for her answer. And lost in memory, she had almost forgotten his question. "I was beginning to believe I'd never meet someone like you," she said softly. "Not in this lifetime."

Again there was a silence, but his eyes were still focused intently on hers. "Someone like me?" he repeated finally. "What the hell is that supposed to mean?"

His voice was harsh, and she knew she couldn't explain to him what she'd been thinking. She couldn't imagine being foolish enough to confess to the romantic nonsense that had been running through her mind. Or to confess the dreams she had once had.

"As strong as you," she offered. *As good*, her heart added.

His lips moved, pursing a little as if he were thinking about that, and then, in amazement, she watched them lift, moving upward at the corners. Almost a smile.

"But then you've been hanging around guys like Amir," he suggested.

Who probably wasn't good. Or strong. Not any of the things she had once dreamed the man she would fall in love with would be.

"Would you quit bringing Amir up?" she said. Once again she deliberately made her voice teasing. She didn't want to think about Amir. About what a fool he had made of her. She didn't want those feelings to spoil what was happening here.

"Did *you?*" Hawk asked. The smile had disappeared, and his voice had changed. Hardened. It was cold once more, no hint of amusement in this question.

It took a second to figure out what he was asking, and when she did her own smile faded as well. There was nothing she could say about her relationship with Amir that Hawk would believe. Probably no one would believe the truth. It *was* pretty unbelievable, and that also made her feel like a fool. To realize how easily *she* had accepted Amir's explanations.

"Does it matter?" she asked instead.

Hawk's mouth tightened. "It shouldn't," he admitted.

"But it does?"

"Forget it," he said. "Forget I asked."

He turned his head, eyes focused upward again.

"You wouldn't understand," she said. An evasion. And it sounded whining and childish.

"Try me," he suggested, eyes still on the ceiling.

Men weren't supposed to care about the *whys* of stuff like that. It was surprising to her that he wanted to know. Even a little flattering, that whether or not she had made love to Amir seemed to matter to him.

"We didn't have that kind of relationship," she said.

"Why not?" he asked.

They had been engaged, if only for a few weeks. And most people would expect that would lead to some intimacy.

"He implied it was because of his religion." Even as she said it, she felt stupid. Used. Gullible.

"And you believed him."

She could read nothing in Hawk's tone. No skepticism. No mockery. But he was very good at hiding what he thought.

"Because I wanted to believe him, I guess. Because..."

"Because?" he prodded when she stopped.

"Because I didn't feel that way about him."

"You were going to marry him," Hawk said.

Almost an accusation. At least it felt like one. *Because I was alone. Scared. Betrayed. Numb with grief and fear.* And none of those were reasons she wanted to take out and examine. Or expose to someone else's examination. Not even to defend herself from what Hawk seemed to be suggesting.

"It's pretty complicated," she offered instead. Another evasion.

"I'm not going anywhere. Not tonight."

She took a breath. The darkness helped, and the fact that he wasn't looking at her.

"My agent had just died. Someone I trusted.

A…mentor, I suppose. And when he died, I found out he hadn't done some of the things he'd promised to do. Some investments he was supposed to make with the money I'd earned hadn't been made. The money was gone, and at the same time, I realized my career was going nowhere. There was nothing else I knew how to do. I never had anything but this," she said softly.

She touched her cheek with the tips of her fingers, but Hawk wasn't looking at her, so he didn't see the gesture. And he said nothing in response to what she'd told him, his eyes still on the ceiling.

"When Amir showed up," she continued, "marrying him seemed like a good idea. Everyone told me it was. Something safe. Somewhere to go." She hesitated, waiting for some response, some reaction to what she had said, but there was none. "I guess none of that makes much sense to you, does it?"

Hawk would always know where he was going. That incredible surety would never falter. And he had probably never depended on another person in his entire life.

"Maybe," he said.

Comforted a little by the soft agreement, even as grudging as it sounded, she went on, trying to make sense of what had happened, maybe as much for herself as for him. "And then the morning of the wedding, I realized that…what I was doing was wrong. Wrong for me. For him. All of it was wrong. For the wrong reasons. I wasn't in love with him."

The last she added almost as an afterthought. Just in case Hawk hadn't understood the wrongness she had discovered. Finally, after a long time, he turned his head. His eyes moved over her face, again searching. But she had nothing to hide. What she had told him was the truth.

"You want another one of those pills?" he asked.

The question seemed out of context. She hadn't even been thinking about the dull ache in her arm. It was an unimportant background element to the things that had been going on between the two of them.

"I'm…" she began, intending to deny the pain he seemed concerned about. Then she realized that his eyes had lightened and the tightness around his lips had eased. "Why?" she asked instead, suspicious of that relaxation.

"Slow," he said. "I just thought you might want a little something to make this time *easier*, too."

The inflection of the word was mocking. But it was also gently teasing. Inviting her to participate in that subtle mockery. Inviting her—

"But if not, I guess we'll just have to employ some of that old tried and true," he said.

"What's that?" she asked, anticipation stirring.

"You know," he whispered.

He turned his body toward hers, propping himself on his elbow just as she was. They were lying face-to-face. Body-to-body. Hardly three inches between them.

"No," she said, her mouth suddenly almost too dry to get the words out, her heartbeat accelerating. "No, I don't know."

He leaned toward her. She thought at first he intended to kiss her. She couldn't remember that he had kissed her when they'd made love.

He didn't now. Instead, his mouth lowered to the square of gauze he'd placed over her injury. He brushed it with his lips, the gesture tender, especially for a man like Hawk. Then he leaned back a fraction of an inch. His mouth was almost touching the front of her shoulder now.

"Foreplay," he said softly.

The single word was moist and hot against her skin. She waited, wondering if he would put his lips where his breath had touched. Wondering if he'd kiss her there. Wanting him to.

There had been nothing like what he was suggesting in the explosion that had occurred between them before. That had been hard and fast and exciting. Without preliminaries.

And very definitely out of the narrow range of her experience.

"You know what that is?" he asked, his mouth closer than before. Warm breath moved against her collarbone now. Tantalizingly near.

She closed her eyes, anticipation so strong it was almost culmination. She nodded, and then, afraid he couldn't see, she whispered, "Yes."

His hand found her breast, thumb moving back and forth over the pearled bud of its nipple. His fingers were a little rough, their hard masculinity incredibly sensuous.

His palm enclosed, squeezing the soft globe. The pressure was exquisite, pain and pleasure inextricably mixed. The breath she took in response was a soft hint of sound, broken, automatic.

He reacted by easing his body against her, pushing her down to her back, in the most vulnerable position a woman can assume. Open. Unprotected. Unquestioning.

He put his leg over both of hers. The contrast between the hair-roughened skin of his thigh and the smoothness of hers was also sensuous. She expected him to lift his body over hers, as he had done before.

Suddenly, despite her teasing request for slow, she wanted him to do that. To do it quickly. Wanted him to push into her again, hard and incredibly strong. So sure of what he was doing. In control.

That wasn't what he did, however. He eased closer, the front of his body leaning against the side of hers, his erection pressed into her hipbone. His hand cupped her breast, pulling it toward his descending mouth. His lips fastened over the nipple he'd teased, and he began suckling like an infant, the pull of his mouth hard and strong.

The words reverberated in her head. He was exactly that. So hard. So incredibly strong. Exactly as she wanted him to be.

It seemed she could feel the movement of his mouth deep within her body. Moving low inside. The sudden flood of moisture that resulted from that pressure was hot, rich, more profuse than it had ever been before. Readying her trembling body for what she knew was to come.

The glide of his tongue replaced the demanding caress of his lips. It circled, leaving a trail of moisture over all the sensitive nerve endings. Then the warmth of his breath touched where his tongue had been, evaporating the trace of wetness into shivering sensation.

Enough, she wanted to tell him. *More than enough. Now. Do it now. Make love to me before I die of wanting you.*

She said nothing, of course, and his teeth nibbled the hard nub his tongue had created. He wasn't gentle. Again she realized that the feelings he created verged on the edge of pain. Walking that thin, erotic line between agony and ecstasy.

She put her hand on his cheek. Protest or caress? Even she wasn't sure. It didn't matter because it had no effect on what he was doing. And she had known that it wouldn't.

She realized finally that his hand no longer cupped the breast his teeth and lips were tormenting. It was moving instead. Tracing over the bones in her rib cage. Finding with his fingertips the small protrusion of her hipbone. Sliding across the softness of her belly. His thumb dipped into her navel and circled. Slow. Infinitely patient.

Two distinctly different sensations. Almost too much for her mind to hold on to at one time. Too much for her body to bear. His mouth, teasing painfully against her breast. And the slow downward glide of his fingers. Moving so tenderly, so incredibly slowly, over her skin.

She knew what he intended. Again anticipation surged. She was already savoring the first knowing movement of his fingers. And there was no doubt now that they *would* be knowing.

Do you know what that is? he had asked. Foreplay. Now

she knew, if she had not before. He had taught her, a lesson she had begged him for.

The fingers that had been tenderly examining every inch of her skin suddenly invaded. They were long, hard and demanding—as demanding as his body had been before. Only with their touch did she realize she was sore. The pleasantly satisfying soreness that follows hard lovemaking.

It had been a long time, he'd told her. An apology, she thought. But it had been a long time for her, too. A long emptiness, and she wanted him to fill it. To fill her, just as he had before.

His fingers moved in and out as the back of his thumb began to caress the center of her need. All her needs. She knew he could satisfy every one. Satisfy her, more than she had ever dreamed anyone could. She arched upward, trying to increase the pressure. To quicken the tempo of what he was doing.

His mouth suddenly fastened over hers, his tongue's invasion matching the unrelenting movement of his fingers. Waves of sensation roared through her body, touching nerves and muscles in their path with sweet heat. Powerful. Demanding more than she could give.

Too many sensations, she thought again, her brain shattering under their impact, the ability to think spiraling away in the darkness. It was too much. More than she could bear.

The waves of sensation converged into one, lifting her, and she was powerless against its flood. Was drowning in it. Drowning in feelings. Heat. Fire.

Her body arched again and again, fighting it, and then, finally, because she had no choice, simply riding the crest like a spent swimmer. He wouldn't release her. He wouldn't let her go. Again and again he demanded. And every time, her body answered, responding to his touch.

Only when she truly believed she would shatter, as her mind had done, under the repeated ecstasy, did he relent.

His head lifted, his lips hovering an inch above hers. His fingers stilled, allowing her body to slowly descend from the mountain of sensations he had built. Her breathing eased, and finally she found the strength to open her eyes. To look into his.

"Too much," she whispered. It was the last rational thought she had in the maelstrom of feelings he'd created.

"No," he said softly, shifting his body. "Not nearly enough." He pushed into her, the size and strength of his erection almost frightening. Almost.

His hips began to move above her in the darkness, the dampness of his chest clinging to the softness of her breasts and stomach. And she was aware of the other wetness. *Too much,* she thought again. *Too wet.*

His movements were controlled, powerfully driven by the muscles in his thighs and buttocks. Deep enough to take her to the edge of pain. And then the long, slow withdrawal. So slow. Anticipation building again. Waiting for the next downward thrust. Bone against bone. Hard and hot and deep. So deep.

Although she would not have believed it to be possible, the same sensations that had destroyed her intellect were building again. Swelling from the inside outward. Clawing this time for release, a release that was nowhere near. Too wet. Too slow.

Now, she thought. Her demand, and unspoken. *Now.* She lifted trembling legs, unsure her exhausted muscles would obey the command of her brain. She wrapped them as tightly as she could around his waist, drawing him to her. Into her. With his next thrust, so deep she knew he had touched the walls of her soul, she cried out.

Still he didn't give in. His control. His decision. Slow withdrawal. A small seep of cold air between the hot slickness of their skins.

Desertion. Just like everyone else always had, he was leaving her. *Don't go,* she thought. *Don't leave me.*

"No," she begged, turning her head against the dampness of his shoulder to gasp out the plea. "No," she whispered again. "Don't go." Her nails dug into the strong, broad back that strained above her. She felt him flinch at the unexpected pain.

He punished her for it, driving into her body until she cried out again at the unrelenting force of what he was doing. Finally, just when she thought she could stand no more, his voice joined hers, at first guttural, hoarse with need, and then triumphant.

The crest of the wave that had carried her alone found them both. And it was strong enough to carry them together this time, their bodies still entwined in the concealing darkness.

Chapter Eleven

The razor was drawn downward again, revealing a path of brown skin in the middle of the white foam. Hawk's eyes were fixed resolutely on the image in the mirror, watching the movement of his hand, following each stroke. As if this familiar ritual, something he must have done almost every morning of his adult life, demanded his full attention.

"Did you know?" Tyler asked him again. "Had you already set this meeting up?" *Before you came to my room? Before you made love to me through those endless hours? Did you know that today this would be over, and I'd never see you again?*

She didn't understand why she didn't pose all those questions aloud. Why she didn't demand answers she was certainly entitled to. Old lessons, maybe. Never forgotten. *Just smile at them, sweetheart, but don't open your mouth.*

"I knew," Hawk said.

Another stroke, pulling the blade downward over the golden whiskers that had brushed erotically against her skin last night. His hand was as steady as it had always been. As steady as when he had held the gun on her that first day. As unwavering as when he'd shot those men in her mother's house in Mississippi.

"Then why?" she whispered.

Not demanding, not even now, she realized. Her soft

question had been almost plaintive instead. Begging him to make her understand why last night had happened. Why he had allowed that to happen if he already knew...

If he already knew she would never see him again. The words echoed painfully in her head, as they had been since he'd told her. To be fair, something she wasn't in the mood to do, he *had* warned her. Only yesterday, she realized, although it seemed an eternity ago. He had told her that after she gave her description of the assassins to the authorities, someone else would provide protection for her. That it wouldn't be him. Couldn't be him.

He had even told her that would happen soon. But still, she hadn't believed it would be like this. This... unexpected. This painful. Especially after last night.

Hawk turned his head, no longer focusing on the mirror, no longer pretending he needed to watch the long, brown fingers direct the razor. The half-finished shave should have made him look ridiculous, but it didn't.

One lean, tanned cheek was completely exposed. The once-broken nose. His lips, which she had thought were thin and hard, and which she had learned last night were not. She remembered the feel of them moving over her skin. Moving under hers. Suckling her breast.

She pulled her gaze away from them. Away from the knot of tension at their corner. And looked into his eyes instead. They were cold. As empty as they had seemed the day she'd met him. Almost as frightening. She had thought, after last night, that she would never see them like this again. Without feeling. Without emotion.

"I didn't mean for that to happen," he said softly.

She was surprised he bothered to explain that much, given what was in his eyes. Given the kind of man she knew him to be. And what he had said was probably even true, she thought, because he had never lied to her before. He had told her all the unpleasant truths her situation demanded. But still...

"You came to my room," she said, hoping for something more. More than this coldness. This *truth*.

"To make sure you were all right."

She shook her head. That was his self-deception. "You didn't have to—"

"I came the night before," he interrupted. "To see if you had a fever. I touched you. You didn't wake up. You didn't even move. Last night I thought you'd taken the pain capsules again. There was a glass of water on the table. The cap was off the bottle. I had no reason to think you hadn't."

Everything he said was logical. He hadn't come to her room with the intention of making love to her. And he wouldn't have if she hadn't invited him to. At least that's what he was suggesting. Maybe it was true. Except, even if it were, she didn't think it changed what had happened between them. To them.

"So what do we do?" she asked.

And waited, hoping that his eyes would soften as they had last night. Lighten with amusement as she had seen them do then. Or darken with passion as they had when he breathed that single, tantalizing word against her bare shoulder. *Foreplay.*

"We go to this meeting. You tell them exactly what you saw. *That's* what we do," he said, his voice low and hard. And then he added, almost spoiling the effect he had tried for, "Because there's nothing else we can do."

"I can think of a couple of things," she said.

She wasn't going to make this easy for him. Despite her inability to rail at him for what he'd done, she hadn't achieved all she had the last twenty years without stubbornness. Without the determination not to let anything defeat her dreams. After all, this was the only one that was left, and she didn't intend to lose it.

Despite the fact that he had said almost nothing to her last night, had made no promises and suggested no future for them together, she didn't believe that what had happened had been only physical. *The last of the dreamers,* she supposed, mocking her naiveté, but for some reason she believed that for Hawk as well, last night had been about more than two bodies in the darkness. About more than satisfying needs.

"Nothing else that will work," Hawk said.

He was still holding the razor, but at least he wasn't using it. At least he was still looking at her. But nothing had changed in the cold blue depths of his eyes.

"I trust you more than I trust them," she said. She didn't want to go into witness protection. She didn't want her life, even with her current problems, to change, to disappear, to be destroyed. And now that she'd found him, she didn't want to lose Hawk.

"I can't keep you safe," he said. "They can. It's as simple as that."

His tone said "end of argument." And she knew she was supposed to shut up and do what she was told. That seemed to be what he expected. What everyone always expected of her. Only this was too important. Too important not to fight for.

"Then I guess I won't be safe. Because...I'd still rather be with you."

He said nothing for a long time. His eyes didn't flinch at the offer she had made. An obvious and unapologetic offer. Made without any explanation to soften the proposal that lay at its heart. Demanding nothing in return. Nothing except to be allowed to stay with him.

"It's no good," he said finally. "It won't work."

His eyes told her nothing, their lightness seeming suddenly as opaque as Amir's had always been, as good at hiding his motives. And she had to wonder about those. Why Hawk was so eager to get rid of her. In such a damned hurry to get her off his hands.

"I'm not asking you for anything," she said softly. "You do understand that? Nothing but to stay with you."

"That's your problem. You *should* be asking," he said.

"What does that mean?" she asked, stung by his rejection. Humiliated by the criticism it implied.

"You were willing to go along with whatever Amir wanted because it was easier than standing on your own two feet. You want to stay with me because it's easier than doing the right thing. Easier than telling the truth about what happened and dealing with the consequences."

"That's not true. And it's not fair," she said hotly.

It wasn't. She had made her own way since she was seventeen. And she hadn't done too badly. Except in trusting Paul. And it was because of his betrayal, she now knew, that she had gone along with what Amir had wanted.

But she had really thought Amir loved her. She had thought maybe that would be enough, as close to the heart of that old, almost-forgotten dream as she was likely to get. She hadn't been able to figure out any other reason for Amir's whirlwind courtship. And she had really tried. But of course, she could never have imagined, not in a million years, that he was simply using her to set up his father. Using her.

"Nothing is ever *fair*," Hawk said softly. "Life isn't. You don't need me. Or Amir. You don't need anybody."

A tough old broad, she thought. Maybe he even meant to be flattering, but this wasn't a matter of need. Maybe she *didn't* need him. But she wanted him. She would always want him.

"One more question," she said softly.

He didn't nod or give her permission, but his eyes didn't release hers. They held on, and so she asked the only question that mattered now. And hoped he'd tell her the truth about this, too.

"If it were different…" she said, wondering if he'd understand. "If they weren't looking for me," she continued. "If we had met some other time, some other way. If all this weren't going on, then…"

She paused, not even sure now what she wanted to ask. He had made no promises last night. Given no commitment. Said nothing besides what his hands and body had told her. And maybe she had been wrong about what she thought they were saying.

"If everything about this was different…" Her voice faded, but she was still watching his eyes. Still hoping for something.

"If we were different people," he said softly.

Not a question, maybe, but she nodded. "Yes," she whispered.

"Then I guess the outcome might be…different, too."

Not exactly all she had wanted. But something. Maybe even as much as a man called Hawk could give. As much as he was capable of giving. That and last night.

And those were, of course, far more than she had had before.

HE HADN'T PARTICULARLY liked this setup from the beginning, Hawk thought, as he pulled the rental car into the underground garage. Despite the fact that it was a little before noon, it was almost dark in this concrete hole, dug to provide below-the-street parking for the tenants of this exclusive office building.

Maybe he hadn't liked the arrangements, but he trusted Jordan Cross. After all, as he had told Tyler at the beginning of all this, eventually you had to trust someone. And if Claire Heywood was willing to help, then he supposed it would have to be on her terms. Despite the premonition that stalked along the nerve endings at the back of his neck. Despite the fact that he knew there were too many factors in this situation he wouldn't be able to control.

Hell, he couldn't even control himself, Hawk thought in disgust. He glanced to his right, toward the passenger seat, and found that Tyler was looking at him, wide violet-blue eyes locked on his face.

What kind of bastard would do what he had done? he wondered again, as he had been all morning. What kind of son of a bitch makes love to a woman he's never going to see again? A woman he knows he's going to hand over to someone else's control in less than twenty-four hours? What kind of man lacks the discipline to deny himself that long?

"Now what?" she asked, seeing his eyes on her. Despite the question, her voice was almost disinterested. Certainly it was without the emotion that had colored the others she had asked this morning.

"We wait here until it's time to go up," he said.

She nodded, turning her head to look out the window on the passenger side of the car. The view in that direction was not all that interesting—an indistinct row of parked cars stretching off into the darkness. A concrete wall.

"Is this where we say goodbye?" she asked, her gaze still directed outside.

Hawk didn't answer. There really wasn't much point in discussing goodbyes. He had never been good at them. And he understood, even if she didn't, that in a few minutes everything she thought she knew about him, all those fantasies she'd dreamed up about why he had come to find her and exactly what he was bringing her here to do, would be exposed for what they were. Myths. Fantasies. Lies.

He could tell himself from now to eternity that they weren't his lies. That he hadn't been the one who had thought them up. But that didn't really matter. She believed them. Believed he was someone—something—very different from what he really was. And considering how al-Ahmad had used her, finding that out would probably have been devastating, whenever and however she discovered the truth. But after what he had done last night…

Hawk took a breath, his chest tight with self-loathing. Just a little discipline, he thought, just some damn self-control, and none of that would have happened. She would have walked away from him today—maybe with regret. With anger that he hadn't told her the truth. But certainly not with what she would inevitably feel after today's revelations.

"Hawk," she said softly.

His eyes were examining his hand, the right one, the one that was still, for some reason, gripping the wheel. At the sound of his name, the only name she knew and would probably ever know, he watched his fingers tighten, brown skin stretching taut around the muscles and sinews and bones that had never before failed him. That had never trembled or faltered in carrying out a mission.

His hand was trembling now. Trembling with need. Trembling because he wanted to touch her. To put his fingers against the softness of her cheek. To touch her breasts. To pull her to him and explain. To tell her that for him last night had been...

Something that had never happened before. Totally out of the range of his experience. With women. With relationships. Not that anything he had ever had with another woman could be called a relationship. There had been nothing remotely like this. Nothing that had ever involved his feelings. His emotions. His mind.

But if he told her that, he knew, it would simply make what was about to happen worse. If it could possibly get any worse.

Another betrayal. Because she had trusted him. With her life. Trusted him to protect her and to keep her safe. Trusted him with her body. Trusted him to love her.

And in the end, Hawk had been no more worthy of that trust than her fiancé had. Or the agent she had told him about. Like them, he, too, had used her.

Sleeve card. Ace in the hole. Those motives, which he had readily admitted to at the beginning of this, were not, of course, what he felt now. But telling her that wouldn't make what he had to do any easier. Or what she had to do. After this meeting, she had to walk away from him. To walk away and never look back. For her sake. To keep her safe. And learning how he felt, knowing what last night had meant to him, would make none of that easier.

"Hawk," she said again, and finally he lifted his eyes from the contemplation of his hand. "It doesn't have to be like this," she said. "It doesn't have to end this way. You said that once I'd testified, it would take the pressure off. That Amir would know I couldn't really hurt him. After that's over, why can't we—"

The knock on the glass of the window beside him interrupted her. Hawk turned his head to find Jordan Cross bending down to peer into the interior of the car. The sickening rush of fear in the pit of Hawk's stomach eased with the sight of the familiar face.

But it could have been anybody knocking on that window—al-Ahmad's men, the company's. Hawk hadn't even been aware that someone was approaching the car, he'd been focused so intently on whatever she had been saying. Like an amateur, he realized.

And that was why, of course, there had never been room in his life for a relationship like this. Because he couldn't afford the distraction. Not in his line of work.

He rolled down the window.

"It's time," Cross said. He had already straightened again, no longer looking inside the car.

Hawk knew that his eyes would be searching their surroundings, examining them for anything out of the ordinary. Anything suspicious. Just as Hawk *should* have been doing.

"What are you doing here?" Hawk asked.

"My operation," Jordan said. "I don't plan on making an appearance upstairs, but I wanted to make sure there was nobody waiting down here for you."

"Risky," Hawk said. They had agreed Jordan shouldn't be connected to him because of repercussions within the agency. Hawk still thought that was the best way to do this.

"Somebody tell you that you were supposed to have all

the fun?'' Cross asked. And then he cleared the amusement from his deep voice. ''Our esteemed colleagues aren't down here. They came in the front. That's what Heywood told them to do.''

''How much does she know?''

''I thought she should know it all. Makes it easier to play the hand if you've seen the cards. You ready?''

As ready as I'll ever be, Hawk thought. He rolled up the window and then put his hand on the door handle. He was aware that Jordan had already stepped away from the car, allowing him room to open the door and climb out. He was also aware that Tyler was still watching him.

This would be his last chance to say something to her, alone and without anyone else listening. Last chance to explain. Last chance to tell her how he felt.

Instead of taking it, the man called Hawk opened the door of the car he had rented at an airport in Mississippi and stepped out into the heat and darkness of a private parking garage in Washington, D.C. The end of a journey.

And his last chance, he thought again, standing up and closing the door behind him. This time he didn't take it. At least, he thought, as he put his hand into the one Jordan Cross extended, he still had enough self-discipline left to accomplish that.

''WE UNDERSTOOD YOU WANTED to talk to my client.''

As she made the opening gambit, Claire Heywood's voice was controlled and professional, sounding exactly like the high-priced attorney she was.

''Your client?'' the assistant deputy director of operations questioned.

''For these purposes,'' Claire said smoothly.

Her long blond hair was arranged again in a neat chignon. Today there were no disordered strands floating around the pale oval of her face. No tears. No black dress. She was wearing a simple red suit that shouted money and power, but it was a nicely discreet shout, appropriate for the elegant office they were in. And her eyes were as dispassionate as her voice.

They hadn't been. Hawk knew from their reaction that she had recognized him from the cemetery. Her pupils had widened slightly when her secretary escorted them into the room. Claire Heywood's gaze had met his, acknowledgment of that recognition in it, maybe acknowledgment of what he had done for Griff as well. Maybe even…gratitude? he thought, questioning the emotions he saw there. However, she had said nothing, gesturing them toward the two leather chairs that were aligned on her side of the wide conference table.

The representatives of the government were already seated on the other side. There were three of them, but Hawk recognized only one man. The others were new or had been pulled in from some other division. It was even possible they were State Department and not CIA.

That was probably the case, Hawk decided, considering the way their eyes examined him, as if he was something that disturbed their bureaucratic smugness. Or frightened them. Like he was some viper that had just come slithering out from under a rock and into their civilized little meeting.

But it really didn't matter what they thought about him. Hawk knew that the man in the middle was the one who counted. The one he would have to convince. The one Tyler would have to convince, he amended, if this was going to work.

Hawk planned to offer no defense of what he had done in Baghdad. As far was he was concerned, that act didn't need defending. He was prepared to offer them proof of the terrorist's guilt, to make threats about going public if he had to, but he was not prepared to beg for their understanding. Not even Carl Steiner's.

Steiner had been a friend of Griff's, and Hawk supposed he had been the logical one to take over the unit after the massacre. Hawk had no way of knowing how Steiner felt about the team or even whether he was the one who had insisted on its dissolution. He supposed he'd find out in the course of this meeting exactly where Steiner stood about a lot of things.

"I think Mr. Hawkins is probably well aware of what we want to talk to him about," Steiner said.

"Why don't we make certain of that?" Claire suggested. "We understand you believe Mr. Hawkins has some connection to the assassination of Sheikh Rashad al-Ahmad."

"*Some* connection?" Steiner questioned, his tone amused.

"Maybe you'd like to characterize exactly what you believe Mr. Hawkins' association to be," Claire suggested.

Hawk didn't look at Tyler. He didn't know if enough had already been said to make her start thinking. To make her start wondering why they were talking about him, instead of about what she believed they were here to discuss.

"I saw the men who killed the sheikh," Tyler said into the small silence that had fallen after Claire's suggestion. "I believe I can identify them."

Steiner's eyes moved to study her face for the first time, and then they flicked back to Hawk's, questioning, before they returned to focus on the woman who had just spoken.

"Ms. Stewart, I believe," he said. "Sheikh Amir al-Ahmad's fiancée?"

"I was," Tyler said.

"I'm sure Amir al-Ahmad would be very interested in learning what you saw," Steiner suggested. "He's trying very hard to track down the extremists who were involved in his father's death, some of whom, he now believes, had infiltrated his own entourage. He is also, I'm told, interested in making public the pictures of the man who set off the fire alarms that day. A man whose actions were captured by the hotel security cameras. He wants those pictures made available to the nation's law enforcement agencies as quickly as possible." As Steiner uttered the last sentence, his eyes moved back to Hawk's.

And you will, you son of a bitch, Hawk thought, *just as soon as you're sure no one can trace the man in those pictures back to the company.*

"Amir is interested in finding out who pulled the fire alarm?" Tyler asked, obviously puzzled.

However, her voice seemed as steady as Claire's had been. As calm and unintimidated. *Maybe,* Hawk thought, *because she still doesn't understand what's going on.*

"As he will certainly be interested in what you saw. I'm surprised you haven't already communicated that information to him. Forgive me, Ms. Stewart, but I understood you were with al-Ahmad's party. In seclusion, I believe, the sheikh said."

Hawk was aware that Tyler had turned to look at him. For direction, maybe, but he didn't meet her eyes. He didn't want to watch what would happen in them when she finally understood.

"The man who pulled the fire alarm," Tyler said, "had nothing to do with the assassination. That was…something else entirely."

"You seem certain of that," Steiner said, his eyes finally leaving their contemplation of Hawk's set face to find hers again. "But then, that is, of course, why Hawkins brought you here, isn't it. To tell us what he *didn't* do."

There was a pause before Tyler answered. "I came here to identify the assassins," she said, her voice low. There was something in her tone that hadn't been there before, however. Some hint of unease. She was disturbed, perhaps, by the direction this was taking.

"Or to assure us that Lucas Hawkins wasn't one of them?" Steiner suggested.

The silence stretched again. Longer this time. The blinds were pulled against the glare outside, and the stripes of sunshine that escaped between them, thin, white and dazzling in the pleasant dimness, fell like bars across the mahogany table.

"Hawk had nothing to do with Sheikh al-Ahmad's death."

"Forgive me, Ms. Stewart, but I'm afraid given Hawkins' past, and his rather remarkable credentials for doing exactly that, not many people are going to believe you. Even we found Hawkins' presence in the hotel that day a little too...coincidental."

"Coincidental?" Tyler repeated.

"A highly skilled...marksman just happened to be in the same hotel when an assassination occurs. A marksman who had that very day returned from the Middle East, where he had killed another man, in much the same manner in which Sheikh Rashad al-Ahmad was murdered. An assassin who was captured on video pulling hotel fire alarms, the effect of which was to empty that hotel of suspects, despite the fact that at the time it had been surrounded by police and FBI agents. Of course your fiancé is interested in this man. Especially considering, I suppose, that you are now traveling in his company."

There was complete silence around the table. It seemed that no one breathed.

"Hawk?" Tyler Stewart said softly. Almost the same way she had whispered his name last night. Except then...

"Would you like to deny for Ms. Stewart the validity of the things I've just said?" Steiner said. "If so, Hawkins, I assure you we'd all be interested in hearing those denials. I'm sure Ms. Stewart would be. Considering her situation."

Hawk had known this moment would come, but as he did with everything that didn't bear thinking about, he had put it out of his mind. Like Griff's death. The end of the team. Losing Tyler.

That was almost a physical pain—the thought of turning her over to someone like Steiner. But Steiner, he reminded himself, was someone who could protect her, someone who could keep her safe.

"I don't deny them," Hawk said quietly, his eyes resolutely on his locked hands, which rested, unmoving, on the mahogany table. "I don't deny that I did any of those things."

things."

Chapter Twelve

"But I had nothing to do with Rashad al-Ahmad's assassination, and you know it," Hawk added softly.

They did know it. Steiner's eyes left no doubt about
what he knew. *And,* Hawk realized, *they don't care about
the sheikh's death. That isn't why they're here. That isn't
why they agreed to this meeting.* He supposed he had
known that all along.

"How would we know that, Mr. Hawkins? Apparently
you've become a man who chooses his own targets. Based
solely on his own judgment. How could we know you
weren't responsible for the sheikh's death?"

"Because you know me," Hawk said. He kept his voice
low, but the bitterness was there. "You have more than
twenty years worth of knowing exactly who and what I
am."

Steiner pulled a file, which had been lying on the table
beside him since the beginning of the meeting, toward him
and opened it. Hawk recognized its type. He had seen others like it on Griff's desk. He supposed all of them had
dossiers like this.

Most of the time they would be locked away, accessible
only to those with a "need to know" about the aspect of
national security Griff's team had dealt with. Now Steiner
was one of those with an official need to know.

"Lucas Hawkins," Steiner read aloud, his voice without

inflection or emotion. "Code name: Hawk. Father: unknown. Mother: Lucille Hawkins. Mother's occupation: prostitute." The black eyes lifted to Hawk's, as if for confirmation of those simple facts. "I believe she died of a heroin overdose when you were seven."

Hawk said nothing, his eyes still meeting Steiner's, his features set. But in his mind's eye was his mother's thin, wasted face, her skin without color except for the brown stain in the sunken sockets around her eyes, which were open, glazed and staring. Just the way she had looked the day he'd come home from school and found her body.

But Hawk wasn't going to give this son of a bitch the satisfaction of knowing he remembered that. Or remembered any of what had come after her death. That long, dark nightmare of abuse and neglect at the hands of the state.

After a moment the assistant deputy director's eyes returned to the page before him, and he began to read again.

"For the next ten years, Lucas Hawkins passed through a succession of over thirty foster homes and various juvenile detention facilities. His longest stay in any one of those was for seven months, when he was nine. He was eleven when he was arrested the first time. Not the last time he was arrested, of course," Steiner added, glancing at the faces of the people aligned across the massive table from him.

Hawk remembered that incident, too. He had run away again, not traveling very fast because his drunken foster father's last beating had broken his arm and a couple of ribs. He had gotten caught stealing something to eat from a convenience store.

The cops had fed him, he remembered, and were amazed at what he managed to shovel down. They kept buying, and he kept eating, trying to make up for the meals he'd missed. They had been kind in a rough way, but Hawk had put up such a fight when they'd tried to take him home that they had no choice but to turn him over to juvenile services. That was the first time he'd ended up in detention. But it hadn't been the last.

"Each criminal offense more serious than the one before," Steiner intoned solemnly, like a master of ceremonies at some macabre awards dinner.

Although his gaze hadn't faltered from its contemplation of the assistant deputy director's face, Hawk hadn't realized Steiner's eyes had returned to the record in front of him until he began to read aloud again. Hawk's mind had been drifting instead, back to those events of almost thirty years ago.

Whatever this bastard wants to tell them doesn't matter, he assured himself. It was ancient history. Unimportant. What he had done for the last twenty years was his life. The important part of it, anyway. Griff had convinced him of that.

"The last of those arrests occurred when Hawkins was seventeen. I won't bore you with the details. It's sufficient to say that the incident involved the infliction of, and I'm quoting the arresting officer here, "grave bodily harm on another minor." I believe all of this is correct so far, Hawkins," Steiner said. He looked up from the file, his brows lifting, but again Hawk made no response.

"Is this necessary?" Claire Heywood asked, her voice tight, revealing emotion for the first time. "I don't think Mr. Hawkins' personal history is relevant to our purposes."

"I had supposed Hawkins intended to make his history relevant. I thought that was the purpose behind this meeting."

"The *purpose* of this meeting is to clear Mr. Hawkins of any suspicion of the sheikh's death. Surely the misfortunes he suffered as a child—"

"I see," Steiner interrupted. "Then you are more interested in current material, I suppose. Of course, the current material *is* the crux of this matter, isn't it, Ms. Heywood. The *real* reason we're all here."

"The reason we're here is because you're trying to set me up for something I didn't do," Hawk interjected, tired of listening to Steiner's crap.

None of this had anything to do with getting Tyler into protective custody. Apparently, however, Steiner was determined they were going to deal with the accusations against Hawk before they could move on to the other.

"I didn't have anything to do with Rashad al-Ahmad's death," Hawk said very distinctly. "And I'm warning you. I don't intend to go down for that."

"So you've brought us your personal witness to prove your innocence," Steiner said, his voice amused.

"Ms. Stewart can verify I had nothing to do with that assassination."

"And that is, of course, why you brought her here. All the way from…Mississippi, I believe. To clear you of that charge."

Another silence, Hawk's this time. He didn't waste much time wondering how they knew about Mississippi. It never did any good to question their sources. And he supposed at this point there was no reason not to admit the truth. By now Tyler would have figured out what was going on. Now she knew why he had intervened that night. And exactly why he had brought her here.

"It's one of the reasons," he agreed. It had been the only one at the beginning, but it was far less important now than the other.

"Then she's very valuable to you," Steiner said. "*If* she can indeed verify that you had nothing to do with that murder." His eyes shifted from Hawk's face to Tyler's. "Are you prepared to do that, Ms. Stewart? Is that why you're here? To clear Lucas Hawkins of that charge?"

Hawk wanted to look at her, to turn his head and find out what was in her eyes, but he didn't. He had done that in the car, and it had been a mistake. It had weakened him. He couldn't afford to be weak now. He watched Steiner's face instead.

"Hawk had nothing to do with the assassination of Sheikh al-Ahmad," Tyler said softly. Just on cue, Hawk thought. "I saw the men who did. I believe two of them were Amir al-Ahmad's personal bodyguards. And there was a man in Western dress. Not Hawk," she clarified quickly. "That man was the one who had the rifle. The one who fired the shot."

"And Hawkins had nothing to do with the assassination?"

"He couldn't have. I saw them all. I heard the gun go off. Hawk wasn't there. He wasn't involved."

"Then why did he set off the fire alarms?" Steiner asked.

"Because I asked him to help me get out of the hotel."

"And why did *you* need to get out of the hotel? That was, I believe, to be the location of your wedding."

"I didn't know who was involved in the assassination. The shots were fired from the balcony of my fiancé's room. I had gone there to speak to him, and when I opened the door, I saw them. Because it *was* his room…" Tyler hesitated, apparently hesitant to accuse Amir without more proof than that.

"I indicated that Sheikh Amir al-Ahmad now suspects some of his own people might have been involved in this," Steiner said.

Tyler said nothing for a moment. Hawk again fought the urge to look at her.

"But it's possible, isn't it," she suggested finally, "that Amir himself was involved?"

"In his own father's death?" Steiner questioned.

He sounds as if that's unthinkable, Hawk thought, but it was an act, of course. Nothing was truly unthinkable. Especially to someone like Steiner.

"Ten billion dollars a year is a lot of incentive," Hawk said. "There are people in this town who would kill you for your pocket change."

"We have no reason to suspect Amir al-Ahmad of having any role in his father's death," the assistant deputy director said. "The extremists had long ago targeted their country for a takeover. And they had made at least two previous attempts on the sheikh's life. Perhaps Ms. Stewart would be willing to make herself available to the new sheikh in order to identify which members of his staff she saw on that balcony."

"Ms. Stewart will make herself available to *you,*" Hawk said. "Not to Amir."

"But I'm afraid we are no longer involved in the investigation of the al-Ahmad assassination," Steiner replied. "Not in any…enforcement capacity."

"What the hell does that mean?" Hawk asked, his eyes narrowing.

"We believe that the action taken against the sheikh represented an attempt to carry out an internal coup. A national matter, probably religious in nature. It is in the best interests of the United States not to interfere in any way with the ongoing investigation of the sheikh's death. An investigation being very competently carried out by his own countrymen and their appointed agents."

"They killed a man on a New York City street," Hawk said. "They blew away a visiting head of state right in the heart of our largest city. Are you saying that's none of our business?"

"Visiting is, I believe, the operative word here," Carl Steiner said, his voice expressing disinterest. "A *private* visit. Which was not State Department sponsored. Or sanctioned. Perhaps if they had requested security…" He shrugged, letting the suggestion trail, his dark eyes meeting Hawk's.

They were triumphant, Hawk realized. The nausea that had formed in Hawk's throat when Steiner suggested Tyler make herself available to Amir for questioning was joined now by a prickle of ice skating along his spine.

"However, there are other matters which we, as representatives of the United States, are still very much interested in resolving,'' Steiner continued. ''Matters having to do with this government's authority. With…obeying orders,'' he said almost delicately, his black eyes still locked on Hawk's.

''The assassination in Iraq,'' Hawk said, laying out the accusation Steiner was dancing around, probably because of Claire Heywood's presence. They had wanted Hawk for that all along. They were determined to rein him in. Maybe even to punish him for going against orders.

''Unless, of course, Ms. Stewart is prepared to provide an alibi for that murder also,'' the assistant deputy director said.

''You know why I went to Baghdad,'' Hawk said.

''I know you had been told *not* to go. And told that your target there was off-limits.''

''My target there,'' Hawk repeated mockingly, ''killed Griffon Cabot and five others in a senseless massacre of innocent people who were on their way to work. I knew who ordered that attack. You knew who ordered it. An international terrorist with enough blood on his hands to float a couple of battleships.''

''Someone who was off-limits,'' Steiner said again.

''Is he right?'' Claire Heywood asked softly.

Steiner's eyes shifted to her, and in them was surprise. ''Right about what?''

''About the man in Baghdad being responsible for the Langley incident?''

''We have no proof of that,'' Steiner said.

''I have proof.'' Hawk's voice was calm and emotionless again. He had himself under control. He could do that as long as he didn't think about Tyler. He had to convince Steiner to put her into protection, and if the price of that was to let them have him for what he had done in Baghdad, then so be it. ''Do you really want proof?''

''You may present it. It will have to be analyzed, of course,'' Steiner said.

Hawk laughed, the short sound devoid of humor. ''*Ev-*

erything has to be analyzed," he said. "To see who we might offend. To determine if our so-called allies will approve. Whatever happened to right and wrong? Whatever happened to doing the right thing, the right thing for *this* country, and letting the chips fall where they may?"

"And you intend to determine what is right?" Steiner asked. "You and you alone will make that decision? The world is more complicated, Mr. Hawkins, than your narrow vision of it."

"Only to you," Hawk said. "Only to bastards like you and your pious bureaucratic brotherhood."

No one said anything for a moment. Steiner's eyes were angry, but still confident. And why the hell shouldn't they be? Hawk thought bitterly. Steiner held the winning hand. He had apparently known that since the beginning. Because he really did know all about Hawk. All the psychological babble that they had collected on him for years. Somehow they had put that together with the fact that he had taken Tyler Stewart with him from Mississippi and kept her with him. And this time, by putting two and two together, they had somehow arrived at the correct conclusion.

"What do you want?" Hawk said finally. It was time to give in to the inevitable and make the deal.

"We want you to agree to answer some questions about what happened in Iraq."

"And where does this questioning take place?" Hawk asked, simply as a matter of form.

"At one of our secured facilities. You will be well treated. I think you know that."

Fed and clothed and housed, Hawk thought, at the expense of the state. Not much different from getting the little pension he'd lost. "And what do *I* get in exchange for my cooperation?"

"We're not offering you a deal."

"You better be," Hawk warned softly.

"Certain terms were set when you agreed to this meeting," Claire reminded Steiner.

"The situation has changed," he said.

"You son of a bitch," Hawk said, his voice filled with cold hatred. The men on either side of Steiner shifted uncomfortably, but he seemed unaffected.

"What do you want?" Steiner asked, his voice amused again.

It was almost as if he were making a concession. One that they all would know he wasn't compelled to make. As if the agency was no longer worried about whatever threat Hawk might represent to them, but was willing to give a little out of the goodness of its heart, a concept Hawk knew to be a joke. Or as one might concede some advantage to an outmatched opponent, simply to be sporting.

Even as he was thinking that, Hawk was amending his demands. After all, there was only one that mattered. And there was no reason why Steiner shouldn't grant it, especially if Hawk gave them what they wanted. It would be no skin off his nose, and he would leave with what the company had sent him here to get.

"Ms. Stewart tells her story about what she saw to the proper authorities. Ours, not theirs," Hawk said. "Then they take it from there. The agency sees to it that the assassins can't possibly find her. You keep her hidden for as long as it takes to track them down."

"Witness protection?"

"Whatever you want to call it," Hawk agreed. *Whatever will keep her safe.* "But she doesn't tell that story to al-Ahmad. She tells it to our people. And then she disappears until you catch the assassins."

"Of course," Steiner agreed softly. His eyes fell, the dark lashes hiding the sudden gleam of satisfaction that had clearly been in them.

And why the hell shouldn't he be satisfied? Hawk thought. He had what he had come for. He had Hawk.

Hawk didn't know what the outcome of this agreement would be for him. It didn't really matter. It wasn't as if he had had a whole lot of other plans for the future.

"And we want the tapes from the security cameras. All copies of them, and those pictures are not to be made public," Claire Heywood said, her voice clear and decisive again. In charge. "And whatever material that file contains."

Steiner looked at her, almost for the first time since she had opened the meeting. His lips twisted, a small mocking expression of amusement. He closed the file and pushed it toward her across the expanse of the table.

"That's the last of it, you know," he said.

"The last of what?" Claire asked, pulling the file to her.

"The last records of a man called Hawk. As far as the government is concerned—as far as the world is concerned—" he amended, "Lucas Hawkins does not now and never has existed."

They had erased everything, Hawk realized, chilled. He had known they would doctor the records so that there would be no connection between him and the agency. But this...

He supposed he should have known. When they released those pictures from the hotel cameras, they would want to be absolutely certain that nothing could possibly be traced back to them. No matter who was doing the tracing.

"You can't do that," Claire said.

Hawk wondered if she really believed what she had just said. Because, of course, they could do anything they wanted. He'd thought she knew how things worked here. He did. They could do any damn thing they wanted. To him. To his life.

"We already have," Steiner said. "What you hold is all that remains of Lucas Hawkins." His eyes came back to Hawk's. "Talk and be damned," he challenged softly. "There is nothing left, not one line of print, not one computer reference, not one pay voucher, not one record in any file anywhere that can be used to verify your existence. Much less anything you *claim* to have done during the last ten years. The only thing that going public about those things will garner you is a hell of a lot of enemies. People have long memories when it comes to murder.''

''I never *murdered* anyone,'' Hawk said.

''That's a matter of semantics, isn't it,'' Steiner said. ''Or maybe a matter of your politics.'' He stood up. Surprised by the abruptness of the movement, the men on either side of him hurriedly rose also.

''Do we have a deal?'' Hawk asked.

''You walk out that door with us, and we do.''

''Those aren't the terms we agreed to,'' Claire said angrily.

''Conditions have changed. You no longer have anything to bargain with. No one will believe whatever stories you tell.''

''They may believe the story I tell,'' Claire said.

''Let it go,'' Hawk said softly. ''It's over.''

He wouldn't allow Claire Heywood to sacrifice herself in a crusade she couldn't win. None of them would win in that case. He put his hand on the edge of the table, preparing to push out of the plush softness of the big leather chair. The sense of fatigue that had haunted him after Baghdad was overwhelming again.

Tyler's fingers were suddenly on top of his. They were cold, but not trembling. He almost pulled his hand away. Almost stood, ignoring the entreaty her gesture represented. Something prevented him. Maybe his fatigue. Or the knowledge that this was the last time he would see her. Or maybe, once again, as in that dark bedroom last night, his self-control had broken. He turned his head slowly and met her eyes. In his was nothing that he didn't intend to be there. And in hers...

''Is what he said true?'' she asked.

What part of it? Hawk wondered. *Calling what happened in Iraq a murder? Saying I no longer exist? All of*

*those things he read out of my file? What he implied about
my reasons for bringing you here today?* But of course,
there was some element of truth in all of those. Enough
that he supposed it didn't matter anymore about the parts
that weren't true.

"Yes," he said simply.

She slowly removed her hand from his, putting it in her
lap with the other. He could still feel the imprint of her
fingers, however, burning against his skin. *Last time,* he
thought. *Last touch. Last chance.*

Then the man who had been called Hawk stood and
followed Carl Steiner out of the room. He didn't look back.

"WHAT DO I DO NOW?" Tyler asked finally into the silence they left behind. "I thought…" She hesitated, unsure
of all her conclusions. Confused by the abrupt ending to
this. For one thing, no one had taken down a word she had
said about the assassination. They hadn't seemed even remotely interested in the story she had come here to tell.

She thought she had been following the conversation,
despite the references to people and events she had no
knowledge of. The man who was in charge had agreed to
put her in Witness Protection. Which was exactly what
Hawk had told her would happen. Nothing else, however,
had been anything at all like what she had been led to
expect.

"They'll send someone for you," the blond woman beside her said softly. "Until they do, we just stay here. I'm
Claire Heywood, by the way," she added, holding out her
hand.

The handshake was awkward because of their positions.
They were still sitting on the same side of the conference
table, the chair Hawk had occupied during the meeting
between them.

"You're Hawk's lawyer?" Tyler asked hesitantly.
There had been no introductions. She had assumed that
everyone else in the room knew one another.

"Not really," Claire said. "Just…a friend, I suppose. A friend of a friend's," she added after a moment.

"Then you knew what that was all about," Tyler suggested.

"Some of it," Claire agreed.

"Hawk killed a man in Baghdad."

"Yes," Claire said. Her voice was softer than it had been before, almost reluctant.

"But why?" Tyler asked, shaking her head. "That's not…I mean, I know that he's…" She almost said "dangerous." He was. She had recognized that from the beginning, but she had thought that was because of his job. Because of being an agent. Now she wasn't sure exactly what he was.

It had gradually become obvious that Hawk hadn't been sent to Mississippi to rescue her. He hadn't come to protect her from the people who were hunting her. Or even to bring her here so she could identify them. That identification had been made only because she had pushed it into the conversation, and no one had seemed really interested.

According to the man in the middle, Hawk had brought her here to clear *him* of the assassination of the sheikh. But he had never indicated to her that he was a suspect. He had saved her life, but apparently even that had been done for his own purposes. Not because he was acting under orders or investigating the assassination, but because she was the one person who could prove Hawk hadn't done it. Which meant, she supposed…

That he had been using her, she acknowledged. And it also meant that nothing of what she thought she knew about Hawk was true. At least not his motives for doing what he had done. And one of those involved what had happened between them last night.

"Who is he?" Tyler asked, pulling away from the pain of that. She was trying to understand what Hawk had done and why. And trying not to judge until she knew everything.

Claire didn't answer for a moment, her eyes filled with sympathy. And when she did, it really wasn't the explanation Tyler had asked for.

"He's a man who believes that in order to keep this country safe, sometimes someone has to do things…" She hesitated before she went on. "Things the rest of us don't always approve of. Or understand. Things that may, on the surface…" She paused again, her eyes full of some emotion Tyler didn't understand. Maybe some of the same confusion she was feeling.

"But he *is* a government agent?" Tyler asked softly.

"Yes," Claire agreed.

At least she hadn't been wrong about that, Tyler thought. At least he was one of the good guys.

"A very specialized agent," Claire said.

"He kills people," Tyler said simply. "Officially kills people, I mean."

Claire's eyes reflected a touch of shock at her bluntness, but that gave way almost immediately to amusement. "You don't find that…repugnant?" she asked, accurately reading her tone.

"I've known a couple of people the world would probably be better off without, and my circle of acquaintance isn't all that large," Tyler said.

She was finally beginning to put some of this into perspective. Hawk was a government assassin. That's why he had been an immediate suspect in the sheikh's death. That's why just his appearance on the hotel security tapes had made them think he had something to with it. And that's why he had come to find her. Because she was the one person who could prove he didn't.

He hadn't told her the complete truth about who he was. And there was really no reason why he should have. She didn't imagine he just went around announcing something like that. As Claire Heywood suggested, there were plenty of people who would find that to be repugnant.

"If you consider all that goes on in the world," Tyler

said, "all the crazy people like Hitler who get into power and then decide they can do anything they want to... I guess it isn't too hard to understand why the government would feel that some of them have to be stopped."

"And that makes sense to you?" Claire asked softly. "It makes sense for Hawk to be the one to do that?"

"It makes sense to me that *someone* has to do it."

Claire held her eyes, searching them.

"You think...what Hawk does is wrong?" Tyler asked.

"I don't know," Claire said. "I thought I did. There are certainly laws against it. Strongly stated national policies. But...I had a friend who believed as you do. That occasionally *someone* has to do it."

"Hawk's friend? The friend of a friend?"

Claire nodded again. "Hawk's friend."

"I don't think he has many," Tyler said.

He had always seemed so alone to her. Maybe that had even been part of his appeal. His aloneness. His emptiness. Always before she had seemed to gravitate to someone who would take care of her. He had accused her of that. And yet in Hawk...

She realized suddenly what she had been thinking. And the incredible flaws in her reasoning. Hawk didn't need *her* to take care of *him*. Hawk didn't need anyone. He never would. He had made that abundantly clear.

He believed in standing on his own two feet. Just as he had told her she had to do. It hadn't been a fair criticism of her life, but he didn't really know her life. What it had been. Why she had done the things she had. Trusting Paul. Agreeing to marry Amir. Loving Hawk.

Loving Hawk. Suddenly her vision blurred, Claire Heywood's classic features disappearing behind a mist of tears. Tyler had never told him that, and she wondered now if it would have made a difference. Wondered if he really hadn't known.

Considering the things in the file Claire Heywood was holding, it was possible he hadn't understood. Possible that he hadn't known he could be loved. She understood that feeling all too well—wondering how someone could find you worthy to love. She had wondered that about Amir. Had wondered why in the world, out of all the women out there, he would love someone like her.

"Do you think that, while we're waiting, I could read that?" Tyler asked. She reached across the space and touched the manila file with the tips of her fingers. "If it's not…classified or something?"

Claire hesitated a moment, and then she pushed the folder along the table. "It probably is," she said, smiling, "but I don't think that matters much now."

Tyler thought about what she already knew. About the things this file contained. The things that had been read aloud today. Bare bones of a story she could certainly put flesh to. A history of pain and deprivation that made her own life seem privileged and protected. At least someone had loved her. At least there had always been a home to run to. A sanctuary.

And for Hawk… With trembling fingers, Tyler Stewart opened the file they had been given. They were still shaking as they fanned the stack of papers the folder contained.

And her eyes, when she raised them to Claire Heywood's, were again touched with moisture. "There's nothing here," she said softly. There hadn't been. Not one written word. Every page of the final file on Lucas Hawkins was totally blank.

Chapter Thirteen

Three weeks later

"So you can see that there really is no reason for you to remain here any longer," Carl Steiner said. "And I'm sure you'd rather be somewhere else," he added, smiling at her.

"Are you saying that Truett actually confessed to planning the sheikh's assassination?" Tyler asked, trying to make sense of something that seemed unbelievable. After all, she *knew* Malcolm Truett. Maybe the CIA could believe it, but she found the scenario Steiner had just outlined to be incredible.

"He'd been working for the extremists long before he became Amir al-Ahmad's personal secretary."

"But why would he become so involved in the internal affairs of a place halfway around the world? In a religious struggle that didn't even involve his own religion?"

"He believed the Ahmads were raping resources that belonged to the people of their country, and that those people were getting far too little in return. There are those, Ms. Stewart, who are altruistic enough to go to a great deal of trouble to attempt to right the perceived wrongs of the world. The English have a reputation for idealism."

"But he must have known that Amir would step into his father's place. That nothing would change."

"He was hoping for something more. An uprising, encouraged by the fundamentalists, as soon as news of the sheikh's death reached his homeland. With Amir out of the country for the wedding, it was the perfect opportunity for them to act."

"But they didn't?"

"Apparently not. Not that we're aware of. Maybe Truett's plans weren't that extreme. Maybe he simply believed he could influence the son as he couldn't the father. Perhaps the new sheikh *will* be more progressive regarding his people's needs."

"I didn't think the extremists were interested in progress," she suggested quietly.

"I'm not sure exactly what they're most interested in. Maybe Truett saw his involvement with the extremists as a means to an end. We may never know what his real motives were."

"What will happen to him?" Tyler asked. Despite the Westernization of Amir's country, the penalties for treason there were harsh. And primitive. That was one of the things that had stuck in her mind from her reading—how traitors were punished.

"Mr. Truett has already chosen his own punishment."

"I don't understand."

"He committed suicide shortly after he signed his confession. The sheikh wasn't prepared for such an act of desperation and hadn't taken any measures to prevent it."

Maybe Truett's suicide wasn't surprising, considering what he could expect at the hands of Amir's courts. The unbelievable thing to Tyler was the whole idea of Truett's guilt. The concept that he had been responsible for the sheikh's death. Amir had warned her, however, that politics in the region were often deadly. So she supposed anything *could* be possible.

"Then who were the men I saw? The ones on the terrace of Amir's room?"

"You were right about that. Two of them were members of Amir al-Ahmad's personal guard. Fortunately, through

Truett's confession, they've been identified and sent home to stand trial. All but the shooter himself. He hasn't been found. Some professional they hired. Totally apolitical.''

"Someone who kills for money?" Tyler asked.

"Not as unusual as you'd imagine," Steiner said. "In any case," he concluded, standing up, "I think you are safe to assume your life can go back to normal. Back to what it was before you opened that door and saw the men on the balcony that day.''

Back to normal, Tyler thought. *Back to what it was before you opened that door...* She took a deep breath, thinking about her life. So many things had changed there was almost no life to go back to. At least nothing she wanted to go back to.

"Is there anything else?" Steiner asked kindly.

He hadn't had to come out to the safe house where she was being kept, and explain the situation to her. They had all been kind, the men who had guarded her these last weeks, but they hadn't talked to her about the assassination. No one had questioned what she had seen or asked her to identify anyone.

However, neither had Steiner again suggested she tell Amir what she saw. He had abided by the agreement made in Claire Heywood's office. And now that agreement was ended. The assassins had been caught, and so Tyler had nothing to fear.

"How can you be certain that Amir had nothing to do with his father's death?" she asked.

"We did our own investigation, of course. According to the terms of our agreement.''

The agreement with Hawk, she thought. The deal he had made with them for her safety. Apparently Steiner had stuck to the terms they'd hammered out.

"We found nothing to tie al-Ahmad to the plot against his father," he continued. "Instead, everything we discovered pointed to an attempted fundamentalist coup.''

"But you can't be absolutely sure?" she asked.

"If I *weren't* sure, Ms. Stewart, I wouldn't be suggesting this," he said, smiling at her.

"It doesn't feel right," she said softly. "Not Malcolm."

"It's hard to judge the depths of someone's political beliefs and commitments from a social acquaintance. Would it make you feel better to see the material we have tying him to the extremists? Those connections are fairly well documented. And besides..." Steiner hesitated a moment before he went on. "It's over. As far as the world community is concerned, the assassins have been caught. Amir al-Ahmad is going back to his country to make sure things stay calm there."

"So...it doesn't really matter any longer what I might say," she suggested. "Is that what you're telling me?"

"It no longer matters to anyone what you saw that day," he agreed, "or what you say about it. You have no reason to be afraid."

Which was essentially what Hawk had told her. Even if Amir were guilty, once he realized she couldn't hurt him there would be no reason for him to have any further interest in her.

"However," Steiner added, perhaps reading the doubt in her eyes, "if you're uncomfortable with the situation, we can provide a more...permanent arrangement. A change of identity or relocation, at least. Most people in your situation would resist something that drastic, which is why I didn't propose it to begin with. And I really don't think it's necessary, Ms. Stewart. If I thought you were in any danger, I'd never have suggested this."

She nodded. What he said made sense. It made sense even if Amir had been involved, and with Steiner's repeated assurances, she was beginning to question her feelings about that. After all, it was entirely possible that when she had realized marrying Amir was a mistake, she'd transferred her sense of wrongness about that to the other situation. To the assassination.

Maybe Malcolm had even been trying to foster that belief by what he had said to her that day. Maybe he had been so desperate to get her away from the area that he had given her the passkey to get rid of her, afraid that she might see or hear something that would make her suspicious.

And as for Amir's claim that she was grief stricken and in seclusion, which had seemed to be even more proof of his guilt, maybe that was nothing more than his overweening pride. He would never admit that his bride had simply run away on the day of their wedding. It was entirely possible it had all happened exactly as Steiner indicated.

"Is there anything else?" Steiner asked again.

"I don't suppose there is," she said reluctantly, trying to think what came next.

"Someone will drive you to the airport when you're ready," he said. "We'll provide a ticket for wherever you want to go. It's the least we can do in exchange for your cooperation."

Although she couldn't quite figure out what cooperation they wanted to compensate her for, she couldn't afford to turn his offer down. Her options were pretty limited. She could go back to New York, she supposed, but she didn't have enough money to pay last month's rent, much less this one's.

She needed to sell her furniture and sublet the apartment. The furniture should bring in enough to pay off some of the bills. And there was the house in Mississippi, of course. Selling it wouldn't realize much, but enough to pay off the rest of what she owed on her credit cards. And enough to keep her afloat until she could figure out what to do with the rest of her life.

Suddenly an image of that sagging front porch intruded into her thoughts, along with the remembrance of the spreading oak that shaded it and the old-fashioned swing. The scent of honeysuckle drifting in with the evening breeze. Her mother's voice, calling her home from the darkness.

"Covington," she said softly.

"I beg your pardon?" Carl Steiner said.

She looked up, surprised to find he was still there. Surprised she had spoken the word out loud. "Covington, Mississippi," she said. "I think that's where I start."

"Start?" Steiner repeated.

"The rest of my life," she said, smiling at him.

"YOU'RE NOT SUPPOSED to be here," Hawk said.

He hadn't moved, other than to lift his head from the pillow to see who had come into the room. Fingers interlocked behind his head, he was stretched out on the bed, staring at the ceiling. He had done a lot of that during the weeks they had held him here. A lot of thinking. Remembering. And none of it had been easy.

The muscles in his stomach had tightened, however, as soon as he recognized his visitor. He didn't want to hear whatever Jordan Cross had come to say. He could tell that by what was in the gray eyes.

"Jake pulled this location out of the computers. I told the guys outside that Steiner sent me to question you, but they're probably busy verifying that right now, so we don't have long."

"And when they find out he didn't send you?" Hawk asked.

No one had questioned him about anything. They weren't interested in why Hawk had gone to Baghdad. He had known that all along. They were holding him as an act of discipline. And he supposed he was lucky they were doing it in a safe house rather than a prison. When Steiner had said a "secured facility," that's what Hawk had been expecting.

"By then we'll be gone," Jordan said.

"I made a deal. I can't *be gone.*"

"He let her go," Jordan said.

Hawk's body came off the bed in one fluid motion. "What the hell do you mean, he let her go?"

"Amir al-Ahmad's secretary confessed to planning the assassination. Right before he conveniently committed suicide."

"His secretary," Hawk said disbelievingly.

"Male type. English. Supposedly the mastermind of an extremist coup."

"Supposedly?"

"Jake says the background on that is manufactured, created after the fact. Probably by al-Ahmad."

"And Steiner didn't bother to check it out?"

"All I know is he considers the case closed. *And* the assassins duly caught. So…"

"That stupid son of a bitch," Hawk said softly.

Jordan's eyes hadn't changed, and Hawk still didn't like what he was seeing in them. "Where is she?" he asked.

"Jake says she took a flight to Mississippi. This morning. The agency paid for the ticket."

"I hope you brought some money," Hawk said, starting toward the door, "because I doubt they're going to pay for mine."

"There are four of them out there," Jordan warned. "You want some help?"

Hawk turned, his blue eyes resting briefly on Jordan Cross's face. "Only if you want to give it," he said softly.

"I didn't come out here for the scenery," Jordan said, and realized this was the first time he'd ever seen Hawk laugh.

SOMEONE HAD CLEANED UP the mess. They hadn't repaired the damaged wall or replaced the bullet-scarred door frame, but the debris on the floor had been cleaned up. And the blood.

Standing now in the afternoon sunshine that was painting patterns of light on the old wooden floors, Tyler realized that it all seemed like some long-ago nightmare. Like a bad dream. As unreal, in a very different way, of course, as the few days that had followed it. The days she had spent with Hawk.

She put her suitcase down on the sagging mattress. It was the same battered case she had bought in the New York pawnshop that day. She'd been carrying it around since, with the same items of clothing she'd bought at the airport stuffed inside.

She walked over to the windows and pushed them up. It seemed hotter inside than out, and the bank clock she'd passed on the way had read 97 degrees. With the house closed up, that probably meant the temperature in this room was pushing 100, despite the shade the oak provided.

Which meant she'd spend another night tossing and turning in the heat. When Cammie sent her the money from the sale of her furniture—if there was anything left after she paid Tyler's rent and the utilities—the first thing she was going to buy was a window unit for this room. Then at least she'd be able to sleep.

She walked back to the kitchen. She had set the groceries she'd picked up on her way home on the wooden table. There was only one sack because her cash was running low, and she didn't want to put anything else on her credit cards unless she absolutely had to. As it was, she had two rental cars sitting out in the gravel driveway. She'd have to figure out a way to get those turned in. And think about getting some kind of secondhand car of her own for transportation to and from work.

Thinking about that, she took the local paper out of the grocery sack and laid it on the table before she put the few things she'd bought into the refrigerator. There had to be some job she could do listed in the want ads, even if the position was only temporary. Until she could find something better.

And there was a junior college less than fifteen miles away. She might be the oldest freshman on campus, but she liked the idea of going to school. Of picking out classes. Of studying for them. She had always wanted to go to college, but there had never been time. Now there was time for a lot of things.

She had already invited Cammie for a visit. Which meant, she supposed, that she needed to do something about making this place a little more inviting. Guest worthy. An update was definitely in order, she thought, looking around the kitchen.

Fresh paint would help. Some inexpensive fabric she could make into curtains, using Aunt Martha's old pedal machine. They'd be pretty simple, given her level of skill, but they would be bright and clean. And a coat of wax on the floors would cost her nothing but elbow grease. Maybe a wallpaper border at the top of the freshly painted walls. *Yellow for in here,* she thought, *and for the bedrooms...*

Her eyes dropped from the border she was envisioning just below the old-fashioned acoustic tiles and found a man standing in the door that led into the house from the porch. Just where the robed men had stood the night Hawk had rescued her.

This one wasn't wearing a robe. He had on a business suit and white shirt, but he was one of Amir's bodyguards. One of the two who had been in the hotel room that day. One of the two who had, according to Steiner, been sent home to stand trial for the assassination. She recognized him immediately, and in his dark eyes was a mocking acknowledgment that he had known she would.

He was holding an automatic weapon, holding it loosely and with a great deal of confidence. She thought it was the same kind that had cut the wall above her head to ribbons that night. She watched it swing away from her as he turned, allowing Amir to brush past him and walk into the kitchen.

"You have certainly proven to be a *most* unsatisfactory fiancée, my darling," he said. "An enormous amount of trouble."

There were several men behind him, Tyler realized.

More of his omnipresent bodyguards. However, they were all in Western dress today, which would be much less noticeable here than the *dishdashas*. With them was the other guard she had seen in Amir's suite that day. The day his father had been murdered.

"They told me you were going home. That it was all over," she said.

Amir's dark head tilted, questioning. "Over?" he repeated.

"The CIA told me about Malcolm."

"They bought into the idea of Malcolm as the mastermind?" he asked, his voice amused. "That's rather entertaining, isn't it?"

She had been right all along. She had known in her heart it was Amir. But Steiner had seemed so sure, and now it was too late, she thought, a layer of ice forming around her heart, seeping outward to chill the blood in her veins.

"You, on the other hand, didn't buy into that, did you?" Amir suggested, still smiling. "That's all right, my beloved. It really doesn't matter what you believe. Or what you say. It never mattered, I suppose, but it might have been a bit awkward—at least socially—to have my fiancée suggesting I had killed my own father. I really don't like things that are awkward or unpleasant. You know me that well, I think."

"I won't say anything," she promised, her voice soft with fear. She hoped he could read her sincerity. She had done the right thing. She had gone to the authorities and had told them what she'd seen. Even what she suspected. No one had been interested in listening to her.

"Oh, I'm sure you mean that. Just as I'm sure Malcolm meant well when he stupidly gave you that passkey. But you see, that wasn't what I had told him to do. And I also don't like people who don't do what they're told. Exactly what they're told. You, however, always did. So you have one last job to perform, Tyler, and then..." Amir paused, his smile widening beneath the soft dark mustache "…then, my darling, it really will be all over."

"What do you want?" she asked, wondering what that phrase implied. Afraid that she knew. She could feel the paralyzing force of her fear, but she fought it, trying to think.

She had run from them that night. There had seemed to be a chance then that she might be able to get away in the concealing darkness. But now, in the daylight, running seemed pointless. And she remembered the bullets hitting the frame of the door, the pain in her arm and a gun, such as the ones they now held, totally destroying the wall above her head. She had survived that night only because of Hawk's intervention. And now there was no Hawk to help her. There was no one to help her.

"A final appearance," Amir said. "It will be just another performance for the cameras, Tyler. You've done a lot of those. And all you have to do this time, my darling, is smile."

WHEN THEY REACHED IT, the little house was empty. The door was unlocked, and Tyler's suitcase was on the bed in the bedroom. There was some food in the refrigerator and the local paper was spread out on the kitchen table. The windows in the bedroom were open, the heated air filled with the scent of honeysuckle that climbed, wild and unrestrained, over a hedge just outside.

"Maybe she's at a neighbor's," Jordan said. "Out to eat. Something harmless."

Hawk knew what had prompted that remark. It seemed too peaceful for anything to be really wrong. There was nothing here but the distant sounds of children playing. The scent of honeysuckle drifting in at the open windows. Age-yellowed lace curtains occasionally moving in the heavy air. An old house set under the shade of a big oak. Peaceful. As long as you didn't notice the scars that pocked the bedroom wall.

"Call Jake," Hawk ordered. "Tell him we need to know *exactly* where al-Ahmad is right now. And we need his itinerary."

IT HAD FELT STRANGE to be dressed again in these clothes. They were some of the things Amir had chose for her trousseau. Tyler was aware of that as they put them on her, but the whole time it felt as if they were dressing a mannequin.

They had even brought someone in to fix her hair and her makeup. The hairdresser had tried to talk to her, but what they had given her was so strong she hadn't been able to formulate any answers. After a while he had simply done what he had been instructed to do and had left. She was still sitting in the chair where they had placed her, looking into the mirror. Looking at someone who was a stranger.

Since they had given her the shot everything seemed to be happening to someone else. It was as if she were in someone else's body, watching these things being done. She closed her eyes, fighting the nausea she had experienced ever since Amir's physician had plunged that needle into her arm. She had fought them, as long as she was able, but it hadn't done any good, of course. She hadn't been strong enough to win.

Hawk could have. He would have fought them for her. But Hawk wasn't here, she remembered. He had left, like everyone else, and she would never see him again. The sense of his loss was strong enough to push into her consciousness, past the effects of the drug.

Amir was saying something, she realized. His voice came from a long way away, distant and hollow, echoing in her head like the voices in dreams. He wasn't speaking English, she finally realized, so surely he didn't expect her to answer.

Then someone else responded. Someone nearby. The doctor, she recognized, turning her head toward the sound of his voice. He was standing at her elbow, shaking his head. Amir gestured, and the doctor helped her stand.

When she was upright, her head swam, and she swallowed hard, denying the building nausea. She swayed a little and one of the bodyguards put his hand under her other arm. Amir crossed the distance between them and caught her chin in his fingers, turning her head to make her look into his eyes.

"You will smile," he said loudly, his tone menacing, despite the fact that he sounded as if he were talking to a not-very-bright child, "when and if I tell you to."

She tried to make her eyes defiant, but the sickness pushed into her throat and her knees were so weak. She was cold and spasms of shivers racked her body. If he turned her loose, she was sure she'd fall.

"Do you understand me?" he demanded, still speaking too loudly, his voice echoing in her head. She should say no, but she couldn't remember why. And it was so much easier to agree. Then maybe he would leave her alone and stop shouting at her.

The doctor said something else, the unfamiliar words fluttering at the edge of her fogged mind. Amir answered him with an expletive from his own language that she had heard him use before. Then he leaned close to her face, close enough that she could see the pores in his skin, the individual hairs in his black mustache. He spoke very distinctly.

"You will smile and wave when I tell you. Do you understand me, Tyler? Because, my darling, if you don't, the doctor will give you another shot, which he says might stop your heart. And you don't want that to happen, do you?"

She shook her head slowly, moving it against the hard pressure his fingers were exerting on her chin. She didn't want her heart to stop. She didn't want to die. *Hawk,* she thought again, and felt the burn of tears.

The fingers holding her chin tightened painfully. "You

will not cry. I do not want them to see tears. I want them to see a very happy woman, smiling and waving as she departs for what will be her new country. Do you understand me, Tyler?''

Smile, Tyler. She had known all along that's what Amir would tell her. *Smile at them, but don't open your mouth. Just smile, and it will all be over. If you smile at them, everything will be all right.* It always had been.

And after all, she thought, she knew how to smile. For the cameras. For everyone who was watching. *Smile and it will all be over.* Slowly, watching his cold black eyes for approval, Tyler nodded.

Chapter Fourteen

The metal steps to the private jet seemed miles away from the limousine, but she had realized when they helped her from the hotel and into the car that her depth perception was distorted by whatever they had given her.

She closed her eyes against the late afternoon glare and swallowed, trying to produce some moisture in her dry mouth. At least the nausea was a little better, and she wondered if that meant the drug was wearing off.

She knew what Amir wanted her to do. He had explained it several times during the ride over from the hotel. They would go up the steps to the jet together, turn at the top and wave and smile for the assembled media. *"Smile, Tyler"* drifted through her head again, seeming so familiar. And…distasteful.

Someone opened the door on her side of the car, and Amir was there, holding out his hand. She wondered what would happen if she refused to get out. If she refused to walk with him up those steps. Refused to get on the plane.

Almost as if he had read her mind, Amir said, his voice low and angry, "I'll have you carried on board if I have to. I'll tell them some story about stress and exhaustion. But if you force me to do that, Tyler, you'll be very sorry. Do you understand me? I promise you'll be *very* sorry," he warned.

She believed him. His eyes, as cold and as black as she

knew his heart to be, *told* her to believe him. She wondered why she had thought Hawk's eyes were cold. They weren't, not compared to these, but she obeyed Amir because she knew she had no choice. She put out her hand, and he pulled her from the car.

She swayed against him, fighting vertigo, nausea, an inability to move or to think. He put his arm around her, his left hand cupping her left elbow.

"Walk," he ordered. "And smile, damn you. Smile, my darling, or I promise you you'll be sorry you were ever born. Very sorry you ever stuck your nose into things you don't understand. Things that don't concern you."

She wanted to argue. Wanted to deny that she had done anything wrong, but the words wouldn't form. It was all she could do to concentrate on putting one foot in front of the other, even with his supportive arm around her waist.

The journey to the foot of the metal steps was endless. He had given her sunglasses in the car, to cover the too-wide dilation of her pupils. To hide the effects of whatever they had injected. But still the glare and the heat reflecting off the tarmac were making her sick.

"I can't," she whispered, looking up from the foot of the stairs to the open door of the plane. She couldn't climb those steps, no matter what Amir did to her or threatened to do. And she was beginning to realize that once she was on board the jet, he could do anything he wanted to her. No one would ever know what had happened. No one would ever see her again. She would simply disappear into that unfamiliar world she had feared from the beginning. The world where Amir's word was literally the law.

"I can't," she said again, trying desperately to think what she could do.

Amir turned around to face the crowd, carrying her with him, almost lifting her and propelling her at the same time with his grip on her arm. She could see the muscle jumping in his jaw as it clenched. He was furious, but she knew she couldn't get on that plane.

They were facing the assembled throng of reporters, too many for this location normally. He must have arranged for some of them to be here in this small Mississippi city. Arranged for them to come out on a hot afternoon to see this performance.

"Smile, damn you," he demanded, the words hissed under his breath. His own smile was broad and obviously false. Obvious at least to her. His right hand, the one that was not gripping her arm hard enough to bruise, lifted to wave at the crowd.

That gesture provoked a flurry of flashes from the cameras. Their lights seemed to explode in Tyler's eyes, blinding her, even with the protection of the glasses. It was all too much for her sensitized senses to deal with. The heat and glare. The noise. The smell of jet fuel. All of it too much.

The pressure on her arm increased. She whimpered with the pain, but the sound was lost in the roar of the jet engines behind her. No one heard her. No one would hear her if she cried out for help. He had planned it this way, of course.

So it was up to her. She had to get away from him. Break his grip on her arm and run toward the crowd. Surely he wouldn't shoot her in front of all these people.

After all, Amir was safe. He had nothing to fear from her. Someone had told her that. Nothing to fear. But if he shot her, then they would know what he had done. On some level she realized that the effects of the drug were wearing off. She could think again. Form words. Take some action. And she had to. It was her only chance.

She struggled, trying to pull her arm from his hold, but she seemed to be powerless against that relentless grip. Her struggle had no effect, except to cause Amir to pull her body closer to his, holding her tightly against his side. To the watching reporters, it must have appeared to be a spontaneous and loving embrace, because he continued to wave at them with his other hand and the cameras continued to flash.

He said something. Not to her, she knew, because it wasn't in English. She didn't understand until the doctor moved into her field of vision, the sun glinting off his wire-frame glasses. He carried his bag in one hand, and even as she watched, he reached inside with his other hand. His back to the crowd as he walked, he took a syringe from his case. It was full of the colorless liquid with which they had injected her before.

For a moment her heart stopped, just as Amir had promised, but then she realized that was only her fear. He hadn't touched her. The doctor was walking toward them from the limousine, and Amir was still crushing her against his side, waving to the crowd. The noise of the engines was deafening. And the glare of the sun blinded her.

What was happening seemed to be occurring in slow motion. Like a nightmare, she thought. The final one. Because when he reached her, Amir's doctor would put that needle into her arm, using his body to shield what he was doing from the cameras. Then somehow, probably with the doctor's help, Amir would get her on that plane. And it would be over. Everything, all the dreams, would finally be over.

Hawk, she thought. All the dreams, including that one. But Hawk had left her, just like everyone else in her life had left her. Because she wouldn't stand on her own two feet. Because she went along with what everyone told her. Because he thought she wasn't strong. And now she would never get the chance to prove to him that he was wrong.

Last chance, she thought. *My last chance.*

Maybe because she had stopped struggling or maybe because the doctor was so close, Amir's grip on her body loosened minutely. She looked up at him, eyes narrowed against the sun. He was looking out into the crowd, still waving. Still pretending this was what he wanted them to believe it was—a gloriously happy couple on their way to begin a new life together.

She turned away from his false smile and realized the doctor was almost there, the syringe he held concealed in the palm of his hand. Amir's men were standing by the limousine, their white robes billowing in the hot air, blown by the jet engines. And there was another guard, she knew, waiting at the top of the stairs. That was always the way they did it. He would have a weapon hidden in the plane beside him, ready to protect Amir in case of trouble.

She remembered the heat and fire of the bullet that had hit her arm and the devastation on the bedroom wall, but she blocked those fears from her mind. *Last chance* echoed in her head, and gathering every ounce of resistance in her drugged body, she shifted her weight to her left leg and kicked Amir as hard as she could in the shin with her right foot.

The blow seemed without force to her, but he reacted with surprise, just as she'd prayed he would. His hold on her body slackened even more. She twisted free and staggered past the doctor, who grabbed at her. She managed to sidestep him, but she stumbled as she did. She somehow regained her precarious balance and began to run toward the cameras. *Smile, Tyler* floated through her head, but she wasn't smiling, of course. She was running for her life.

Her legs kept refusing to obey the commands of her brain. She staggered drunkenly across the tarmac, the crowd wavering in and out of her vision. They looked distorted, their mouths opening and closing like beached fish, but she ran toward them, fighting to stay upright. Fighting to stay alive. Fighting to stay on her own two feet.

She didn't make it. Her right leg folded under her suddenly, and unable to regain her equilibrium, she pitched forward to the ground. She got her hands out to break her fall, but she was down. And despite how much she wanted to live, she knew she wasn't going to be able to get up again. Not in time to keep them from reaching her.

She was still looking toward the crowd, and from where she lay on the ground, she stretched one imploring arm out to them. Appealing for someone to help her. Surely someone would see what was happening. Surely now they knew what Amir was doing.

Instead they began to run away from her, scattering in a panicked flurry, like doves in the middle of a hunt. Running from something. She turned her head to see what was happening behind her. Both Amir and the doctor had been coming toward her, just as she had known they would.

But for some reason their forward motion had checked. Amir shouted something, and the doctor started forward again. As he did, a spray of fragments kicked up from the tarmac in front of his feet. He had stopped again, jumping backward, before Tyler heard the crack of the rifle.

Rifle, she thought, her dazed brain beginning to understand why everyone was running. *Rifle,* she thought again, turning her head, eyes searching the roofs of the terminal and the towers. Someone was shooting at Amir and his men. Someone...

ANOTHER JOB, Hawk thought, the crosshairs of his sight holding a second on the doctor before they lifted to Amir. Al-Ahmad's handsome face was suffused with color. He was clearly furious. Hawk watched as he gestured to someone behind him.

"The one on the steps of the plane," Jordan warned. "He's got a weapon."

Obediently Hawk lifted the scope, finding the figure in the doorway of the plane. He was pointing a Uzi toward the woman on the ground, hesitating to fire only because Amir and the doctor were in his way. And as soon as they realized that, Hawk knew, the man at the top of the stairs would spray the runway.

That man was shouting something now. Through the

scope, Hawk watched his mouth moving, opening and closing on the words. Telling the others to get out of the way? Surely Amir wouldn't be stupid enough to order them to kill Tyler in front of all these people.

But maybe he thought he could get away with that. After all, he had gotten away with killing his own father. All he had to do was shoot her and get on that plane and fly away. He could worry about a story to explain it all later. Tie her to the plot somehow. Only this time, Hawk thought...

The man he was watching brought the gun into firing position, and in response Hawk squeezed the trigger. Same slow squeeze as always. He was surprised that his hand wasn't trembling. It had trembled that day in the parking garage, but now it was as steady as it had always been.

Another job. Another target. Danger passed. Threat resolved. Lives saved. Or in this case, Hawk thought, life saved. One solitary life. That of the woman he loved.

He watched as the man he had shot tumbled off the metal platform that had been rolled up to the door of the plane. Hawk took his eye off the scope and looked down on the scene unfolding below, the characters in the drama slightly distorted by the heat waves shimmering up from the tarmac.

The Uzi bounced down the steps as the robed figure rolled bonelessly behind it. Hawk's gaze moved back to Tyler, struggling to get up. *Someone will come to help her,* he thought. *Someone out of that crowd will realize what's wrong.* He had, simply by watching her walk beside Amir from the limousine to the foot of the steps.

They had drugged her to make her carry out this farce. A performance for the press. For whoever Amir believed might still care about his role in his father's death. He apparently hadn't realized that no one cared. Just as no one cared enough to come to the aid of the woman who had finally managed to push herself up to her hands and knees.

There was movement to Tyler's left, and Hawk pulled

his eyes away from her figure. He couldn't think about her as a person. Not about what she was feeling. Not about going down to her. His job was here. The important job. At least for now.

What he had seen peripherally was Amir, bending to pick up the Uzi that had fallen almost at his feet. He had stooped, lifting the weapon and then turning toward the barriers that had been created to keep the media at a distance.

Hawk put his eye again on the scope, lining up his target in the crosshairs. Even as he did it, he couldn't conceive that Amir would be foolish enough to shoot. He had nothing to gain by this and everything to lose. Nothing to gain...

Apparently Amir al-Ahmad didn't realize that. Or he no longer cared. In Hawk's sights, the sheikh's face was a distorted mask of fury as he aimed the weapon. Aimed it right at the fallen woman. A woman who had defied him by running away from him in front of all those people. Spoiling the picture he had wanted to create for the media.

Hawk's finger tightened against the trigger, steady and unhurried, and suddenly a small, dark circle appeared in the forehead of the man in the crosshairs. The Uzi continued to fire as Amir fell forward, squeezing the trigger in a reflex motion as he died. Bullets hit the tarmac, sending up sprays of dust and debris wherever they struck.

Hawk forgot to breathe as he watched them, praying to a God he didn't know for a miracle he didn't deserve. Still praying when he pulled back from the scope, and his eyes, unaided by artificial magnification, found the woman they had sought.

On her feet. Moving again in a slow stagger toward the terminal. Still alive.

"Give me that," Jordan said, taking the rifle from Hawk's hands.

Now they were trembling, Hawk realized, shaking with

fear. Shaking with the need to touch her. To hold her. To verify what his eyes were telling him.

"I'll take it from here," Cross said.

Hawk turned to look at his friend, and watched the gray eyes lighten and the well-shaped lips curve into a smile at what was in his face.

"You know what will happen if you do this," Hawk said.

"I'll tell them Steiner sent me," Jordan said, his smile widening. "Go on. Get her out of here. I'll handle the rest."

"I can't let you," Hawk said. He knew what it would do to Jordan's career. They had already destroyed *his* life, but so far he had managed to keep Cross almost in the clear.

"I told you. It just speeds up the inevitable," Jordan said. "Besides, Griff was my friend, too."

He was looking down at the runway, rifle held at the ready. Perhaps his aim wasn't as deadly as Hawk's, but then no one else on the tarmac below was attempting to move toward the weapon lying beside Amir's body. And if they somehow found the guts to try, a bullet in the ground nearby would probably put an end to that bravado.

After all, the sheikh was dead. There was no one to give them further orders. Without Amir to urge them on, neither the doctor nor the bodyguards by the huge black car seemed particularly eager to challenge the skill of the unseen shooter.

"Go on," Jordan said again, his voice soft. "And Hawk?"

Hawk had already begun to move, but he stopped, his eyes shifting to the man who had been beside him almost all the way.

"Godspeed, my friend. And good luck," Jordan added.

The man called Hawk nodded, the movement small. Contained. Both acknowledgment and thanks. Unspoken. As always.

Then Jordan Cross's gaze fell again to the runway. Crouching low, Hawk began to move, across the rooftop and toward the door that would lead to the service stairs they had climbed to this vantage point. There were debts to be paid, he thought, no matter what Jordan said. Debts to Cross for taking the blame for this. To Jake for tracking down the flight plans Amir's pilot had been required to file. Hawk wouldn't forget what he owed to either of them. He never forgot those things.

Hawk heard feet pounding across the roof behind him. Airport security had finally arrived. He also heard Jordan's shout of identification. "Jordan Cross. This is a CIA operation." Jordan was CIA, of course, and more importantly, he could still prove it. Hawk couldn't have. Not anymore. That was why Cross had taken the rifle from him.

Imagining Steiner's reaction to the uproar this shoot-out would cause, a small satisfied smile flickered at the corners of Hawk's lips as he began to descend the concrete stairs.

EVERY TIME SHE OPENED her eyes, he was there. Watching her. Or holding her. Through the bouts of nausea, she held on to what was in his eyes. To something he had never allowed her to see in them before. And he cared for her through the long dark hours with the same tenderness with which he had once made love to her. The slow time. She smiled, remembering.

"What's so funny?" he asked, his voice soft and intimate.

That shouldn't be surprising, she supposed, since he was lying beside her on the bed. They were in a motel, she guessed, allowing her gaze to move around the room. She remembered the beige-tiled bathroom. Typical motel. He had carried her there a few times. Literally carried her. And she supposed she should be embarrassed to have him take care of her in those very intimate ways. But she wasn't. She wanted him here. She wanted Hawk beside her. Whatever the situation.

"Not very much," she said softly, cupping his cheek with her hand. His skin was unshaven, and she liked the brush of the golden whiskers against her fingers. Evocative of that night.

"How do you feel?" he asked.

He was lying on his side, one arm under his head. She had to turn her own head to see him, but at least she could do that now without setting off the nausea.

"Like a couple of Mac trucks ran over me, and then rolled back and forth over the dying body a few times."

He reached out and touched her bare arm. She flinched a little. That was one of the bruises she'd gotten fighting Amir's guards, she supposed, looking down at the place his fingers had found. She was wearing only her underwear, she realized, but she couldn't remember undressing. Or remember Hawk undressing her. She thought she might like to be able to remember that.

Of course, she didn't remember much of anything after the injection. And all of what she could remember was hazy, like something that had happened a long time ago. Or had happened to someone else.

But she remembered Hawk finding her, appearing out of the crowd at the airport like a miracle. She remembered him picking her up and carrying her in his arms through the terminal building and outside. He had told someone he was a doctor. Since they couldn't possibly believe what he *really* was, that was probably as good a lie as any.

She didn't remember much of anything else until she woke up in this room, and Hawk was taking care of her. Caring for her as her mother might have long ago. His hands, long, dark and so strong, had been as gentle as hers.

"Thank you," Tyler said softly, fighting tears that she recognized, due to the lingering effects of the drug, were too close to the surface.

"For what?" he asked, his voice amused.

"For everything," she whispered. "For coming to my rescue again. For this. For…being here."

"Go back to sleep," he said, dismissing her gratitude.

"You'll still be here when I wake up?" she asked, her eyes searching his. He had never lied to her. He hadn't told her everything, but what he *had* told her had always been the truth.

"I'm not going anywhere," he promised. "Not without you."

The tears threatened again, but they were different tears. Happy crying, her mother used to say.

"I'll be here when you wake up," Hawk said softly. "I'll be right here beside you until you tell me to go away."

She smiled at that, but she didn't tell him why. She'd tell him later, she decided, holding the blue eyes until her heavy lids drifted downward. Once or twice she forced them up again, just to be sure he was still there. To be sure he wasn't a dream. And she would find that same surety in the steady blue gaze. Finally, trusting in what he had promised, she slept.

"I WAS PLANNING to make new curtains for in here," Tyler said, watching Hawk's face. He seemed so out of place here. Alien to this rural peacefulness. To this little house. His life had been so different.

Of course, she admitted, for the last twenty years, so had hers. But this would always be home to her, and so she felt as if she belonged. She had wondered, even when she suggested they come here, if it would ever feel like that to Hawk. Like home.

"And I want to paint the walls," she added, when he didn't respond. "And the ones in the bedrooms, too."

She knew she was talking about things that couldn't possibly mean anything to a man like Hawk. Domestic trivia. They hadn't even discussed what came next, if anything, but still she couldn't seem to do anything about the hope that had been growing in her heart. A hope that Hawk would want to stay, now that it was over.

"It is over, isn't it?" she asked, needing his reassurance. "I mean…Steiner won't expect you to go back? He won't try to make you, will he?"

"We had a deal. Which I honored until Steiner broke it. He's got to know from what happened at the airport yesterday that he didn't fulfill his part. I don't think they'll come after me, but…if they want to, Tyler, they can find me anywhere I go. I don't intend to run from them. Or to hide."

"But you *think* Steiner will leave you alone."

"I think even Steiner should have trouble sleeping at night when he thinks about what he almost let Amir do to you," he said, his voice bitter.

She nodded, remembering what had happened. And thinking about what *would* have happened if it hadn't been for Hawk. She thought about expressing her gratitude again, but he wouldn't want to hear that.

She took a breath, her eyes finding the mark the bullet had made on the door frame. She wanted every bit of evidence of the nightmare they had lived erased. Even the scars, if possible.

"And I want to do something about the damage to the wall in the bedroom," she said.

"Are you expecting me to offer to fix that?" Hawk asked, his lips touched with the small smile she had seen there too seldom.

Exactly what *had* she been expecting, she wondered, when she suggested they come here? "Do you know how to fix it?" she asked, smiling back at him.

"I don't know anything about taking care of a house. About paint. *Or* fixing walls."

She nodded, but she didn't say anything. This was up to him. His decision. His choice. And whatever he decided, she would learn to live with it. On her own two feet.

"If there's a hardware store in town," he said, his eyes

still on her face, "maybe somebody there could tell me what to do."

She nodded again. "Probably," she agreed.

The silence stretched.

"You haven't even asked about the other," he said finally.

"The other what?"

"Why I didn't tell you the truth," he said.

"I guess you had a good reason. And...I didn't tell you the truth, either. Not at the beginning."

"I was afraid you'd think I was like him."

"Like Amir?" she asked, her voice puzzled. "Why would I think you were like Amir?"

Hawk hesitated, and his lips tightened a little before he answered. "I thought you'd think I'd just been using you."

"Were you?" she asked.

"At first."

She nodded again. "Well, at first I was using you, too. That's how you got involved in all this. I guess I can't blame you for doing that. I got you into it, and I was the only one who could get you out. It just made sense that I do that."

He said nothing for a long time, so long that she wondered if she'd said something wrong.

"And the other?" he asked softly.

"The other?"

"Making love to you."

"Were you just...using me then?"

"No," he said. "That was never what that was about."

"What *was* it about?" she asked, and held her breath.

"What I said, I guess. Making love to you."

"No ulterior motives," she said, remembering to breathe.

"A couple, but not any you need to worry about."

She laughed, and watched his eyes lighten. The corners of his hard mouth moved. Fractionally.

"And I want a wallpaper border," she said. "They probably have those at the hardware store, too."

"With instructions?" he asked.

"I don't know. But it can't be too hard. If everybody else can figure it out, surely the two of us together…" She hesitated, wondering if she had overstepped some invisible boundary. No commitments had been made. Not about anything. Not even about wallpaper.

"I think the two of us together can probably handle most things," he said. "Even wallpaper. If you want to try."

"If *I* want to try?" she asked.

"You heard what Steiner said. I don't have a lot of experience at…families. Or homes. I guess I'm not…a very good risk at any of those."

She nodded again, her throat closing at his unemotional dismissal of all that pain. She conquered the tears he wouldn't want to see. Hawk wouldn't want her to cry for him, ever. But for a man like Hawk to make a commitment of this kind, a commitment to build a home—and a family—together, would take an enormous amount of courage.

"Are you saying you *want* to have a home? And a family?" she asked. She needed to be sure she understood before the dream got totally out of control.

"I'm saying I want *you,*" he said. "No ulterior motives. But…no restrictions either, I guess. I figured you'd want both of those."

"Yes," she said softly. "I want it all. All of the above. And I think we probably better hurry about at least one of them."

His eyes changed, darkening a little, and his head tilted. "The wallpaper?" he asked innocently.

"No," she said.

"I didn't think so."

"But…I guess we could take a look at that wall before you go to the store."

"The one in the bedroom?" Hawk asked.

"That's the one," she acknowledged. "Ulterior motives," she added softly. "I guess I should warn you. Mine may fall into the category of…using you."

He nodded this time. "You still have that wedding thing?"

"The bridal gown?"

"That's the one," he said, deliberately mimicking her comment about the wall.

"I hocked it," she said.

He laughed, and she decided she really liked hearing that.

"The last of the romantics," he suggested.

"The last of the dreamers," she corrected. "Why did you ask about the dress?"

"I thought the hardware store might know about churches, too," he said. "And about preachers."

"Are you proposing to me, Lucas Hawkins?"

"I think that's exactly what I'm doing," Hawk said.

"Then do it right," she demanded. "I want it done right."

He laughed again and closed the space between them. He took her in his arms and kissed her on the mouth. Not particularly passionate or possessive, but just…right, she thought. Just exactly right.

"Tommy Sue Prator," he said, his mouth moving against her cheek, "will you marry me?"

"Just as soon as you fix that wall," she whispered.

"Then I guess we better go take a look at it," Hawk said. He bent, slipping his right arm under her knees. He carried her through the door with the bullet-scarred frame and into the bedroom. Just, of course, to look at the wall.

Epilogue

"You do know what this means?" Carl Steiner asked, his finger tapping the grainy black-and-white photograph at the top of the stack of newspapers on his desk.

Jordan Cross glanced down at the picture, then wondered why he had bothered. It wasn't any different from the others he would find in that stack. Jordan was in almost all of them, of course. Along with scenes of the carnage at the airport.

What had happened there was the most exciting thing the locals had seen in a long time. Amir had deliberately gathered as much of the media as he could round up on such short notice, so there were a lot of cameras in that crowd. Apparently they were all snapping when Jordan and airport security stepped through the door to the staircase that led down from the roof.

At least none of them had gotten a good shot of Hawk, Jordan thought philosophically. He was sorry that hadn't been the case with him, but he had known exactly what he was doing when he had taken that rifle out of Hawk's hands. And he hadn't hesitated.

Griff Cabot had been his friend. Hawk had taken the heat for what they *all* had wanted to do to that bastard in Iraq. And Jordan was more than willing to take the blame for what Hawk had done yesterday.

"I suppose this means my services here are no longer

needed," Jordan said, lifting his eyes from the photograph to meet Steiner's.

"I'm afraid that's the least of it," Steiner replied, leaning back in his chair and tenting his fingers.

"The *least* of it?"

Maybe Steiner really didn't understand what the team had meant to them. If that was true, it was pretty damned ironic that he was the one who was now in charge.

Missing Griff had eaten at Jordan's gut the last six months, of course, but that had been more about personal friendship than any kind of professional anxiety. They had all known things would change with Griff's death, but for someone like Steiner to come in here—

"I'm afraid that as a result of what you did yesterday you've acquired a whole lot of enemies," Steiner said, interrupting that train of thought. "All of Hawk's. Al-Ahmad's followers. And the agency's enemies, as well. You've become our...public face, so to speak, and you'll probably spend the rest of your life looking over your shoulder to see which of those is after you."

Steiner lifted his hands, tapping the tips of his steepled fingers in front of his mouth as if he were thinking. Jordan waited, not sure where he was headed with this. Other than to try to frighten him.

If that was what the assistant deputy director was attempting, it wasn't having much effect. Nothing Steiner was saying was news to Jordan. He had recognized all these things yesterday. *Before* he'd made his offer to Hawk.

"Of course, there *is* a way to keep you safe," Steiner said. "Something we've certainly done before."

"And what is that?" Jordan asked, interested to hear what his new boss was proposing.

"A new face," Steiner said, looking down again at the stack of papers. "A new identity to go with it."

"I'm not sure I'm all that tired of the old one," Jordan said carefully, controlling his inclination to laugh.

They'd gotten rid of the problem Hawk represented by

destroying his identity. Apparently, they intended to do the same thing to Jordan. Give him a new face, a new ID. And a new life to go with it. All *outside* the agency.

There wasn't much doubt now where Steiner was heading. Of course, they had all understood that the team, as they knew it, was doomed. But this…

"And *I'm* not sure you really have much choice," Steiner said softly. "After yesterday, you'll be a marked man, Cross. Hunted for the rest of your life. I'm simply offering you an out. My best advice is to take it. With the skills you've learned here, you won't have any trouble starting over."

Starting over. That was an opportunity a lot of people would love to have, he supposed. Jordan Cross wasn't sure he was one of them. But from the look in Steiner's eyes, he also wasn't sure he had much option. They would cut him loose with all the enemies Steiner had warned him about on his tail, or they'd do exactly what they'd offered. Give him a new face and a new name.

With all that had taken place recently within the agency, so much had changed already about his life. Griff's death. The dissolution of the team. Hawk's "disappearance."

Jordan wasn't sure what there was left here to hold on to. Except an identity that would be, he knew, just as dangerous as Steiner had promised. At least what they were offering gave him a chance.

"Okay," he said softly.

"I don't think you'll ever be sorry," Steiner said.

And of course, Steiner would be wrong about that, as well.

*Now that you've read the first book of
Gayle Wilson's exciting new series,
look for her next* MEN OF MYSTERY,
THE STRANGER SHE KNEW,
coming May 1999 from Harlequin Intrigue.

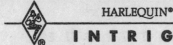

Amnesia...
an unknown danger...
a burning desire.
With

HARLEQUIN®

I N T R I G U E ®

you're just

A MEMORY AWAY

from passion, danger...
and love!

**Look for all the books in this exciting new
miniseries:**

Missing: One temporary wife
#507 THE MAN SHE MARRIED
by Dani Sinclair in March 1999

Mission: Find a lost identity
#511 LOVER, STRANGER
by Amanda Stevens in April 1999

Seeking: An amnesiac's daughter
#515 A WOMAN OF MYSTERY
by Charlotte Douglas in May 1999

A MEMORY AWAY—where remembering
the truth becomes a matter of life,
death...and love!

Available wherever Harlequin books are sold.

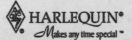

HARLEQUIN®
Makes any time special ™

MURDER AT THE MOVIES

CHARLENE WEIR
GEORGE BAXT
MAXINE O'CALLAGHAN

MURDER TAKE TWO
by Charlene Weir

Hollywood comes to Hampstead, Kansas, with the filming of a new picture starring sexy actress Laura Edwards. But murder steals the scene when a stunt double is impaled on a pitchfork.

THE HUMPHREY BOGART MURDER CASE
by George Baxt

Hollywood in its heyday is brought to life in this witty caper featuring a surprise sleuth—Humphrey Bogart. While filming *The Maltese Falcon*, he searches for a real-life treasure, dodging a killer on a murder trail through Hollywood.

SOMEWHERE SOUTH OF MELROSE
by Maxine O'Callaghan

P.I. Delilah West is hired to search for an old high school classmate. The path takes her through the underbelly of broken dreams and into the caprices of fate, where secrets are born and sometimes kept....

Available March 1999 at your favorite retail outlet.

COMING NEXT MONTH

#513 THE STRANGER SHE KNEW by Gayle Wilson
Men of Mystery
Ex-CIA agent Jordan Cross was given a new face and a new life.
What he didn't know was that his new identity belonged to a man
with dangerous enemies—and now he's put an innocent woman and
her children in jeopardy.

#514 THE BODYGUARD by Sheryl Lynn
Elk River, Colorado
J. T. McKennon was everything a man was supposed to be. Loyal,
strong, responsible and determined—not to mention the way he could
kiss. And as a bodyguard he was the ultimate protector. But as far as
Francine Forrest was concerned, he was the one brick wall she could
not move. Without him she'd never find her kidnapped sister. But
could she avoid falling in love with him in the process?

#515 A WOMAN OF MYSTERY by Charlotte Douglas
A Memory Away...
More than muscles and a handsome face, Jordan Trouble was a
professional protector. And while the cop in him wanted to know
what caused a beautiful woman's amnesia, the man in him wanted to
know how she did what no other had—made him feel alive again.

#516 TO LANEY, WITH LOVE by Joyce Sullivan
A note from her supposedly dead husband sends Laney Dobson's
world into a tailspin. But the clues she and Ben Forbes follow lead
to the revelation of a lifetime of deceit—and unexpected passion in
Ben's arms.

Look us up on-line at: http://www.romance.net